# Border Line

Hilary Custance Green has previously published two novels, *A Small Rain* and *Unseen Unsung*. Both reveal her love of music and celebrate the resilience of individuals faced with challenges in the modern world.
Hilary has also worked as a sculptor and research scientist.

For more information see Hilary at:
hilarycustancegreen.com
greenwritingroom.com

Also by Hilary Custance Green

A Small Rain

Unseen Unsung

# Border Line

Hilary Custance Green

 Threadgold Press

First published in 2014
Threadgold Press

ISBN 978-0-9560127-2-2
Copyright © Hilary Custance Green 2014

A CIP catalogue for this book is available from the British Library

Cover design by Amy Green
Typeset by Anthony Furness & Threadgold Press

Printed and bound by CPI Group (UK) Ltd, Croydon CR0 4YY

Threadgold Press
threadgoldpress@waitrose.com
hilarycustancegreen.com
greenwritingroom.com

### Rehearsal

*...for an exercise*
*I look at his hands*
*to improve our relationship*
*onstage?*
*...*

*Eleanor Green*

AUSTRIA

HUNGARY

+ Moravske
Toplice

Kranska Gora +
+
Vršič
Pass
+ Visevnik

+ Bled

Slap Rinka

+ Logarska
+ Luče

+
Ptuj

+ Kobarid

+ Bohinj

+ Volcji Potok

ITALY

+ Ljubljana

SLOVENIA

+ Žužamberk

+ Otočec

+ Predjama

+ Divača
Trieste + + Lipica

CROATIA

Adam, 33, woodworker

Anita, 54, carer

Bedrich, 57, car hire manager

Ben, 36, something in IT

Daniel, 36, drama tutor

Grace, 35, geographer

Imogen, 72, retired academic

Kip, 22, ambulance driver

Leon, 44, unemployed

Lindsay, 23, student

Vicky, 39, biologist

# Border Line

I *am* in my right mind.

It seems important to mention this because I sense my right mind slipping away – a sea-change over which I have little control. Before this goes too far, I need to record a transformation of a different kind; one as joyful as the distant sail to a castaway. Somewhere, no doubt, a butterfly flapped its wings to kick-start events. For me, the beginning is a freezing April night when the enchantment to come is way beyond the horizon.

## Devon – Day nought

The smoothness of the mouse under my hand is comforting. When I turn it over, its crimson underside glows like a living organism – an illusion of heat. I look up at the screen again and there's a pop-up message blinking at me. It says:

> ‹Before you make any final decisions, please contact Daniel, I may be able to help you.›

My hand jerks away in case I respond by mistake. There's an address, an email and a phone number. No purple flashing banners or suggestive graphics and the wording quite restrained; yet I feel exposed, watched from inside the screen. I hit the close button and breathe more easily.

The whole village is asleep. I'm sitting in Dad's old wicker chair looking up Dignitas on the internet. If I have a choice, then dying in a dignified manner with someone at least within earshot would be better than vomiting alone in my bedroom. Having no visible illness or injury I don't qualify for Dignitas, but I have to start somewhere. The founder has written an essay on why we should be able to choose when we die. Many people make failed attempts and end up injured or in mental homes. I worry about that.

The heating went off hours ago; my nightwear is poor cover and the weave of the chair is printing on my skin. I should go to bed.

I'm not as alone as I thought in wanting to opt out, though apparently seventy per cent of people who get a green light from the Dignitas clinic never actually take it up. Some who get as far as Switzerland change their minds at the last minute and come home.

I wish I owned slippers. I could fetch a pair of socks, but I daren't stop now. There's a Pied Piper drawing me on from website to website. I can't help believing there is help or an answer somewhere out there.

&lt;Before you make any final decisions, please contact Daniel, I may be able to help you.&gt;

Again? I scrunch myself in the chair so I can hold my feet in my hands and rest my chin on my knees. This way the cold has fewer entry points as I watch the screen. The message blinks, but doesn't move. Who is Daniel? Is he offering a quicker route? Is he hoping to cure me of my foolish intentions? Perhaps he's religious. Most likely he wants to relieve me of my money and leave me washed up and still alive.

Of course he could be – no, he's likely to be – something rather more sinister. I dream up a sadist with a taste for human flesh. I've given him my home address and here he is on my doorstep. I'm several minutes into this scenario before I stop myself. Feeling shaky and foolish, I'm a finger click away from the close button. Yet this Daniel is the only person in the world who knows that I want out, and he sounds... well his words are not unkind or unbelieving.

Somewhere, maybe in my wardrobe, I'm sure I have an old hot water bottle.

I half expect the message from Daniel to vanish or expand, but twenty minutes later it's unchanged. Apart from the risk of encouraging a psychopath if I'm stupid enough to communicate with him, there's also the danger someone could invade my computer. I copy the contact details, delete the message and sleep the computer.

The hot water bottle is not in my wardrobe, or anywhere else I can think of. I settle for socks and a cardigan under the duvet. Sleep would be good, but it mostly comes with dreams attached. It's nearly 2 am.

Who could possibly mind if I go? In World War II more than forty million people killed each other on purpose. Who could object if one more insignificant human departs? It's true, though, that I could be accused of ingratitude. I'm not hungry or homeless. I have a job. A plate of seafood risotto still brings water to my mouth. In the swimming pool I sense the same physical satisfaction with each long pull of the water. But... there's no way to wipe my mind clean.

Absolutely it's my own fault. By wrecking other people's lives – by wrecking my brother's life – I have wrecked my own. If I reach for a tin of beans on a shelf, it's Oscar's five-year-old hand I see. If I lie on the beach in the sun and shut my eyes, I hear his voice nagging me to come and play. I'm so obtuse it has taken me more than fifteen years to work out that there's only one way to achieve silence for us both.

As I lie trying not to think of Oscar, out of nowhere comes an image of where I put the hot water bottle. I stuffed it in a bag of soft toys under the stairs because of the bunny ears on the cover. I leap out of bed and unearth it. Trembling with anticipation, I boil a kettle, fill the bottle and wrap myself around its hot body. Then, as I pass the computer on the landing, I can't resist un-sleeping it. The bottle is now under my feet, the water slurping gently back and forth like a colicky cat. I type:

    <Dear Daniel, who are you? If your offer is
    to find a simple and relatively dignified way
    of quitting this life, I would be glad of your
    help. Please don't reply if you have any other
    project in mind. Grace>.

I delete Grace and type in my initials GEM instead. I dither over changing 'dignified' to a more honest 'painless', but lose interest as I am not really planning to send it.

I have another reverie. Daniel is someone who fills people like me with peace and lets us cut loose from our lives without hassle or even pain. He has a doctor's know-everything eyes. This image is more improbable than the cannibal one, but there *are* good people in the world. I save my email as a draft and return to bed.

I fall asleep for a little while. I am inside a tree; trapped, still and watchful. I don't mind, this is a decision-free position. When I wake up I remember enough to wish I could climb back, but that seems to be my ration for the night. It's past 4 am.

I get up, refill my bottle, un-sleep the computer again and look at my draft email. I log on to my rarely-used webmail, type in Daniel's address, paste in my message and hit the Send button smartly. My stomach lurches. I am not absolutely sure I meant to do that. I sometimes switch on the kettle when I meant to open the fridge.

I am a little pleased too; I made a decision. On my way back to bed I hear a ping, and tip-toe back to the screen:

<Dear GEM, this is precisely what I have in
mind. Go to my website - see below - and type
in your password which is GEM. Daniel>

I enter the site, wondering if my computer is now infected.
There's a picture of Daniel. He looks marginally more like a doctor
than a cannibal. Actually his image is folk-singer – unruly hair,
dreamy eyes; not that anyone would put up their own picture
if they had sharpened teeth and a wolfish smile. This little Red
Riding Hood walks straight into the den. The website is abnormal-
ly plain. Daniel doesn't employ expensive IT consultants – a lone
predator. It reads:

<Dear Visitor, every year I take a few com-
mitted people on an expedition. Our purpose is
to find a quiet place where individuals who
have concluded that they no longer wish to
live can find a secure way out, in company and
without fear of returning or being damaged and
surviving. We set about this in a way that is
not suitable for everyone. I would need to understand you and your motives before suggest-
ing that this is the route for you. Also, you
would need to be able to trust me before you
commit yourself. This will take a while. Each
year some of the people who come with me change
their minds and choose to return home.
    You can write anything in the space below if
and when you wish. Daniel>.

I return to my lukewarm bed and sleep deeply until the alarm rings.

Over the next few weeks I email, write and finally phone Daniel. He
has a not-quite-English accent. He's not offering a quick or a cheap exit.
Nothing will happen until September, an eternal six months from now.
Then there will be three communal weeks in Slovenia to live through
before we travel across a border to our final destination. Slovenia? Other
people? Exhaust fumes in the car would surely be easier, if only I were
more competent.

Daniel doesn't want money. He will book hostels etc for this period,
but we have to pay directly and not through him. So what does he want?
He emails:

‹Dear Grace, if you are choosing to give up on life, I want you to experience the last three weeks fully, to know yourself, to know others and to be sure of what you are quitting. I will need you to commit yourself to playing the games and doing the exercises I give you.

I need only your willingness, I will not force you or anyone to do anything you dislike. In return I promise you the quiet, comforting exit you so desire. You may change your mind at any time, though this will be entirely your decision.

You want, understandably, to know what I get out of it. I want to carry out my work; some might call it a vocation. I have no religious affiliations but I think we all have the right to choose. My training is as an actor and a therapist. I care about people.›

Rationally I should press Daniel for answers to hundreds of questions, but I ache to have this decision out of the way. I *want* to be convinced. I can't stop myself from trusting him and, when he accepts me, I dance a little jig. I have accomplished something. Someone at last believes that I mean what I say.

I patrol my half-a-house in its muddy Devonshire village looking at what I have to lose, then set about wrapping up my life. I pack some photos of my father, my brother, my mother and a couple of boyfriends, along with some personal letters, into an old leather suitcase of Dad's. There's only one photo of me and it's at the worst age, fifteen, and in shorts; I am tall and knobbly-kneed. I never threw it away because Dad is beside me, laughing, with my crazy hair blowing across his face. I wander round the house with the weight of this case stretching my arm. I have in mind to drop it in the river but this seems over-dramatic. Someone might discover it prematurely. Instead I climb into the loft. Light is leaking through the joints between the slates, and the bird droppings suggest a bigger gap somewhere. I push the case into a corner of the eaves.

Selling my half-a-house is easier than expected. Then I rent it back from the new landlord, who merely wants the investment. There doesn't seem much else to do. I have distanced myself from friends over the years. Boyfriends have come and gone. One or two persisted, but at what point in a relationship do you mention that you have caused your brother's death? I only tried it once. Oscar's tiny spirit floats between me and any man who comes too close. Besides, guilt is a hungry beast; it has eaten into the spaces where love could grow. I am tainted with it – an unlovable human incapable of loving anyone. Of course love is not essential to life. In some ways it's the ultimate luxury, but something in me has rebelled and I am unwilling to continue the trek in its absence – in the certainty of its continued absence.

This is my last day at work. I don't think anyone will miss me. Although map revision is often communal work, I've always had the corner desk, so no one consults me as they pass by. I have the feeling that I'm simply a shadow to my fellow workers, not a full inhabitant of their world. I register a couple of new roads on a housing estate outside Milton Keynes; I update the carriageway status of a revamped section of the A303; I answer an email from a victim of a persistent SatNav error. I take large-scale maps of Slovenia and print them off on A5 paper to keep with me on the journey.

Now I'm sitting staring out at Exeter's respectable office fronts. I've booked an extended holiday supposedly in Trieste. My large and small rucksacks are at my feet. Ought I to be feeling something? There are no butterflies inside me, no tendrils of melancholy, only a vision of stillness. In the blank spaces of my heart I'm trying – really trying – to experience some regret. I did love my father but it is two years since he died. I phoned my mother last night to say I was thinking of working abroad. She said 'Really, darling?', but didn't ask where. She, along with my boss and my landlord, thinks that I'm off on holiday. But, like my brother, I shall come no more, never, never...

Twenty-one days to go.

## Trieste – Day one

My first impression is that I'm involved in some kind of a hoax. The only blue coach in the car park at Trieste station looks like a Dinky toy – not a mini-bus but a pint-sized twenty-passenger version of the real thing with pairs of seats down one side, singles down the other and four seats in a row at the back. There's no sign of our leader, Daniel, so, following my instructions, I put my large rucksack in the miniature hold and board the coach.

In spite of the joke transport I don't really believe that I've sunk my savings into a scam. Daniel has answered every letter, email and call I have ever sent him, so by now I would trust him on the nuclear button.

The few faces I spot as I climb the steps have a blitzed look about the eyes. Not surprising since we are, I assume, all heading in the same direction. They also have that same slackness about the jaw that I can feel as I un-grit my teeth. I choose an empty single seat near the front and drop onto it.

Looking round again I see and pass over a woman in her forties; I'll never reach middle age. In the next row is a fair-haired teenager, brown eyes wide with anxiety. She looks too young and pretty to be wanting to end her life. She's dressed up for a day at the office – cream blouse with a collar frill. In front of her is a rumpled man plugged into his iPod, he looks like someone you might see on a pavement with a dog and penny whistle.

The teenager is so very skinny my mind slides off sideways to a girl with anorexia I saw years ago. She had a heavy pregnant bulge on a frame where the only other bulges were the outsized knuckles of her joints. This memory diverts, like a train over points, to another image, a café in Exeter five years ago.

I recall sitting in that café practically levitating with relief. I realised that I had a choice; I could decide never to have children. I could duck that terrifying responsibility. I remember the espresso machine beside me, burnished and humming. Opposite a young man was speaking shyly into his mobile, his eyes lit up over something only he could hear. In the window two women leaned towards each other, chuckling at their own jokes. The beauty of it all had me gasping. My crack of laughter made the poor barman jump. Years of anxiety drifted off with the steam from my coffee.

I snap out of my trance as the coach vibrates to the tread of a new passenger. He has to duck as he climbs aboard. On his way down the coach he looks left and right, giving me a considering glance before his eyes settle on the more appealing, brown-eyed girl. His self-assurance does not fit with my image of a bunch of losers heading for the exit. His presence is distracting. I find myself absurdly reviewing the contents of my rucksack; these don't compare well with the outfit the girl is wearing. Setting off on a journey to that bit of the map "where the dragons be", I didn't feel any incentive to pack more than basic comfortable clothes. I haven't even attempted to tame my hair today. I only have to last three weeks and take part in whatever activities Daniel asks us to do during that time. No pressure to pretend any longer, to put on a show, to get a life. I plan to walk quietly to the end of the plank and then sink without trace – problem solved.

Another man is swinging himself up into the coach; he slips into the driver's seat. He is, like the song, *Young, black and beautiful* – no, I've got that wrong – it's *Young, gifted and black*, that's it. In the glimpse I have I reckon he's barely within driving age. Well that doesn't matter much either. Seconds later I'm blushing; like the victim of subliminal advertising, I'm humming the song. I pray the driver is out of earshot.

The only other sound in the coach is the whispering of a couple near the back. All the other occupants are single and silent. After one glance through the windows I find the scale of the outside world, individual mountains into which you could tuck the entire Cairngorms, too unnerving. Letting my fingers trace the gold threads in my scarf, something they do with or without my permission, I close my eyes and drift off.

The little coach is rocking again and I can hear a familiar voice. A man in a soft brown jacket is leaning over talking to the person on the seat in front of me. He has a very faint foreign accent. Then he turns to me. His eyes are bluer and wider than in the photograph, his hair is still uncombed and he moves with a sort of slow motion that suggests he is at ease with time and space.

'Hello Grace, I'm Daniel.' He bends over to look out of my window. 'You see that bigger peak on the left, you'll be able to watch it all the way. We'll stop at the border in half an hour, then lunch near Divača after we've picked up our last passenger, Adam.'

Obediently I gaze out at the faraway peaks and feel myself shrinking to a speck; safe, small, inconspicuous. As Daniel moves on down the coach I cannot control my grin of relief. All these months communicating with him means that he knows I cannot sew on a button or organise a funeral; that I cry if I watch small children playing, bite my nails, have a terror of hornets and the stench of rotten fruit and that nylon sheets give me a rash. He knows I'm a killer. I've handed my life, even my death, into his keeping and having seen him I know I'm utterly safe. He can't be more than mid-thirties, but looks as tired as a man should, given the weight of my life and of everyone else on the coach. He has the eyes of a screen Jesus, all-seeing and profoundly kind. I imprint on him, happy to follow blindly like a newly-hatched duckling.

From Trieste we start climbing up into the mountains. Like a distant sea, I can hear plaintive murmurs from the older couple at the back; no one else is speaking. At the Italian border Daniel has a word with the driver then gets off the bus. The driver walks past me and once again the voice of Nina Simone leaps into my head, *"Young, gifted and black..."*, and refuses to be suppressed. He introduces himself to the whispering couple as Kip, and shows them a map. I get out one of my books of maps. I know I've left work forever, but I can't stop myself. I like to track my movements on the paper surface of the globe. The backs of the maps are blank and I start to jot a few notes about our journey on them.

Two Italian border guards climb into the bus, chatting to each other. They glance round and we all start pulling out passports. With a gracious wave of the hand, and without interrupting their conversation, they both descend again and Daniel reappears. 'That seems to be the Italian frontier done.' He stays on his feet as Kip drives on and moments later two more guards in different uniforms get on. These, a man and a woman, greet us individually in English, inspect our passports enthusiastically and depart smiling. A buzz comes into the bus. We are crossing the border between choice and a done deal.

Even as I think this, Daniel is bending over a previously hidden, white-haired woman, 'This is now Slovenia. If you choose to go back, it'll be as easy as coming in, you know.'

I don't want to know. I want a conflagration of boats so final that I never have to make another choice in my life. It's only at this point that I begin to wonder what exactly Daniel will be doing with us for these twenty-one days in Slovenia before he sees us over another border. He mentioned games and exercises. I have worrying images of people spread out in a field doing aerobics or playing rounders. My preferred options have always been swimming or jogging solo.

As if he's tuned into my brain, Daniel adds, 'For the time being there's no need to think about anything except, perhaps, what you might like for lunch.' Obedient again, I realign my focus to the here and now.

An hour later we stop outside the train station at Divača. One man is sitting on a bench in the shaded area outside the station reading a paper. He doesn't look up so the coach waits.

The couple from the back of the coach, in their fifties or even sixties and both comfortably stout, get off and wander over to a big steam engine sitting on a disused bit of line nearby. The man on the bench doesn't even glance at them. All I can see is a hollowed profile and paper-thin hands. He might be twenty-five or even forty. After a minute Daniel gets off the bus and goes over to him.

'Adam?'

The man leaps half way out of his skin. Daniel puts out a hand, but Adam avoids it.

'Adam, it's me, Daniel.'

'Yes,' he says, not smiling. He has a snapped shut face – don't talk to me, don't touch me. He picks up his bag and follows Daniel back onto the bus. He sits near the front without looking at anyone. That's it, that's the last of us.

## Divača – Party game

We stop at a chalet-style restaurant a few miles on from Divača. The intense green of the fields disconcerts me; too fresh for the end of summer. We file off the coach and take surreptitious stock of each other. I'm not good at assessing faces on sight. Mostly I like people when I get to know them, but strangers rarely strike me as enticing. We stand around in uneasy silence. Only the tallest man and the tiny, white haired woman, who peers over her glasses, chat as if at a cocktail party. The rumpled guy takes his earphones out. In a soft Northern burr, he asks my name and how far I have come.

Daniel gathers us round a couple of tables below a steep, green alp. The sun is blazing and, although it's early September, the air smells like June in Hampshire. He says, 'We'll order lunch shortly. First I'd like you to meet each other.' He holds up some bits of paper. 'This is an old method for identifying your opposite number – if you happen to be a spy.' He's smiling at our raised eyebrows. 'If you need to meet up with a particular person, but this individual is a complete stranger and other people are anxious to impersonate this stranger, you need a device to ensure that only the two of you communicate. I've got some old paper bus tickets here and I'm going to give each of you half a ticket. There are ten of you.'

The rumpled man is counting heads. 'Surely...'

Daniel puts a hand on the driver's shoulder. 'Kip's not only driving; he's on the same journey as the rest of us...'

The woman of the elderly couple puts a hand over her mouth. 'But he's so young!'

'... so that's five tickets.' Daniel is tearing each one roughly in two. 'The trick is to find your other half – that is to match up the torn edge of your ticket with the torn edge of someone else's. For today it's important that you try out every ticket. Don't leave anyone out, even if you think you've found your match. Tag that person, but keep on trying. Don't worry about anything else today except names. Everyone has a story and we'll come to these in due course. Leon?' He leans towards the rumpled man, 'Can I borrow your hat?' He takes the navy baseball cap, revealing Leon's balding head, and upturns it, dropping in the handful of torn tickets. 'There.'

He shakes the cap and offers it round. I don't know how he does it, but Daniel has the kind of smile that is contagious and we all wander about in the sunshine, tickets in hand, wearing childish grins.

This playtime among strangers is part children's party, part blind date. One half of a bus ticket is much like any other, matching them proves more difficult than it sounds. In seconds I'm adrift in a blizzard of names. Leon, in spite of looking like he can't work a washing machine, turns out to be best at matching the pieces, but it's the tall guy who seems to dominate proceedings. His name, as befits his blonde, well-heeled appearance, is Benedict, though he wants to be called Ben. Hearing him talk unsettles me. His intonation is shot through with expensive schooling and the certainties of privilege. He's making a play of secretively checking his ticket with a singular-looking woman. I've dubbed her "The Badger" in my mind; she has a white stripe in her hair, jogging bottoms and a purposeful manner.

Everyone manages a bit of party spirit except our last passenger, the ultra-dour Adam. One sight to enjoy is the slight girl, Lindsay – all big brown eyes and straight honey-coloured hair – looking startled as the driver leans over her and joins her half-ticket to his. They are by some way the youngest two and both sound like Londoners. He takes her hand and leans over in a mock bow; she flushes, looking almost happy.

For the first time it occurs to me that I'm on holiday. I look round to see if others are having the same revelation. For the most part people are wearing effortful half-smiles. In my dream world my ticket will match with Ben's who, in addition to his other assets, has attractive sea-coloured eyes. Even as I watch him walking towards me, the female half of the only couple pops up at my elbow, waving her half-ticket.

'You must be my match, I think you're the last one left. I'm Anita,' she points to a big sleepy-looking man in his fifties, 'and that's my husband Bedrich over there. You are...?'

'Grace.'

'Grace?' She wrinkles her nose. 'You look very pre-Raphaelite, if you don't mind my saying, and with a name like that... I mean. Are all those curls real?'

I wish I could think of a matching reply. I look at her arms heavy with bangles, her belt with a big gold buckle and the handbag with its clinking chain – a would-be Carmen? In the end I sketch a smile and mutter, 'All Mother Nature.' This pigeon-holing of my appearance always disconcerts me. Apart from the corkscrew curls, which are dark brown with only a touch of red, I can see no connection.

Uncomfortable now, I quail at the forced intimacy ahead. I'm in a confusion of strangers and, except for Daniel, can't spot any potential friends. There's a sparkle about the tiny white-haired woman with clever eyes called Imogen, but she's definitely older than my mother; none of the women look close to my age. I see no soul-mates among the men either. Even Ben, with his beautiful manners, is not really my kind. Given our purpose (or mine at least) we should as a minimum appear odd, like Lindsay, for instance – a twitching gazelle on the lookout for lions.

Of course we might all be here for different purposes. Daniel could have told each one of us a different story. The whole thing could be a set-up for some weird crime. He mentioned spies – perhaps this is a recruitment drive for a suicidal mission for Queen and Country. Or... I gasp at my next thought and when I look up I find the last arrival staring at me. Turning quickly away I see Ben raising one golden eyebrow.

'What's the joke, Grace?' he asks.

'Oh nothing, I just had a crazy thought.'

'Like what?'

I shrug, 'What if some people-traffickers are waiting for a consignment and get us lot instead? We're a rather mixed bag.'

The rumpled guy cracks a laugh, and Ben produces a grin of real amusement, as do some of the others, but The Badger woman, with the unlikely name of Vicky, looks less than amused. Lindsay gives a little shriek, which could mean anything.

Daniel lifts his beer, 'Quite a thought, Grace. Actually we're less mixed than we appear. We probably have more in common than, say, the average church congregation. We'll soon feel more homogenous – more of a group – too. How are you doing with names?'

I look at the assortment of humans around me. When I see a place name it lodges solidly in some compartment of my brain; I can remember and locate several thousand of them – it's my job. People's names seem to pass through leaving less trace. You would think that people, being solid and present, would be easier to track down than dots on a map. I look back at Daniel and my ability to lie withers, 'Um, yes. I'm not brilliant at names, I might need a day or two to get eleven, well ten not counting mine, attached to the right people.' There are nods all round.

He opens his palms. 'It doesn't matter. Some people register names quickly; others struggle to put a name to their cat. It *really* does not matter; we have twenty-one days to get to know each other. That's the important thing.' He leans down to his small rucksack. 'Anyway, while we're waiting for the food to come we'll get a little exercise. Everyone round in a circle. Stand next to the other half of your ticket. So Lindsay, Kip, Bedrich, Leon, Vicky, Ben – is that right Ben not Benedict?'

'Yup.'

'Imogen, Adam, Anita, Grace and myself, Daniel – or Dan if you prefer.'

Definitely Daniel to me; there was a scary Dan at school.

He slips a tennis ball out of the rucksack, calls out, 'Leon!' and throws it across the circle.

After a moment's pause, Leon calls out, 'Bedrich,' as he throws.

Bedrich catches the ball, mutters, 'Anita,' and passes it swiftly to his wife.

I'm distracted by Daniel's rucksack into thinking of Mother's bottomless bag in the Swiss Family Robinson and then I remember that Daniel is half Swiss. I don't hear Anita call my name and of course I fail to catch the ball.

I'm not the only games duffer; The Badger, Vicky, has butter-fingers worse than mine. Her jogging outfit is misleading. I try to concentrate when Daniel tosses the ball. After a couple of minutes he makes us swap places. Ben already knows all our names, others, like me, are still floundering. I worry when I see little Lindsay beginning to stagger on her heels, but her mobile phone rings and the game breaks up.

I'm mildly happy and breathless in a way I haven't felt for years. Ben has a healthy flush and looks as though he's attending a tennis party. On the other hand, Anita is scowling at her husband and Adam, our newest passenger, looks about as happy as a bridesmaid who's stepped in a cowpat.

## Lunch – Questions

As we settle at a couple of tables for lunch, I find myself opposite Lindsay, hunting for a safe topic that we might have in common. Luckily, Ben sits down next to me, compares his mobile to hers and has her laughing in minutes. Then Imogen asks a crucial question.

'Daniel, tell me, for how long have you been taking people like us abroad?'

'This is the fifth year.'

'Why Slovenia?' Ben asks.

'Well, as you know, I'm both Swiss and English and spent my childhood travelling across European borders. I find everyone I meet here exceptionally helpful. Also, although it's only the size of Wales, it's got everything; mountains, seaside, wilderness, ancient cities.'

As he pauses, Ben presses, 'And?'

Daniel gives a tiny smile. He continues, 'Slovenia also has several specific advantages for us. Most of you have never been here before and you don't speak the language. Though I gather you have some Serbo-Croat, Ben. And Imogen,' he smiles his appreciation, 'has gone to the trouble of acquiring some.'

Bedrich protests, 'These are advantages?'

Daniel folds his hands like a peaceful uncle about to tell a bedtime story. He says, 'I can see that the idea sounds counter-intuitive, but I want to avoid provoking memories.' He looks up, his eyes stopping on something distant, we all follow his gaze. There's a pony and cart heading up the path behind the restaurant. Daniel laughs out, putting his head in his hands, then looks up, purses his lips in a little huff and admits, 'I'm a fool; seeing that cart being drawn uphill, I am instantly seven years old again. Memories lurk everywhere for all of us. Still, for you I'm hoping for an unexplored backcloth to our games, I want to give you fresh surroundings for the next three weeks.'

'Our last three weeks.' Anita corrects him.

Daniel nods. 'Then there's the language. With any familiar language, you would hear it around you and without meaning to, you would listen. Obviously you will learn to recognise simple greetings: *doberdan* – good day or *hvala* – thank you, and the other words on the list I sent you, but the rest will be no more distracting than wallpaper, I hope.'

I clap a hand to my mouth. 'Daniel, I'm so sorry, I never looked at that list of words.'

'Don't worry, Grace, you can forget everything you haven't done and start anew today.'

Lindsay puts up her hand like a child, 'Do... did people change their minds? Did they all go across the final border or did some of them go home?'

Daniel smiles straight at her. 'I won't be talking about earlier expeditions, but yes, some people go on and others go home. You choose.'

Leon unplugs his iPod. 'I've chosen. I'm not going back. I can't go back.'

Several of us nod. Ben says, 'Me neither.'

Daniel repeats, 'You choose.'

Vicky wants to know about the games. 'I'm not very good at physical stuff; will we be doing a lot? It's not like Outward Bound courses is it? I mean, you're not going to make us abseil down cliffs or anything are you?'

Daniel grins at her. 'Absolutely not. These games and exercises are about getting to know yourselves and each other. I'll ask none of you to do anything you can't cope with or are afraid of.'

With everything Daniel says, I relax another notch. I'm beginning to get a sense of why we all trusted him. I don't feel so... so anchorless now he is with us.

Lindsay looks relieved. 'I thought it'd be like school games.'

Daniel shakes his head. 'No, these are more fun. I learnt them when I did some drama training; they help actors release inhibitions and find their way into new or alien emotions. Others come from my therapy training, but they do the same job. There's no reason why you shouldn't enjoy these three weeks.'

I almost laugh at our faces receiving the news that we might enjoy the last three weeks of our lives. Apart from Imogen and Leon (with his fixture earplugs), the others could not look more appalled if he had promised daily thumbscrews. Even Anita's large husband Bedrich, who appears so sleek and sleepy, the kind of guy who never quite lifts a finger, lets a spasmodic twitch cross his face. I hope someone will ask what kind of therapy Daniel trained in, but no one does.

Ben, beside me, mutters, 'Games? I've been down some weird paths but… Jesus!'

Imogen says, 'Any more advantages, Daniel?'

He grins, 'I see I'm not going to get away with any fudging with you on board, Imogen. OK. Slovenia has a lot of borders. As you know this is not my first expedition. I can't repeat myself without making national authorities uncomfortable. At the end of our three weeks, we can book into a self-catering house, in one of four countries, all no more distant than a couple of hours driving.'

A shadow passes across the faces in our circle.

After a moment Ben says, 'Well, now I know you've got the logistics zipped up, I need food to sustain me until we get there.'

We titter, as if he has said something clever. It's a relief to see plates of pasta starting to arrive. Leon is going on about Wynton Marsalis, the jazz trumpeter, who is apparently performing in Ljubljana next week. I'm happy to listen to Leon. Inside his jumper, all frayed at the neck and the cuffs, there's a solid sort of man, with a soothing northern rhythm to his voice. He's talking to Bedrich whose eyelids fascinate me; they droop further and further then, with a millimetre to go, they pick up again. I listen to one and watch the other until I spot an ant attempting to negotiate my empty beer glass.

I'm separate from these people. My role, as always, is outside the action like a spectator on a film set. I concentrate on the ant. It's only a dab of an ant, nothing big or exciting, but it has the equivalent of a tree trunk in its jaws. It's also a daft ant; it loses its grip on the spar over and over again, it trips over it and has to realign everything. Finally, big excitement, it gets the thing airborne. Seconds later, it slips down one of the gaps in the table and the spar gets stuck. Now it's reversing. As the idiotic creature arrives back where it started from, I have a sense of fellow feeling. I'd help if I had a notion of where it wants to go.

I'm still sitting nose to nose with the ant, when I hear a snort. I jerk and knock over my empty glass. It's Adam; he has lowered his newspaper long enough for me to make a fool of myself.

He picks up the glass and gives me a half friendly grin, 'Sorry I made you jump.' Then he returns to his paper. This is the first whole sentence I hear out of him. I decide to give him the benefit of the doubt for a bit longer.

As Lindsay comes to the end of her third phone call and the white-stripe woman checks her mobile, Daniel says. 'Shall we agree what we want to do about mobiles. Apart from the exercises, during which they need to be off, it's up to you. We can have them on all the time, or with us but switched off, or kept in our hotel bedrooms. What do you think?'

Imogen doesn't have a phone, nor, amazingly, does Adam. I do wonder if he is a lot older than he looks, which is thirty plus, but in the midday light his skin looks enviably clear except for the unused laughter lines. Bedrich and Anita have left theirs at home on purpose. The others want their mobiles with them but switched off. Lindsay puts hers away with a distinctly wistful look.

I put a hand into my bag as they talk, but I already know. My phone is sitting on the hall table at... not home, I don't have a home any more. In December the landlord will come looking for his money and find himself the owner of a confused wardrobe, a thousand maps, a two-foot stuffed wallaby, a rusting Renault and a mobile phone. I did remember to empty the fridge, so at least it shouldn't smell too bad.

### Names and maps

I sleep most of the way to Ljubljana and stand groggily through the formalities of the hotel reception. I hear Daniel say, 'We'll be staying here for the first week, so make yourselves comfortable. Does anyone else, apart from Anita, want a list of names?'

'Yes please.'

'Me, too.'

This is quite funny. All the women have asked for a list, but none of the men. Do they remember better or care less? I'm not sure Leon, plugged into his iPod, has even heard Daniel. Imogen is tapping him on the arm. It turns out he does want a list. Anita says her list is for Bedrich, who never remembers anything.

As Daniel writes down our names, The Badger frowns at me, muttering, 'It's all very well to say that we need to concentrate on names *today*, but there are people at work whose names I still can't remember after two years.' Then she stumps off.

I don't know what to say. I've had six months to get Daniel sorted: kind eyes – they look tired though – I guess he's older than me, perhaps as much as forty. The revelation face-to-face is that he moves like a dancer, comfortable in his own skin. Imogen is easy too: tiny, the oldest person by some way and she has dimples – a feature I've always envied. Ben, ah Ben: difficult to miss, with his green eyes, olde English confidence and a massive dictionary under his tongue.

Daniel stops writing. 'OK, that's five, no six with Leon.' He waves his pen towards the lifts. 'Go and settle in, I'll come to each of your rooms with a list in the next few minutes.'

In my room I start to unpack. I manage to get my wash-bag and pyjamas out, but then I can no longer resist. My fingers search out my last indulgence: five large scale (seriously large scale 1:10,000) maps of Slovenia. I unfold the first great crackling sheet and spread it over the bed. As I flatten the folds, the south-west quarter of Slovenia takes shape under my hands. My world becomes a maze of tiny contour lines, blue water zones and names, names, names. I crouch at the bedside, pen poised above the map, warmth invading my chest, as I start to plot our journey so far.

Daniel's knock on the door makes me jump. He hands over the list, raises his eyebrows at the map on the bed, nods and says that supper will be downstairs in an hour's time.

After he goes, I look at the list. I find it comforting to see his handwriting again. It's been such a feature of my life these last months. In this printout age it's an extra pleasure. I scribble a word or two beside each name.

Adam – the guy we picked up in Divača
Anita – bangles and husband
Bedrich – sleepy eyes, wife
Ben – tallest, green eyes
Daniel
Grace

18

Imogen – dimples, white hair
Kip – driver, *'young, gifted and black'*
Leon – earplugs, northern accent, nice voice
Lindsay – pearly fingernails, v. thin
Vicky – Vicky The Badger

Before I forget, I draw a quick plan of the bus and jot people's names in their seats. I look at this sketch in disbelief. These are the people I have been planning to meet for the last six months? I can see that I'm a misfit among misfits, and yet I must endure this. Today's stilted conversations are my – our – lot for another twenty days and then it will be over.

It's a relief to return to the map. I could happily spend the whole three weeks just getting to know its hills and valleys, its delicious names and history-packed borders. I do finally reach the bottom of my big rucksack and there they are – the pills. Ever since Daniel gave me the medicine list, I've worried about mucking it up. All the "mgs" and "NSAIDs" look like code, things I could easily get wrong. Three of the packets are open from that time, nearly two weeks ago now, when I phoned Daniel because I wanted it all over that night. He didn't tell me not to, but he said the pills might not work on their own. He will have some others with him. We talked about… I think we talked about the power cables running near our village. They hum. I don't mind, but the two boys in the other half of my house grumble about the noise every time we meet. We don't meet often.

It's a strange thought that in the last twenty-four hours I have exchanged Devon and its power cables for a hotel in Ljubljana. I am too tired to care. I think I'll do without supper and go to bed. I have my pyjamas in my hand and an absurd temptation to curl up among the contours of the map still open on the bed, when there's a knock on the door. The Badger is standing there offering me a toothbrush. We stare at each other.

She says, 'Oh! Sorry, I'm so sorry. I thought this was um… the other girl's room.'

There's only really one other "girl". 'Lindsay?' I suggest.

'That's it, Lindsay. You see, on the coach she told me she forgot her toothbrush. I always carry a spare. She must be next door. Sorry.' She turns away, then stops and says, 'I'm going down to supper when I've handed this over, you coming?'

'Well, I… yes.' I drop the pyjamas and grab my bag.

No toothbrush? I sympathise, but wonder what else Lindsay might have forgotten. We knock on the room next to mine and she opens the door an inch, so all that's visible is the bushbaby brown eyes. Seeing us and then the toothbrush, she lights up, opens the door, thanks Vicky and we all troop down to the restaurant.

Lindsay is clutching her list and says, 'Isn't Daniel kind? I told him I'm not good at names and he didn't even laugh, he said to set myself a target and learn two a day. I'm starting with the older lady as I've never met an Imogen before and you, Grace, because I wish that was my name.

I'm trying to think of a reply, when Vicky says, 'It's a pretty name and it suits you, Grace. But for myself, I'd rather look pretty than have a pretty name.' She sounds matter-of-fact, but looking at her homely features, I struggle to think of a truthful compliment in return. Before we can respond she says. 'It makes all the difference to have the names written down. It's like a map, each name occupies a particular space on the page, unlike people who move around, change their clothes and generally confuse you. If, say, the tallest man, Ben, is not in the room then the last guy, Adam – you can't help but wonder what's bugging *him*... where was I?'

'If Ben's not in the room?'

'Oh yes, then maybe Bedrich, who's twice as wide as Adam, is the tallest – and so on. I don't suppose it really matters though. Surely we can muddle through another twenty days together and then it'll be over.'

I nod, a little startled to hear this echo of my own thought.


## Kip

Later, after supper, we follow Daniel into warm, strangely-scented streets, with their quixotic buildings; all blessedly unlike Devon. For a few minutes I genuinely forget our purpose. We settle at tables in a café near Presernov Trg – the main square – behind the statue of the local hero and poet France Preseren.

Daniel bathes us in his smile and says, 'Each one of you will get a chance, when you're ready, to talk about why you're here. It won't always be easy to understand other people's motives unless you have similar experiences in your own lives. The important thing is to listen and accept that each one of you has reasons for your choices, whether or not you're able to express them.'

Our driver, Kip, jerks to his feet. 'I'll do mine now.'

Standing there in his dark anorak, with his cropped curly hair, soft features and slight build, he looks all defiant teenager.

Daniel puts a hand on his arm. 'There's plenty of time ahead, Kip, but would you be happier talking now than another day?' Kip nods. 'Fine, go ahead then.'

Lindsay mutters, 'God, that's brave.'

Kip flicks her a glance. 'I just want it done.'

I look round, relief shows on most of the faces. He must be seriously courageous. He looks half anybody else's age. He's the only black person in the group – probably in the whole of Slovenia, as far as I can see. I imagine walking down the street in an African town. I'd feel isolated, uncomfortable, even scared. Kip's voice suggests a confident Londoner and he has good looks on his side, but his eyes narrow in a cynical gleam as he scans our faces.

There's a lull as drinks and wildly exotic ice creams arrive. I gaze at the tiny drops of strawberry juice laced and twirled across the mounds of white cream thinking how exquisite they are. When I raise my eyes again I see Ben gazing speculatively at Lindsay. Well, we have twenty more days before we cross the last border and stop being interested in anything ever again.

Our double table occupies a corner of the café. As Kip walks round the table, exclamations over the ice creams cease. He leans over the greenery edging the balustrade and gazes into the Ljubljanica River. 'Looks cool and soft down there, be a nice way to go.' He turns to face us. 'There's nothing much to tell you. My kid brother had ALL – Acute Lymphoblastic Leukaemia. He had it on and off with remission from when he was seven. By the time he was thirteen and I was fifteen he needed a bone marrow transplant to survive. I had matching tissue. I could've saved him, but I didn't, I refused. He died.'

Both Anita and Imogen open their mouths but make no further progress. No one knows how to break the kind of silence that follows. Daniel says nothing. He must, of course, have asked all his questions in advance. Kip hitches himself onto the balustrade edge and sits looking at us, with a shrugged I-told-you-so expression.

At last Leon pushes away his glass and says, 'He might have died even if you had donated.'

'Yeah, the consultant told me. He also said that Mark would definitely die if I didn't.'

'Are you able to tell us why you refused?' Imogen asks.

Kip turns to her with a glinting smile. 'I can give you reasons. I can even make them sound real good, but I know when I'm telling... when I'm making excuses.' He looks out towards the statue and frowns. Kids are shrieking in the square and bats wheeling above them. He waits for silence. 'Mark'd been ill on and off since he was little. You've no idea how many holes they made in his body. Lumbar punctures, plasma tests, blood for this, blood for that, day after day until they put in a thing called a central line – they fixed a permanent tap into his heart vein. He had chemotherapy, of course, not once, but over and over. He lost his hair, it grew; he lost it again. Every day he swallowed pills – mouthfuls of plastic and dry pellets. There were a million things he couldn't do, people he couldn't meet, places he couldn't go.

'His remission times got shorter and shorter. He told me he wanted it to stop. He lay there in his bed, his skin like some old candle, and begged me not to donate.' Kip runs a hand over the soft fuzz of his head and adds, almost by the way, 'Our mum had died the year before.'

There is a small movement as Lindsay puts her hand to her mouth. Kip's lashes drop onto his cheek as if they are simply too heavy, but a moment later he goes on. 'Mark told me he'd only tried so hard to get well for her, but now she'd gone he wanted out. Dad and I could get on with our lives, he said, not have to live in hospital, or live with half the hospital in our front room.'

Kip looks round our circle, then his face splits with unamused laughter and he shrugs. 'I told you it'd sound good, but I've really thought about it. If I had Mark's life and thought Mum'd died because of the stress of looking after me, and there was Dad stressed out and breaking up over Mum... what'd I do? This guy, my *little* brother was like a man in his thinking. Sickness grows you up awful fast. He loved us, he handed me a get-out pass.' Kip looks over at the statue, his lips pressed tight. 'What he really wanted was for me to be Mum, fight for him, make him want to live. Dad was too beat up over Mum; Mark knew it was me or no one. I failed him, see.'

Imogen gets up; she goes to lean against the wall beside Kip. She looks tiny and silvery beside him. 'You don't know, do you? You don't know for sure. When my sick husband said he wanted to go he really meant it.'

22

'Sorry, lady, your husband wasn't thirteen years old. I do know. That's why I'm here.'

Kip is silhouetted against the light, so it's difficult to see his face, but his body stiffens and his voice has an edge to it. 'I know what he wanted; I know what he needed. I went along with what he told me because *I* couldn't face him going through the pain. You've no idea how he hurt, how much he needed Mum. *He* could bear it, I couldn't. One tough kid, huh?'

Imogen persists, 'You say he was mature for his age and he asked you to refuse, maybe he really meant it.'

Kip waves her suggestion away. 'Sure, I fooled myself into thinking stuff like that, but I knew him from the minute he was born; I *know* what he wanted.'

'Why didn't he just refuse treatment?' Vicky wants to know.

Kip's body sags now, he runs a hand over his face and I remember that he's done all that driving today. He answers, 'Hospitals are weird. Mark was underage; they didn't think he could make that kind of decision himself. They'd have listened to Dad, but Mark and I knew we'd never persuade him to agree to let Mark die. If I'd donated they'd have made Mark go ahead with the op.'

I recognise in Kip's voice the hours of self-questioning; the slammed doors on all the better exit routes. He sounds almost middle-aged. I feel sad that he should give up on life, but I guess it's his business.

'But your dad?' Lindsay asks, a choke in her voice.

'I haven't seen him in four and half years. I don't blame him. When I refused to donate he told me to get out and stay out. He wouldn't listen to Mark. He knew what Mark really wanted. He let me visit until it was over, then he wanted me gone.'

Anita waves a bangled arm. 'Well I think Lindsay's right, you should think about your dad, he might regret what he said one day. Your following Mark won't make anything better for him.'

Lindsay gasps, 'Oh, I didn't mean…'

Kip puts out a traffic-stopping hand. 'It's OK. Dad's got my married half-sister. She's got kids. He'll be fine. I remind him of Mum and Mark. With me gone he can start clean.'

Lindsay leans across the table. She sounds surprisingly emphatic for such a fragile creature. 'But he'll think it's his fault if you go and… if you just disappear.'

'I don't suppose he'll know.'

'But I thought… Daniel didn't you say relatives will be told?'

'They will, Lindsay, but it's up to Kip to choose what he does with his life and that includes who gets notified.'

'Aye but…' it's Leon. He waves his iPod at Kip. 'I bet your Dad hurts too. And I wouldn't be too sure your brother didn't mean what he said.'

Kip's chest heaves and he slumps against the wall. 'Jesus, I'm not sure of anything back home. I'm just sure this is the right thing to do now. This'll tidy up the mess. I'm extra, the family don't need me, I don't reckon anyone does. Anyway the decision's made. I don't suppose any of you lot are in a position to know or tell me anything different. What should I live for? I don't feel nothing. I don't want friends; I don't want family. I don't want to live with me.' He clears his throat and straightens. 'I'm sure you lot're all great guys, but you're not going to change my mind.'

Daniel intervenes at last. 'Kip, tell us about Mark. What did you do when he was well?'

Kip looks up at the statue in the square and I think he won't answer, but then his eyes crease in their first warm smile. 'Fishing, mostly. When he was well enough, we'd go, all three of us, Dad, Mark and me, with Catch 21 – it's a sort of angling club for everyone in London. We got to fish in the Mount Pond on Clapham Common. That was the best. The worst was fishing in the swamp that was Camden Lock before they cleaned it up. We were really thick; we caught zilch. A stickleback would be a rare sighting. Mum said it gave her man-free time. I went along for the cider. Dad'd let us have half a pint of cider each. I reckon he thought it was non-alcoholic. But Mark, he really cared where we fished; he minded about his kit and all. After he got ill, Mum and Dad would spend everything they had on getting him this amazing gear, even a 12 foot Delta Carp Rod.'

'Didn't you mind – about the rod, I mean?' Lindsay asks.

'Nope, I'd rather have cruddy fishing tackle and no leukaemia than the other way round. Hey, what's up?' Kip leans towards Lindsay, who is wiping her eyes on her sleeve. He sits back again as she holds up both hands.

She whispers, 'Nothing, nothing.'

Daniel touches her shoulder. 'Lindsay?'

Ben, who is sitting beside Lindsay, hands her a beautiful white hanky and she looks around, startled by the attention.

'I don't know really. I hate that Kip's mother died and that his brother died, when he might have lived, and that Kip's going to die too, and his father will think it's his fault and I can't bear that Kip watched his brother get all those presents. And I know it is stupid to cry about things that are nothing to do with me.'

I can almost hear a collective sigh of envy as Daniel smiles at her. 'Lindsay, you can cry about anything you like. We all have to do with each other now.'

Anita speaks up, 'Kip what do you do for a living?' We all rustle forward again.

'Ambulance driver. I've been trying for a paramedic course for the last four years. I got a letter from my headmaster about my GCSEs. They're not great; I did them when Mark was real sick. When I started with the ambulances you could progress through the service, now they want A levels as well.'

I hear sympathetic murmurs. I can see that his work must remind him every day of his brother. Anita opens her eyes at all this, as if it reminds her of something. She is about to speak, then Bedrich puts his hand over hers. She twitches and her bangles clink, but she remains silent.

Vicky shakes her head. 'Well, I'm glad you're driving us, but you could do good if you lived.'

After this the talk veers off into people's jobs. Leon was in the army, which explains things a bit. His clothes are rough, but there's a sort of competence about him. He checked the coach when we arrived earlier and reunited me with my map pad and Lindsay with her umbrella. I shouldn't wonder if Leon has been in a conflict, maybe Northern Ireland.

My eyes close, but inside is the image of Kip; a dark profile against the bloom of the lamplight over the river. His lashes and lips are dipping and lifting with his story, his voice sounds now softer now harsher, like sea over pebbles. I'm worried about the questions no one asked. Most of the group, Adam excluded, said something, but our comments chipped at the edges of Kip's story and never addressed his real dilemma. I have the feeling that every-one was engaged in a weird exercise, an attempt to wrap him up in moral cotton wool, something nebulous and comforting. We failed to ask crucial questions, such as what happened to his Mum.

Suddenly I have an urge to tell my story, I want to shock the others with reality. Kip's guilt seems so passive, so forgivable – not for leaving his brother to die, of course – but if his crime is to fail when faced with Solomon's choice then surely no one can blame him. He doesn't deserve to die. He's young and likeable and if he gets to be a paramedic people will need him.

Deserve to die? An odd concept, no one has made him come on this journey. Like me, he feels guilty about his brother. Surely he's as free as me to choose what he does with his life. The session leaves me with another undercurrent of anxiety; how will I cope with the likes of Vicky or sleepy Bedrich, or any of these strangers, quizzing me about my brother?

I must have made a sound because when I open my eyes I find Adam looking at me, one eyebrow raised. Hoping for some fellow feeling, I start a smile but his eyes slide back to the inevitable newspaper and I feel silly.

I need this day to end. Some of the others spent a night in Trieste on the way, but I've travelled from Devon non-stop and I'm wiped out. Ben's fair head is bent persuasively over Lindsay's and Leon is holding court with Kip and Daniel. He's urging them all on to a nightclub. A nightclub! I haven't been in one of those for ten or more years.

I decide to go to bed. Imogen, Vicky, Bedrich and Anita vote the same way; I have joined the geriatric club. We gather to set off and Ben tries to persuade me to swap groups; perversely, I cling to my decision. Adam slopes off independently.

As we walk towards the hotel, Vicky talks about donating bone marrow or kidneys. Imogen regrets that the way we are planning to die – using pills and away from a hospital – means that our bodies will be of no use to anyone. Anita and Bedrich walk behind us and don't join in. I don't mean to, but I find myself confessing how much physical pain scares me, and how relieved I am that we're going to take pills. I'm sure Vicky thinks I'm very feeble, but Imogen is kind. Most people are braver than I am.

We stop so that the other two can catch up and I can't help gazing into a shoe shop window, all lit up with a row of green shoes and then a row of red ones, so different from English displays. I think of Christmas. The half-empty streets are cooling now and dim; they use neon sparingly in Ljubljana. People still wander easily, including family groups. The few lights reflecting in the river look so beautiful they hurt. I make my standard self-check about whether I really want out of all this. I breathe deeply. If only I could

26

go like this, now, between one breath and the next. I feel foolish; so many people across millions of years have already had this thought. We walk, my new companions and I, past the sweet smells from café kitchens. A strange appetite has sprung up in me, I'm hungry again. Imogen and I share a pastry and eat as we wander home. Imogen, who must be at least seventy, starts giggling.

## Ljubljana city – Day two

Someone has moved my bookshelf. At least that's what I thought at first, then I wake up properly with a whoosh of adrenalin. This lingers as I dress for a new day in a new city with new people. I peer down at the street from my hotel window recalling Kip standing in the lamplight last night talking about his sick brother. If he had the money, would he study for his A levels and get on the paramedic course? I still have money from the sale of my house, but I've left everything for my mother. I owe *her* really, not someone I met yesterday for the first time.

Downstairs the sun is streaking into the breakfast area. Those of us who went to bed early last night are bright with tourist anticipation. Some of the others from the clubbing contingent look frankly weedy. Leon has come to breakfast shading his eyes. Lindsay, too, looks brittle; of course that may be the norm for her, she may be, as Vicky claims, a recovered anorexic – all seven and a bit stone of her. Kip strolls in, looking ultra cool in dark glasses.

I mutter sympathetically to Lindsay, as we wait for the bread to toast. She looks in wonder at Leon, a sausage halfway to his mouth, and tells me that he was paralytic at 2 am last night. Apparently Adam was also at the club, but sitting in a corner reading a book.

We gather after breakfast and every time I look up I see Daniel's compact frame in its brown jacket as he wanders amongst us patiently shuffling our needs and abilities. Imogen wants to go to the flower market. Most of us aren't bothered where we go; we're happy to be led anywhere, happy to smell the air in this luminous city.

Vicky, in the same grey tracksuit as yesterday, map in hand, mutters, 'Shall we find a bus? The market's a heck of a way off.'

We all look at Imogen, though to my mind she looks fitter than, say, Vicky or even Lindsay in her dinky skirt and heels. Imogen turns her face up to the sunlight. 'Let's just walk slowly. I need to give last night's ice cream a run around.'

Lindsay turns down Ben's company to go off shopping with Leon, Anita and Bedrich, and we all arrange to meet up in a couple of hours at the market. Unfazed, Ben turns to me. 'Shall we take the scenic route? I'll fall asleep if I walk at Vicky's pace.' I find myself whisked away from the others, which suits me fine. Communal arrangements make me feel herded.

We wander off and get lost. As Ben talks – and he does the talking – I remember the boy from Eton who came to our office for work experience during his holidays. They both show a sort of unashamed presumption of cleverness and competence. In Ben's case I have a feeling it might be justified, yet, if so, why is he on this trip? Maybe he's doing research into suicidal types. Perhaps he works with Daniel – no, that doesn't feel right.

'Wakey, wakey Grace! I shall have to hold your hand if you cross roads without looking.'

'Oh, sorry, I was... thinking of something...'

'...other than my scintillating conversation?'

He's laughing and doesn't seem to mind. We stroll down streets of buildings with walls of coloured tiles in kaleidoscopic patterns. One wall – the unlikely home of the Cooperative Bank – has stunning geometric Moorish doodles on a rose madder background. Dazed, we progress to the subtler architecture of the University district.

The big soft civic buildings of Ljubljana rise up all round us. In the strange limbo we now inhabit, I feel like a visitor from space. The city, this thriving capital, seems to doze in the mid-morning September sunshine. The streets are so quiet you can hear telephones ringing and keyboards clacking through open windows. We hear a nearby piano played with sweeping brilliance and stand mesmerised on the pavement. Another couple pause nearby. As the piece finishes, Ben gives me a quick hug of solidarity. We wait, but there's no more.

I begin to feel undone by the heat and Ben's easy company. I want no confusions in these last weeks, nothing to deflect me from that straight road to freedom. But just as the music has brought easy tears to my eyes, Ben's relaxed charm and long stride, which he halts at intervals to let me catch up, eat into my resolution. We fetch up quite fortuitously on time and at the right place – Preseren Trg, the main square. Quite overcome by our cleverness, we clutch each other in triumph.

From the square we wander across the Triple Bridge and turn towards the market. At most I'd expected cheery displays of lilies and tulips along with the damp earth and gardenia smell of a flower shop; what I actually experience is an invasion by blooms – a simultaneous assault on all the senses. The flower section fills a small square and a narrow street alongside the cathedral. Stalls are crammed with buckets of flowers, flanked by tables on which lie intricately made posies, starry with white and red-beaded blooms.

Petunias and roses, delphiniums and daisies, banks and banks of them fill up my vision. I'm giddy and want to lie down and inhale for hours. The others drift in, mouths agape, and even Adam's eyes widen as he observes Imogen wandering, drunk with pleasure, from stall to stall.

## Imogen

We find a café, but it's a while before we can tether Imogen to a seat. She's tiny, barely reaches my shoulder. There's something taking about her face which makes her age irrelevant. She has traces of dimples and a brightness about the eyes to which we all respond. She starts to talk almost immediately. 'Stewart and I met at University. We were the original postgraduate students, taking Kant and Ryle to pieces in the small hours, convinced we had the answers.' Her eyes crinkle. 'If you have an intellect, you have to work so much harder for sex. We debated all night, trying to find good reasons to get close to each other and yet keeping the paragraphs rolling between us like drawn swords. There was never any question for either of us; in spite of this we took weeks to achieve even our first kiss.

'Flowers were part of it. We went to choose some flowers for my landlady who was in hospital. We walked all through the market in Oxford, sampling blooms. We kept rejecting our choices in order to go on looking and smelling. We bought too many: mimosa, freesia, lily-of-the-valley. In early March the air had a bite to it, but in the covered part of the market it was warm and damp and the smell was Dionysian. We still talked Wittgenstein and Descartes, but the discussion became sporadic.' She shakes her head, lips pressed. 'We even struggled with topics such as the origin of certain plants, about which we couldn't have cared less – funny, this later became a lifelong obsession for both of us.'

Imogen bends her snowy head and fingers the texture on the leaves of the cyclamen in her hands. She looks up at us almost shyly. 'We were unbelievably naive. I'm not sure we even knew what our bodies were trying to tell us. I do remember that when my hand closed round Stewart's as we were taking a bunch of narcissus out of a bucket, I felt as though I'd touched a hotplate and I jumped. He looked startled too. I could see him digesting my reaction and the heat washed through me again.' Imogen smiles into her memory.

'We took the flowers to my landlady, but something had changed between Stewart and me, we didn't know what to say to each other. I had this foolish notion that we'd exchanged all our important ideas and might never see each other again. So I got glummer and glummer and Stewart, so he told me later, nearly ran away. We cycled back to my place and were sort of saying goodbye, when he put his hand on mine on the handlebars. It was an experiment, apparently. He wanted to know if he would have the same reaction he had observed in me when I touched him back there in the flower market. I remember gasping in surprise and then he kissed me.' Imogen hides her face in the flowers.

I glance round the group. What I see in most people's faces looks like envy, but maybe Imogen perceives something else, because her voice becomes dry. 'So why is this old bat telling you about being kissed? I'm trying to make sense of my actions in a way that will make sense to you. Stewart and I were married for forty-four years. We didn't bother with children. It didn't happen and I don't think either of us minded very much. We were so busy, you see. Time sort of flowed past us as we tried to make sense of the world. I doubt the history of philosophy will mean very much to any of you, but believe me it was bread, milk, and children to us.'

'We had other interests in common, we used to go plant hunting in the French Prealps, the Béarnèse Mountains or the Pyrenees; one foot in front of the other, always hoping that round the next boulder the purple starfish heads of *Soldanella Alpina* will peek out of a crack.' She stops once again to fondle the leaves in her hand and stare into her memory. 'We were happy all those years. I don't know how many other people can say that.

'Then about eight years ago Stewart started to get pains in his chest. We thought at first that he might have heart problems, but the GP checked him out and he seemed fine. He had always coughed at lot, but that winter it got worse and didn't improve in the spring. He began to lose weight.

'He had lung cancer, of course. He hadn't smoked for thirty years, but when we first met he'd been a heavy smoker. This is a very common story, so common that we'd talked about it in the abstract over the years. We'd concluded – no extreme treatment unless there's a genuine prospect of full recovery. We'd also decided to go together.'

Imogen pauses, but only, as far as I can see, to confirm her memory. 'Yes, we planned a double suicide. A year or so after diagnosis, it became clear that treatment was no longer keeping the disease in check. There was no chance of a cure, nothing except a lingering and painful deterioration to inevitable death. We talked about what next. We stopped all medication except painkillers and took ourselves on holiday in the Scilly Isles. We sat there on a bench in the splendid Tresco Abbey Gardens, with the great pink blooms of proteas all around us watching the swallows dipping and diving above. Stewart decided the time had come.'

Imogen blinks into the distance, looking distressed for the first time. She adds emphatically, 'I had no problem, *no problem at all*, with this decision. However, Stewart was not happy in spite of all our discussions. He was troubled that here I was, still fit and several years younger than him, yet preparing to commit suicide with him. This was the first...' she looks up, surprised, 'this was the only serious disagreement we ever had. Before this we could always talk things through, agree to disagree or find common ground. On this one subject we simply took opposing positions, with no meeting point. Anyway he said he would honour my choice.' She snorts. 'Honour! What a fool I was. At least I think it was intentional, though I'll never be sure. He had engineered it so that he would be the one to make the final move. Never mind the details; he died and I survived.'

She shoves the plant in her hand down on the table as if suddenly disgusted with it. 'He thought I could still enjoy life after he'd gone, if I only put my mind to it.' She half smiles. 'That was so like Stewart, he believed you could do anything if you put your mind to it. Well, I've given it five years. No one can say I haven't tried. I've had enough. There's no one to care more than a little now, that's one of the rare advantages of age. I've had an excellent run, now I'm going for the final rest. That's it. Any questions?...

Oh sorry, old habits die hard… Oh dear, I am getting into semantic loops here. Never mind, let's have another wander in this glorious place.'

For all her warmth and accessibility Imogen comes over as someone who inhabits an intellectual plane out of reach of most of us. We look at each other. None of us has the appetite for an argument with her. Anyway, why should we; it's her life. I even envy her that she can choose *after* having had it so good.

I spot Anita whispering furiously to Bedrich, but it's Vicky who speaks, 'Imogen, are you still working in your field?'

'Well, I'm retired, but I have a research Fellowship. I've recently wrapped up a collaborative project so all is tidy.'

'It seems a bit wasteful, if you're still doing good work, but obviously it's your choice.'

Leon asks the boldest question. 'Imogen, I'm not being rude, but can I ask, are you taking your life to prove your husband wrong? I mean to show him that you were right and couldn't live without him?'

'As he's not here to appreciate such a gesture, that would be pointless. Anyway I would so much rather have proved him right. I don't like waste, but I can find no point in being unhappy.' She looks at our sceptical faces. 'OK, I'm not unhappy in the sense that I am visibly weeping my life away. The wound is… internal.' She puts her palms together then presses them to her mouth.

I imagine my face registers the same bafflement as those around me. Imogen is one of the most confident, self-sufficient women I've ever met.

She looks at our faces with those bright, penetrating eyes and nods. 'All right, I *will* try and explain. I did my work independently, but Stewart was my sounding board, the other half of my mental squash court.' She stares out at us over her hands. 'Oh dear, it's so difficult to convey loss. Imagine living in a house where the outer walls have been blasted away. There is nothing left to lean against, nowhere safe to lie down, my thoughts and therefore my body are unanchored. Add to that various physical systems starting to pack up and I'd simply rather not *be* any more.'

Leon speaks tentatively, 'What about helping other people with difficult lives? I mean you've already helped some of us.'

'Thank you Leon, it's kind of you to suggest this, but I lack the necessary altruistic streak. I can help people I like, but most of those who need help are not so easy to love. I'm not patient. Anyway, I've made a considered decision. The one thing in life that no one can take from us, at least while we are well enough to be in control, is the choice to stop living.'

On reflection I suppose this is a cheering thought, given our current mission. People can stop you doing almost anything, they can coerce you into doing things you don't want to do, but trying to force a fit person, who doesn't want to, to stay alive, is tricky. Anita is looking unhappy, even disapproving, but says nothing.

I find Imogen's story unsettling on a different front. I assumed that everyone on this journey would be guilty in some way. Imogen appears to be wholly innocent. I don't believe that Kip, whatever he thinks, has committed any crime either. I look round wondering if I'm the only bad person here. Even Adam, leaning over to smell Anita's bunch of freesias, doesn't quite look the part; perhaps I don't either.

## Beliefs

We order lunch, but while we look at the menu a discussion springs up between Anita and Leon. Anita, it turns out, is troubled by religious worries. She seems to think suicide might possibly be acceptable to God if it's a compensation package, as in giving up a life to pay for another. Bedrich agrees vigorously; this is a bargain they can understand. Clearly no life is owed in Imogen's case and this troubles them.

Imogen's dimples reappear. 'Relax, Anita, your scruples don't apply to me. I'm an atheist.'

I feel, rather than see, Daniel picking up the thread. I had foolishly assumed that no one with beliefs would come on an expedition like this, but I should have remembered that religion is very sticky stuff. It clings even to those who think they have seen the light of reason.

Lindsay is leaning towards Imogen her face glowing with certainty, 'But you must have some belief, you're so… good, so thoughtful.'

Imogen replies, kindly, but firmly, 'Thank you, but I think perhaps you are conflating morality with faith. I have no belief in any supernatural power, but I do adhere to a set of morals.'

'But morals are from the Bible.'

'As in The Ten Commandments? Well they're there, but the writers of the Bible didn't invent the rules for good behaviour.' Imogen smiles, 'Lindsay, tell me, do you think that no one was faithful, kind or unselfish before the Bible existed?'

Lindsay is shaking her head. Anita chips in, 'The Bible is The Word of God. From birth we carry our Original Sin and we need guidance to keep Satan out. Without the scriptures and priests to… to shepherd us, people would… would commit crimes, they would be led by the devil, thinking only of themselves.'

Imogen nods, 'Well, I agree with you, Anita, that humans are naturally geared to look after themselves, but I differ about where the guidance comes from. Leaders in all cultures across time have made rules about how we behave. To me the Bible or other religious tracts are more like political ideologies.' Imogen looks at her audience and stops. 'Sorry. Put it another way. Are you only good to please God and earn yourself a nice spot in Heaven?'

I'm not the only one that laughs as Anita jingles with shock.

'You should not speak so, Imogen. Of course I want to please God, but you must do good deeds without expecting rewards.'

Lindsay speaks up again. She looks so doll-like her interventions are always a surprise. 'I try to be good because… because people matter, because people can get hurt. I care about people.'

Imogen nods. 'Precisely. So do I. For me there's no afterlife, no father figure to lavish forgiveness and no salve for my conscience. What matters is here and now.'

Vicky interrupts, 'From an evolutionary point of view, God is simply a way to explain things humans don't understand, and of course a kindly authority to take on responsibility when it all gets too much.'

As Bedrich lays a pacifying hand on his wife's arm, Leon's deep voice intervenes. 'Give over, folks. We're not in school any more. I reckon Lindsay's right and one commandment pretty much covers them all – be kind to others.'

A waiter begins to lower plates of steaming food in front of us and Ben, who has been playing with his mobile, inhales with satisfaction, 'The gods be thanked. For what we are about to receive…'

I can't help laughing and Leon snorts. Anita is whispering furiously to Bedrich.

As we progress to coffee and then onto the coach for a short trip out of town, the religion theme rumbles on. Adam stays out of it, naturally. Lindsay says she attends Quaker meetings. I give her a mental point for this; it's about the only form of religion I can stomach.

Kip says he doesn't do religion, likewise Vicky, Ben and myself. Daniel too, has no God, but could happily, he says, be a Buddhist. The rebirth side of that is a problem for me. Leon is more or less Church of England. Anita and Bedrich are the only Roman Catholics. Given the church's views on suicide, I'm amazed they've come at all. They will, according to their faith, be committing themselves to eternal flames by their actions. I'm extremely curious about what they might have done to invite such a fate.

In the coach Vicky, who likes to get to the root of things – more and more like a badger – sits near Anita and Bedrich and I hear her asking, 'Surely, if you commit suicide it's a mortal sin. However unbearable you find this life, the one you expect on the other side – the Roman Catholic version of hell – will be much worse.'

Daniel suddenly intervenes, 'Perhaps this question can wait, Vicky, until we understand better the pressures Bedrich and Anita have to live with. This is a judgement only they can make.'

I shudder. Even thinking about fire does that to me.

By chance, or possibly design, when Kip parks the bus in a lush village about fifteen kilometres out of the city, we find ourselves beside a chapel. It's tiny, bare and quiet. After wandering round, mostly in silence, we gather outside on a couple of benches flanked by massive pots of scarlet geraniums. Lindsay, still puzzled, asks Imogen if she doesn't feel any sense of 'spirit' in the chapel, any feeling that she shares this planet with other beings.

'Such as?'

'Well I... all the things people say they've seen or heard, like visions or messages from the dead, ghosts, angels or even fairies. I don't believe in fairies, but lots of people do.'

Imogen looks at her in amazement, but with a twinkle. 'Leprechauns and dragons, angels and devils? Myself, I think they all come up in the same bucket from the same well – our imagination. I don't know about anyone else's brain, but mine produces very fantastical beings...' I must have murmured because she asks, 'What's bothering you Grace?'

'Mine does too. But what about all those people over all those years believing all those things – that bothers me. Don't you think any of them are true?'

She laughs. 'Well, take your pick, different eras have produced different theories. The Greeks, Romans and Vikings worshipped humanoid gods; Christians believe that Jesus is definitely the son of God; Jews and Muslims believe equally firmly that he's only a prophet –and so on.'

I didn't think Ben was listening, but he says, 'Well sure as heck, none of them are more right than any of the others.'

I put both hands up. 'I can't believe any of it, but it's funny how long it's gone on and how much it varies.'

Imogen chuckles, 'Mmm, think of naiads, dryads and similar animations of nature.'

Lindsay looks round and opens her mouth but Ben speaks before she asks. 'Nymphs – water and tree, to be precise.'

Anita is shaking her head and re-pinning the brooch she wears on her scarf. I imagine her wanting to stick it into Imogen. Bedrich rubs his hand over his hair, heaves himself up and takes her arm; they walk back towards the little chapel.

I look at the pond beside us where a bird, perhaps a moorhen, is bobbing and poking around the edges. There are leaves just under the surface of the water and something is stirring in the shadows. If only water nymphs and tree nymphs did exist it would be a different world. I wonder if there are fish. Kip said he used to go fishing. When I look around for him, I see he and Ben are doing something to Lindsay's mobile phone. Lindsay sits between them, head bent. I envy her that smooth fall of honey-coloured hair, as I grope through my bag for a band to hold back my own unruly mane. I want to lean right over the water. The only other person staring into the water is Adam. His eyes are the water's colour – darkish grey – unless that's merely a reflection.

Imogen, on the bench nearby, peers over her glasses at him and says, 'Adam, oh silent one, do you have a view on these things?'

We are excited for a moment at her daring.

Without a blink he says, 'Same as yours.' Then, to our surprise, he pats the smooth bark of an overhanging beech and adds, 'Though I've a fondness for dryads.' Everyone laughs. Bedrich and Anita rejoin the group and, with the strange swiftness that characterises these first days together, we move on.

Leon pulls the small speakers for his iPod from his pockets. 'Listen, Imogen, Adam, I bet there are some nymphs lurking in the landscape here. It's Debussy, *L'Après Midi d'un Faune.*'

For thirty seconds mesmerizing flute notes hang in the air then, inexplicably, after glancing at Imogen's face, Leon hits the stop button. Vicky gasps as if slapped, and Leon looks at her curiously. Imogen claims to be tone-deaf and Lindsay says she can never get into classical music.

Leon is shaking his head, he leans towards us. 'Listen!' There's a tremor in his voice. 'Listen to the spaces between the sounds,' he insists. '*Listen* to how one sound leaks into the next. Imogen, you only like words? So, pretend it's a book. Sounds make sense too – like grammar. Lindsay, let the notes in, like warm rain on your skin. Vicky, sorry about that, I'll let it run this time.'

He touches the button and the sounds put us all into a trance. I find that I am beginning to like Leon more than I expected. He seems so shabby and careless, then just now he went to the trouble of finding ways into the music for different people. I knew he liked jazz from yesterday, but this is heavy music – though I have to admit it's not bad.

While the music is playing, Daniel crouches beside me and we look for fish. There are little insects walking on the water, they're probably mosquitos or something nasty; still I think they're beautiful. The afternoon sun is so bright and slanting across the water you can see the tiny dimples their feet make on the surface.

Thinking about the religious stuff, I feel a little as though we've been through a sort of staged joust; everyone being so careful on a subject that often makes people fight. Perhaps it's simply that we are all buttoned-up and British. More likely Daniel has been quite selective; we don't have any of those forceful, ranting kind of people with us. I'm glad he included me.

I've become attached to the little pond; a moment ago I saw a spear-shaped plant with its leaves covered in tiny snails. That's something I've never seen before and perhaps never will again. I wonder if Daniel will let us come back here. It's good to sit about sometimes.

At teatime, as we troop into a nearby bar, I leave reluctantly, though I can still see the geranium pots outside the chapel. A young waiter arrives for our orders. Maybe it's because I've been looking so closely at things, but I have a strange moment of déja vu. As the waiter leans over the table to write carefully on his pad, the back of his head, with the hair cut just so, is in touching distance. It's neat, swirled around a point and tapering perfectly into his neck. I have to resist putting out a hand and burying it in the soft texture. Although I set my mind to work, it refuses to track down anyone from my past to explain this urge.

## Honesty

The day already feels very long, but next Daniel takes us to yet another wide area of grass. It's only a couple of hundred yards from our bar, but green as Ireland and empty as the moon. This country is amazing; the land seems to be open to everyone, with manicured grass and bright tubs and window boxes everywhere, and largely unpeopled.

'Grace, are you all right on the ground?' I realise that Daniel has been handing out folding stools. I try to concentrate as he explains, 'This exercise is especially tough when you don't know each other well, but I'd like you to have a go while you're still aware of the surface that you present to the world. Later, when you're closer to each other we would get different results. This is about using others to understand ourselves. How do other people see you?'

'*O wad some Pow'r the giftie gie us / to see oursels as others see us! It wad frae money a blunder free us, / And foolish notion.*'

Daniel nods, 'Exactly, Leon. Robbie Burns spoke a great truth.'

Imogen is staring at Leon. 'Poetry too; you really are a sheep in wolf's clothing, Leon.'

He grins. 'That's it. I didn't even know it was poetry when I was small, it was just what my Gran-da always said. He was a Scot; he'd recite the man if you came within ten yards of him and the sniff of a Haggis could turn him into a preacher. Sorry, Daniel!'

Daniel calls us together. 'We'll start in pairs, but you're going to spend time with every person, so it doesn't matter who you start off with. I want you to tell the person facing you one thing you don't like about their behaviour – *not* their appearance – but how they act towards others.'

More than one set of eyes slide towards Adam as Daniel goes on, 'I want you to look at each person as honestly as you are able and tell them what happens to rub *you* up the wrong way. This could be a big thing, for instance you feel you can't trust your partner – though this is so big and vague, it's better if you can be specific; you could say I didn't really believe you when you said you worked for MI5...'

There he goes again. What is the truth? Am I in some reality spy show?

'… mostly, though, it is the little things that bother us: that someone uses obscure words all the time, or stands too close, or, in my case, that I let out a little puff of air when I am trying to settle myself.'

There's an all-round chuckle, so I'm not the only one to have noticed this endearing characteristic. He grins. 'Really – it irritates some people like crazy. You may find that each partner refers to a different characteristic in you or alternatively that they all pick on the same awkward point.'

Suddenly I find myself confronting Vicky-The-Badger and feel lost. She kneels awkwardly on the grass. Her rounded sensible face sits within a square haircut, with the strange white stripe down one side, like a painting in the wrong frame. I'm a fine one to talk; I've not had a hair cut in months.

'You're supposed to go first,' Vicky prompts me.

Oh dear, I'm not supposed to be thinking about appearance. I don't like or dislike her. She seems a little nosy, perhaps. Too inquisitive is all I can think of. I tell her so; it doesn't seem adequate. Vicky has trouble with my scatter-brained approach to things. She says I'm too vague. I guess this is pretty accurate.

Next I come to Ben. He has a way of diffusing solemn moments and says he doesn't like the colour of my nail varnish; a backhanded compliment as I don't wear the stuff. Daniel, passing by, says, 'Be brave Ben; everyone has some defects.'

So Ben tells me that I'm too easily moved. 'You should have seen your face when Dan was helping that child in the breakfast-room this morning.'

'But…' I start to protest, then stop. As the little boy was struggling, with only one working hand, I assumed that we had all been overcome by his independence and his condition.

'This is the real world, Grace. You wouldn't survive a day in Mumbai.'

I nod and scribble on my pad, then day-dream of Ben sauntering down a street in Mumbai, like a stork picking his way through frantic parakeets.

'Grace?'

'Sorry.' I have to struggle in order to find fault with Ben. He sits watching me; green eyes sparkling, unblemished skin shining.

Once more I fail to get my head round the idea that he isn't along merely for the ride. Perhaps he's a journalist making a secret documentary. I could really bear to know why he's come. I realise that I've been sitting staring at him for too long.

'Ben, I find it impossible to know when you mean what you say and when you're joking.'

'Are you implying that I'm insincere?'

'Yes. No. Yes, I think I am. Or rather I'm never sure.' He doesn't seem in the least put out.

Leon is easy – with his iPod always in his ears you never know if he's heard what you're saying, and Lindsay who treats us all as if we're dangerous animals. I kneel down in front of Imogen and I'm flummoxed. She tips her head to one side watching me, she's so like a robin that I laugh.

When I get to Adam I see, as I did in the flower market, a softening of his shuttered expression. His dark hair has an attractive upright quirk at the front. In the group he remains silent and impenetrable. Face to face, it's as if a blind has lifted a little way. He seems to think I'm often half-absent – he's right, I struggle to hold my mind still in the present. I look up, trying to think what bothers me most about him. I'm reluctant to add to the list he has collected from the others – sullen, surly, hard-bitten, stand-offish. The seconds tick by as I stare at him. He says very softly, 'It can't be that difficult.'

Something about the way he says it, or the way his eyebrows lift, makes me blush. Furious, I rap out, 'Inconsistent. And I don't like the way you hide behind your newspaper, when the rest of us are brave enough to expose our feelings.' His mouth opens and I see a flicker of something that might be surprise or even hurt, then he drops his eyes and moves on to Lindsay.

I'm still only half way through when I see Vicky has finished. I sigh; I am by far the slowest to finish my list. I want to get it right.

On the whole I'm relieved by the results. Vicky, who has studied psychology, goes into this spiel about me being "field dependent", someone who is drawn into and responds to events around them at all times.

'And yet,' Anita points out, 'Grace is often so detached, she misses what is happening.'

'She daydreams.' Ben says, grinning. 'She's distracted by her own thoughts.'

I can only hide under my hair. I watch Anita and Bedrich while my face cools. They have placed their stools at a distance. I do wonder why they came and whether Bedrich is here willingly. They are, or were, in some kind of a car business. Perhaps they've run someone over, or been involved in an elaborate fraud, cheating old ladies out of their nest-eggs. What about Adam? Did he really deserve all those negative comments? Is he the nastiest person here? Vicky's blunt questions make even Bedrich wince. On the other hand Anita tends to bully with a sweet smile, which I find more uncomfortable.

'Grace? Grace come back to us.' Daniel is waving a hand in front of me. I jump, but he doesn't look annoyed and goes on, 'Some of you may be surprised by what others think of you; others may find you are familiar with your own rough corners. You may have chosen not to do anything about these. Perhaps because you feel they are part of your personality and cannot be changed, perhaps you don't wish to change.'

Of course I want to change… that is I would if I planned to go on with my life; there's not much point in changing now. If I were choosing this minute, I'd be back in my hotel room, but there's more to come.

We have to pick on the quality of someone's behaviour that we admire or wish we possessed. I struggle with embarrassment. What is there to like about big Bedrich, for instance? There is too much to like about Daniel, who insists on being part of the task. People say lovely things about Lindsay and Kip but once again Adam comes out badly. I like the way he notices things that I notice, like the pond today, or the ant yesterday. Is this an admirable quality?

Afterwards, when we talk through our lists and Adam reads out my words, Daniel says, 'Grace, when you say Adam notices things you notice, does that mean that you think Adam is aware of others' feelings?'

Since several people have mentioned honesty or frankness as my plus point, I feel under pressure. I push my hair out of my eyes. 'As in having empathy? I'm not sure if that's exactly what I mean. Maybe we are simply interested in the same things, but I suppose that if Adam recognises that I, or anyone, is interested in something and feels interested too, that is empathy... I suppose the answer is yes.' I feel as surprised as everybody else by my conclusion. The others all look at Adam, who seems to be modelling a sphinx.

Later, as we're all sitting down to platefuls of pasta, Vicky brings up the afterlife yet again. She asks Leon, 'If you believe in heaven, how old do you think your spirit will be when you die? The age you died? Newborn? Or some ideal time in between? And will we recognise each other?'

I think she's simply needling him, but Leon puts down his coffee cup to answer. 'I reckon that spirits, if they exist, are ageless. My problem is whether the personality goes with the spirit. Would my poor, claustrophobic aunt be an anxious spirit, for instance? Would a boring person still be boring?'

I think of my skinny, half-grown brother, whimpering and lost in Paradise, then glance over at Kip wondering about his. Luckily he and Daniel are bent over a map.

Anita is firm. 'We will all be released from the burdens and pains of this physical world and, after we have served our sentence in purgatory according to God's justice, we will be placed near our Saviour.'

Ben is checking his mobile, but he looks up casually at Anita, 'Only those of us who have bought into your version of God; the rest of us will be a load of moaning spirits in limbo, isn't that right?'

She turns on him, speaking sharply, 'Religion is not a fit subject for your jokes, Ben.'

He lifts a palm with a light shrug.

Vicky laughs, 'I didn't think I'd get a proper answer.'

Imogen says drily, 'If no one believed in any afterlife, we might be more inclined to respect the living and indulge less in the slaughter of our fellow men.'

Lindsay surprises me, saying, 'I think I'll go on believing what I want to and not worry about other versions.'

By the time we get back to the hotel, I'm thinking how to escape to my room. Only Leon has the stamina for a late night but Imogen and Daniel persuade him to play scrabble. Ben seems to be attached to his mobile in a series of texts. More and more sinister, I think, this will be his girlfriend – presumably ex – or the editor of Hello Magazine. Adam is buried in his book. Anita and Bedrich are sitting in silence until Daniel stops playing scrabble and goes to talk to them. Coming as a pair has actually isolated them; I still know nothing about them after twenty-four hours.

Suddenly Kip appears. His eyes, with their amazing long lashes are gleeful, like a child allowed to stay up late. He waves a costume and towel. 'I've just found out that Hotel guests have the right to swim in the pool of the Hotel next door. You can reach it from the mezzanine floor of this one. Anyone else coming?'

I jump up. 'Give me a second, I'll grab my costume.'

Ben shakes his head with an elaborate shudder.

Lindsay says quickly, 'I'll come too,' and follows me.

The pool is cold but it gives me thirty minutes free. Never since school days have I had so little choice about my physical contacts, my activities or my conversations. I've begun to feel porous as if these people are getting under my skin.

## Ljubljana Castle – Day three

The plan for today is to go, by one means or another, up to the castle above Ljubljana. To get there we must choose between the winding road or the much shorter footpath. The path presents, according to Imogen's guide book, "a considerable vertical hike". As Kip stands looking up buses for the benefit of the less fit members of the group, I observe Ben charm Lindsay away from the group and set off with her. I shrug, half-relieved. Imogen watches them depart while Bedrich mutters, 'Some people have all the luck.'

'What's that?' asks Anita, absorbed by bus times.

I look at Kip. Last night in the pool he and Lindsay were so relaxed together, but if he's concerned he hides it well. Any relationship will be unpleasantly hot-housed in our circumstances. I resolve to keep my distance. We set off walking: Leon, Daniel, and I, with Adam as a detached follower. The others go by bus.

The path is stiff going, between high walls to start with, then through thick, damp woodland. On one side you can get glimpses of the city growing smaller as we ascend. Heavy overnight rain has loosened the grit on the steep upper reaches; we stumble and slip, Leon gives me a hand over the worst patches. Adam overtakes us and I notice that he's limping. Daniel is as surefooted as a cat; he is inhaling the air like someone released from an underground bunker.

I take a much-needed pause to say, 'You look happy, Daniel.'

He grins, 'I always breathe better at a height. How are you doing?'

'Succeeding in putting one foot in front of the other is my achievement today.'

The sun is blazing by the time we reach the summit and find our way into the great courtyard of the castle. The others, including Ben and Lindsay who have walked up the road route and then jumped aboard a bus from half way, have found a double table half in, half out of the main café building. It's surrounded by plants and away from other tourists.

Our walking party falls thirstily into the remaining seats and we have barely ordered our drinks, when Ben, who's been describing the differences between the castle's position and that of the Parthenon in Athens, says, 'I think I could tell you why I've ended up here.'

He looks over at Daniel who smiles and nods. 'That's fine, go ahead, Ben.'

I look at him standing there; he must be well over six foot and muscled to go with it. His hair is a superb dark blonde and attractively wavy too. He wears it a tad too long for my taste. He can't help knowing how good-looking he is – almost a parody of a male model. That's it, he should be advertising Rolexes. I find his whole presence with us disconcerting. What can possibly be so wrong in his life that he wants to quit?

## Ben

Ben pats the jacket pocket over his heart. Then rises and perches casually on the corner of a nearby empty table. Apart from the checking gesture he looks at ease and I think – he's been looking forward to this. He gathers us by eye until he has our full attention. Most of the people on this expedition are going to need winkle pickers to get their stories out of them, but Ben appears to be a natural for public speaking. He probably ran the debating society at university. We all settle back, almost with pleasure, to listen.

Ben smiles disarmingly then admits, 'I thought I was someone special and I found out I was an impostor. The girl I love is married to another man. Everything I care about most and thought I owned, was mine under false pretences. I can't think of any other way to right the wrong except to take myself out of the equation.'

This resumé comes out sounding practised and detached, like a film producer pitching the plot of his latest enterprise.

'I was eighteen before I knew anything was wrong. I'd taken A levels a year early and had a gap year. I had a place to study classics at Oxford and my parents thought it would be good for me to work for six months in Greece. My father had business friends in Athens, so he sorted me out a flat in the city quarter and a part-time job in the Benaki Museum.

'It's an amazing city, Athens, you can walk for hours and see nothing ancient at all, then you turn a corner and go back more than two thousand years in a couple of steps. Coming up here, even though the architecture is so different, reminds me of that time. I didn't know it then, but I was carefree for the last time in my life.' Ben shifts his position; profile-on and blinking, he gazes across the white expanse of the courtyard. Then he turns to us again. 'My father's friend, I'll call him Daddy Patras – though that's not his name – had two sons, one near my age, and we hung out together, swimming on the beaches at Vougliameni, playing volley-ball, drinking a bit, all innocent stuff. You know, the usual things teenagers do.'

Ben stops and for a second I think he's changed his mind about telling us, but he starts again. 'There was also a daughter, Eleni.' He runs his hand through his hair and frowns. 'I was asked to coach Eleni as she intended to study English at University. I went to some trouble. My father had made it clear I was to be especially nice to them.' He smiles and shrugs. 'It wasn't difficult. When I say she was beautiful, I'm not exaggerating. She wasn't dark, like most Greeks, she had hair like... honey?' he looks around, 'a bit like yours, Lindsay.' As he says this, Ben puts a hand up, perhaps without realising it, to his own wheat-coloured head.

'She had a perfect figure, a pretty laugh and her legs were...' He looks up to gauge his audience and meeting Imogen's eyes goes on smoothly, 'like something off a magazine cover. She was spirited and charming and her English was exemplary. She'd already made a start on the literature. At school they'd been set Hartley's The Go-Between. It seemed an odd choice.' Ben pats his pocket again.

'She was nearly seventeen. Her parents were pretty strict; Grand-ma would sit with us during the two evenings a week I taught her. Of course Grandma didn't speak English.'

'I'm not sure how it started, but the Go-Between had some-thing to do with it, we began to plot how we could see each other outside the house.'

There's a whisper and a rustle in the group and Leon speaks up. 'Some of us here haven't read this book. Does it matter?'

Ben glances at Daniel then resumes, 'Well, it's not really important. It's about a boy who passes love letters between an upper class woman and a cowman and, un-surprisingly, it all goes wrong and the boy is scarred for life. Actually it's a clever book about sexual deception and I guess it put ideas into Eleni's head.'

'*Her* head?' chips in Imogen at her driest.

'Well, I mean, I had ideas about her in my head anyway, but not about deceiving anyone. I don't think she would have had any ideas at all without us reading the book together.'

I can't help laughing at this point and he casts me a sharp glance. I shrug and say, 'She went to school, didn't she?'

'Yes, well...' Ben looks a little taken aback. 'Anyway, she said her parents were forever on at her to learn more about her culture, so she suggested that she take me round some museums during my free days. Grandma wasn't up to the travel, so although Eleni's little brother tagged along with us for the first visit, he got bored and we were free of our chaperone from then on. I think the family wanted to stand well with my father too.' A hint of colour appears on Ben's smooth cheeks, 'They may also have thought I was older than I was.'

I find myself contemplating Ben from a new angle. Lying about your age is something any eighteen-year-old might do but it is odd that he needs to pretend to us as well. When my turn comes I'm planning to tell the whole truth out loud for the first time in my life. Easy to think, perhaps I'll run scared at the last minute.

Ben has started again and I may have missed something.

'... well, we did go to museums.' He looks round, his eyes challenging Imogen, and takes a breath. 'Then she had her seventeenth birthday – big celebrations with masses of cousins, aunts, uncles and godparents. She practically ignored me during this party. So when I took her to a museum a couple of days after, I was feeling marginalised, but it turned out to be all part of her plan.

'Eleni said to me. "There, now I'm really old enough to do what I want. But my parents are so old-fashioned; they don't understand.". She was right; I mean girls from her kind of family would get into trouble just holding hands with a bloke. She'd have been in deep... water if she'd been seen kissing anyone. So – and I know it was stupid – we ended up in my apartment. And... well... it was a hot summer and I didn't have enough Greek to get protection... you know.'

'You know… what?' Anita looks honestly puzzled.

Leon makes a humph noise, 'Rubbers, contraception.'

'Why not say so?' mutters Vicky.

'He's being delicate.'

Daniel waves an arm and Ben picks up again. 'She probably wouldn't have known about such things and we were careful. She didn't exactly hold back though and I was very young.'

Imogen adds dryly, 'She was even younger.'

'I know. We should have known better.' He lifts his palm. 'All right, I should have known better. You can guess the next bit. About three weeks from the end of my stay she realised she must be pregnant. We stupidly wasted time on useless remedies and hoping.' He looks into the distance. 'We thought and thought but we couldn't, we really couldn't think of any way out.'

For the first time since he started, I feel sorry for him. I can see him reliving that moment.

'I didn't have big sums of money with me and anyway Eleni cried when I tried to discuss dealing with it. She was terrified of saying anything to her parents. She said her father would kill her, and probably me as well. In the end with only a day or so to spare before I was due to leave, we made a plan. I know it will sound crazy to you now, but back then it was only way out we could think of.'

Ben stops as a load of kids pile out of the castle and fill the courtyard. They make a terrific racket and it seems to take forever before we can hear each other again at our table.

At last he's able to resume. 'Eleni found her passport and her birth certificate. On the day I was due to leave, we all said goodbye and she went to spend the day with a friend. She rang the friend to say she was sick and joined me at the airport. I know it sounds really corny – we eloped. We flew to England, I borrowed a car, drove to Scotland and we got married.'

Vicky is frowning, 'Oh come on, you don't mean Gretna Green?'

'Yup, you can still get married there at seventeen. We did have a problem, though, you need two witnesses and we didn't know a soul. I had to be very nice to the waitresses in the local café.'

He stops. I don't know what the others are thinking but he's so patently not a married man now that I'm appalled by where this story might be going.

'I'm going to get a drink, be back in a minute.' He slips back into the café.

'What about the impostor business?' Vicky wants to know.

'Perhaps getting married in that deceitful way makes him an impostor,' Anita suggests. 'I cannot believe he truly cares for her.'

Anita's right, he sounds very cool about it all. Then maybe that's just his style to keep emotions under control.

Ben returns with a glass of wine in his hand. 'Well, to cut a long story short…'

'Don't do that.' Everyone jumps. Daniel's tone is mild, but the command in it unmistakeable and the fact that he intervenes at all, a surprise.

'Oh. Yes. All right. I just didn't want to be boring.' Daniel doesn't respond to this, so Ben takes a sip from his glass and says carefully. 'Well, I suppose we shouldn't have been surprised, but the next few weeks were hell. Daddy Patras threatened to annul the marriage on the grounds that Eleni was coerced and that I was after her fortune – that was after he had offered to come and sort me out in person. My father was blindingly furious threatening to disinherit me and throw me back where I belonged. I might not have taken this too seriously, but my mother went bananas, begging him not to do it. So I asked where do I belong then? And my father said, "in the gutter" and then my mother had hysterics.' Ben doesn't look up to see our open mouths.

'Next day he gives me my birth certificate.' Ben pulls a folded sheet out of his pocket.

Anita says, 'Oh no!' under her breath.

'They meant it literally; I'm an adopted foundling. They were childless and needed an heir for the name and the estate. The irony is that when I was ten, my mother conceived – she was over forty – and my brother, James, was born. What I thought was mine, really belongs to him.'

The sense of listening to a fairy story is so strong I look round at the others, but a waiter comes over and we have to order some lunch as we've been at the table so long. Leon mutters to Imogen that he doesn't believe a word of Ben's story.

She says, 'A trifle far-fetched perhaps, but there are such people and Ben fits the picture.'

'If it were anyone but Ben,' I agree, 'I wouldn't credit it.'

The waiter goes, Vicky leans across Bedrich to say, 'And so…?'

Ben smiles, but briefly. 'You want the end of the story?'

Anita says abruptly, 'We want to know why you've come with Daniel.'

'Yes, well. Eleni miscarried in her third month, so no one ever knew about the pregnancy. Her father persuaded her to come home and finish her education and I went off to Oxford. Every time we tried to meet up one of the four parents managed to prevent us. It was worse for Eleni, she could only write to me by smuggling letters out via her friends.'

'But that's medieval!' says Vicky.

'Exactly. The letters dried up and then Daddy Patras offered me a very large sum of money to agree to "desert" Eleni. He made it clear that the alternative would be a meeting with his bodyguards. I was allowed to speak to her on the phone for a few minutes and she agreed that this was what she wanted. So... well, I accepted.'

Leon stands up. 'That's all? Didn't you contact her through those friends of hers.'

'That avenue had been cut off a while ago. What could I have done? Of course, in hindsight I've wondered, but maybe that's really what she wanted. Eleni, when I last heard, is happily married with a child.'

Food starts arriving. This is very unsatisfactory as Ben has still not fully explained the impostor stuff and poor Vicky, ever curious, tries to get him to talk. Daniel suggests that we eat first and let Ben finish afterwards.

Finally, half an hour later, Ben picks up again. 'So, Vicky, you want to know why I'm here. Well, from the day of my marriage my adoptive parents have been aching to disown me. They're probably too decent to actually do it but there's something in the estate's entail which means that the eldest legal son, which is me, gets it all. I've talked to a solicitor; there is no way out for them or me. The neatest solution to everyone's problems is that I duck out of life altogether.'

He stops and we all wait. Surely this can't be it? Then Adam stands up abruptly. 'I don't buy it.'

Ben looks up quickly, a tinge of pink staining his cheeks, 'What d'you mean?'

Adam says as though he is talking about the weather, 'I think there's a bit missing. I don't think that would make *you* quit.' He hunches a shoulder. 'But what do I know?'

This is the most words that Adam has so far spoken in sequence, everyone stares, waiting for him to elaborate. He has finished. We turn to Daniel but Ben jumps in to fill the silence.

'Well, that's it. I don't know what more Adam thinks I should add. I can't live knowing that my wife is married to someone else and that my parents are being forced to pass on to a 'stranger' everything that should go to their rightful son.'

Adam's intervention has effectively pre-empted questions, which would now sound invasive. Bedrich tries, 'Ben, have you looked for your birth parents?'

'No.'

This is very unsatisfactory. Thankfully Vicky does our dirty work by asking. 'Why not?'

Ben twinkles at her. 'I was found in a layby and the police got nowhere at the time.' Ignoring our gasps, he proceeds, 'What if my father is right about the gutter? I don't have the right education to deal with that.'

We can see Vicky is going to go on asking so Leon says, 'Did you ever talk to your mum or dad, after they had cooled down, about your adoption?'

'Nope – it was definitely a closed subject.'

I am confused by Ben's story. He didn't even try for the sympathy vote. Yet his crime is another non-crime, unless you count an affair with a willing seventeen-year-old. Then there's Adam's comment; I can't work out what he's implying – rape? Surely not. It seems clear from mutters around me that few of us believe in Ben's noble gesture. Is it simply that we have no conception of that kind of life?

I can't tell if Ben is hurt. Perhaps his laid-back manner is all camouflage. My sympathy, alienated by his story, is veering back towards him after Adam's remark. Still, doubts have a way of germinating.

On the bus after lunch I sit in front of Vicky and Leon. Vicky has no time for Ben's noble gesture. 'Either he's lying or he's mad. We're living in the twenty first century, for chrissakes.'

'Yes, but it's England. People like Ben still lurk in the upper regions of the class system. The brigadier of my old regiment lived in a castle and owned the local village. Don't forget we have a Queen and a House of Lords.'

# Looking at hands

Half way down the castle hill we get off the bus and walk until we find yet another fresh green patch in the middle of the city. I don't think we've met one mean keep-off-the-grass notice in this country yet. The ground feels dry and warm in the afternoon sun. Daniel sits Imogen down on a bench and the rest of us gather round. There's another game in the offing, I can't tell whether my internal jitters are anxiety or anticipation.

Daniel passes round some numbered slips. 'OK, can you pair up. Everyone with an odd number find the person with the number after yours and sit opposite. Now odd numbers pick up one of your partner's hands. Everyone there?'

I have an even number and I've drawn Ben. Yesterday I would have been delighted to face him rather than, say, Vicky or Leon. Today I feel ambivalent. I kneel down on the soft grass, take a brief look into the green eyes so close to mine then pick up his right hand. His skin feels silky against mine, and the nails are perfect. I chew mine, though they're not too bad at the moment, because I cut them drastically short before I came. It works most of the time.

Daniel starts to talk us through, 'I want you to examine this hand as if you have never seen a hand before, have no idea what it could be used for. I want you to think about it in as much detail as if your life depended on knowing *this* hand again. You might even need to recognise it with your eyes shut. Try not to talk except to ask specific questions.'

For a few minutes I struggle, my mind is full of Ben's story. I think of him with the Greek girl, hands undoing buttons and slipping inside a waistband, on a mad drive to Gretna Green, having rows with his parents... then I remember my parents. After that I find it easier to switch off the thought of him and spread out those pale digits. Has he ever done any rough work? They are creamy smooth, the long fingers narrowing at the tips almost girlishly. Mine in contrast are square and functional. He has the lightest down of blond hairs, around the signet ring he wears. On my left Bedrich takes a firm hold of Lindsay's well-manicured hand and out of the corner of my eye I see Anita reach cautiously for Adam's tanned fingers.

I turn Ben's hand palm up and try to memorise the patterns. I imagine being a microscopic animal and swimming along the major lines and then slipping off into one of the hundreds of tributaries. If I stretch his palm the lines turn into pencilled tracery and in the bright sunlight the tiny furrows and ridges of the skin itself, the substance of fingerprints, emerge.

Now the hand is a dead weight, disembodied: a poorly made starfish. I remember, aged five or six, making the discovery that if I repeat a word, say "cup", over and over again it loses all shape and sense, all connection with the world. The hand in my lap now ceases to have a function, an owner, or any kind of meaning. I spread and prod it; there's no reaction. Behind me I hear Imogen and Kip giggling and remember that I have a task. I search more purposefully and find a line across the whorls – a tiny nick on the forefinger.

I look up, Ben appears to be asleep. 'When did you cut that?'

'What? Oh that, I was fifteen, I think; it was a penknife. I was camping and we'd lost a guy rope, so I tried to divide another one in half. I bled like a pig.'

I shut my eyes and try to learn the feel of that scar. When I open them again I can see a light sheen of sweat on his fingertips. Mine are quite damp too, so I wipe them on the grass. I feel weirdly detached. Perhaps there will be more magic when we swap roles. I fan out his fingers and measure them against mine. Bigger, but not as much as I expected. I close up the fingers and feel along the tips; the middle three fingers are curiously similar in length.

'Do you play the piano, Ben?'

'Yup.'

'I think these are musicians' hands, your fingers would spread well on the piano.'

'I never practised enough.'

'Me neither.'

Our concentration breaks as Daniel wanders over. 'Can you bring your examination to a close now.' He waits a minute until we have all laid aside the hands we are holding. 'Now I want you to swap partners. Even numbers pick up the hands of the next odd number up. I feel a bit miffed thinking I have got Lindsay, who is lovely, but whose hands do not hold quite the excitement of Ben's and whose pearly nails are going to make mine look very rough. Only it turns out to be Adam.

Catching a pitying glance from Anita, I grit my teeth. I look up to see Adam's silhouette against the light, then he drops to his knees in front of me. I avoid his eyes and stretch out my hand, furious with myself because it trembles.

He says mildly, 'It doesn't hurt.'

Coming from him this is almost a joke. I manage to look up and give a small grin. His expression doesn't change, but his mouth has relaxed into a look of concentration. He takes my hand and simply holds it firmly for a moment between both of his. This feels, after all, rather comforting.

He examines my hand much as I looked at Ben's. Yet his hands couldn't be more different. The skin is altogether more weathered and he's so thin that they have no padding just skin, bone and muscle. They are more purposeful than Ben's, but then of course he's doing the looking not the being looked at. Perhaps he's older than I first thought, around thirty-five, maybe he works out of doors a lot. I have some idea that he does carpentry. He has square fingers – like mine.

'No scars?'

'On the other hand.' I pass him my left hand, with the rip mark up the thumb.

'Nasty. Barbed wire?'

'No! I mean yes but...' I almost say but not when I killed my brother, but I have not yet told my story. I wish I could get it over with. I feel a sweat break out as my thoughts flounder. My hand becomes slippery which makes things worse. He says nothing, but runs his thumb gently up and down the scar. Then he lifts my hand and I look up. He is bending over it, his mouth relaxed almost tender. He looks as he did when watching Imogen in the flower market. I take a sharp breath, thinking he is about to kiss the scar better.

I must have moved my hand or something, because he lifts his eyes to my face, they widen and go blank. We both look down. I can see his chest moving too fast. Mine is doing the same. I daren't raise my eyes again, fearing his bleak look. I begin to feel suffocated and desperate for the game to end. Then, thinking the poor devil must find this stressful too, I murmur, 'We must be nearly done.'

He curls my hand over into a fist and surrounds it with his own. I feel very small, though he doesn't grip or anything uncomfortable.

I have no trouble identifying either Ben's or Adam's hands later on but continue to feel unsettled around Adam for the rest of the day and he avoids me too. Not that we have ever sought each other's company, but I pride myself that, like Daniel and Imogen, I have not succumbed to the group hostility.

Kip says afterwards, 'I handle bodies all day in my line of work, but this was something else.' He grins. 'I've gone crazy for Imogen's hands. Don't laugh!' He leans over and takes Imogen's wrists, holding her hands up for us to see. 'Look, I can see through her skin. Amazing! We should do this every day.'

Vicky reaches out towards Daniel. 'Yes, yes, I know exactly what you mean, when I looked at Daniel's hands, I just wanted to take him home.'

We all laugh, but Bedrich becomes astonishingly eloquent leaning forward as he talks. 'I have the answer. Once I shared rooms with a sculptor of heads. He had this… philosophy?… that familiarity gives birth to love. You talk to your subject and you watch him – or her; the way his eyebrows move, the line of his jaw and the way his lips push out and turn in and become cheeks. Then you put marks on his face and so gently measure with the calipers. You press the skin to learn how deep is the bone. In time you have touched every portion of his head then – behold! – you are in love with him. My friend would lean over and kiss the wet clay, boy or girl, old or young.'

We all gaze at Bedrich. Even Anita looks surprised.

'Anita did you know Bedrich had shared with a sculptor?' Vicky asks.

'No. Yes. I forgot. We have a bust by Stefan. I don't think it will be worth much.'

I think she is doing the same double take that I do each time I remember that I'm not going home again.

## Lipica – Day four

It's early on the morning of the fourth day and we're gathering to board the coach for Lipica. This is the home, apparently, of some amazing white horses – though horses have never featured in my life. I had my old nightmare last night then, after an hour or so awake, I slept and had it all over again. At breakfast Daniel asks if I'm all right and I nod, afraid I might blub. Kindness? I have become so used to drifting through life feeling, at most, hunger and sleepiness that I have no safe way to handle all these new sensations. My internal circuitry is waking up – a sort of pins and needles of the mind. I wish I were friendly enough with one of the others to talk to them about it.

Daniel looks at me. 'Come and enjoy the horses, Grace.'

I nod and climb into the coach and Daniel sits with me. We talk about Devon and the different landscapes. I've never even ridden a horse. Daniel tells me a ridiculous story of trying to ride a cow when he was about twelve.

'There's nothing to hang on to, Grace, and their backs are immensely wide with bones in unexpected places. I bounced about like a ping pong ball until I fell off and broke my wrist.'

I don't know what Daniel's magic is, but by the time we are driving between the white wooden fences of the Lipica fields two hours later, my stomach has settled. In a distant meadow a ripple of silver catches my eye as a herd of horses changes direction like a shoal of fish. They settle and browse and you can see the odd dark foal silhouetted against its mother. Everything looks wide, spacious and relaxed, but also unreal and cinematic.

As we tour the stud farm, Ben grows several inches, his eyes shine, his hands go out to the muzzles of the Lippizaner mares as though he knows them personally. He says little except to our guide, but his whole body seems to yearn towards the animals. He's suddenly raw – almost unrecognisable. This is the first time I've seen him without a social veneer.

Later, as we watch the demonstration, our hearts thudding with the hooves, I surprise an odd calculating expression in Ben's eyes. I swear he would have been out there riding given half a chance. Seven great white stallions – only the stallions are taught the moves – manes and tails streaming, are skipping in the most unlikely way to the music, like an oversize *corps de ballet*. I almost fall over backwards as they finally rear up, pawing the air with their forefeet. The skill and the scale are splendid but unsettling.

We're so hungry and awed by the horses that we lunch in Lipica and are back on the road without a story or a game. The morning has felt like a holiday, a day full of marvels. For me the horses are a first. Although I've lived in rural Devon for the last seven years, I'm essentially an urban girl. Most of my life has passed in a series of satellite towns, Chelmsford, Hertford, Reading, Guildford, circling around the sun of London. I have seen more mounted policeman on television than the live article. Horses in their great steaming flesh are a disconcerting collision with reality.

Back on the coach Ben is sitting next to Lindsay and I've missed my chance to ask about his relationship with horses. Several of the others are no longer fixed to their single seats. Vicky and Imogen are occupying a pair in front of me. Leon across the aisle is leaning over in rapt conversation with them. Daniel is sitting at the back with Anita and Bedrich. This expedition is like making toffee, all of us are separate ingredients but with Daniel stirring us up together, maybe there will be a chemical change and we will transmute into a new substance; new people.

When we were little I used to make fudge in a steam-filled kitchen with Mum and my little brother. We would make miniature fudge Easter eggs. This was never easy because fudge wants to crumble if you heat it too much – or is it too little? Chocolate fudge comes out best. It is stickier and makes good egg shapes when it cools enough to handle. I liked to experiment with the shapes. I was pretty mean though; I used to make sure I got the bowls to clean out. Oscar only got second lick.

After he was gone I never licked another bowl. I'm not sure, thinking back, that I ever cooked with Mum again either.

'Grace?'

I jump. It's Leon leaning towards me. 'Penny for your thoughts?'

'Um... I was remembering making fudge and wishing I had a second chance to do things better.'

'Better fudge?'

'Well, no,' I shrug, 'but that too.' He laughs, but it's a kind not a mocking sound and I feel better. Then he leans back and plugs in his iPod again.

Remembering being little has recalled the anxiety of my dream again. Will Daniel make us all talk about our childhood in front of each other? I look behind me and he's sitting there his head bent towards Anita. What have any of us done to deserve that he should care about us so much? You would expect instead that he would struggle to even like us.

Another thing I don't understand is how obedient to Daniel we are. Of course he never *makes* us do anything. He simply asks and we can't wait to obey. Perhaps that's how it works, he's hypnotising us into submission. We each tell our story and then go home.

An appalling thought. I have no home to return to. As my skin prickles with sweat I laugh, realising I have just frightened myself needlessly. The last thing I want to do is pick up my old life again.

I look up to see if my laughter has been overheard and there, as often seems to happen, is Adam across the aisle looking up from his paper. I'm beginning to suspect that I'm a permanent source of amusement to him.

I look away and see Lindsay beside Ben near the back of the bus. In spite of his best efforts, she has her trapped animal look on. I've begun to like Lindsay. She makes funny wise remarks and everyone seems to behave more gently around her. I rather hope she will go home. There must be someone at the other end for her because she keeps looking at her mobile phone.

## Back to the city

Half way back to Ljubljana we leave the motorway for a comfort break and I go with Daniel into a small bar. The others gather on a nearby area of grass with a copse of bushes in the centre and kids playing on the far side. Vicky told me later that as they waited, uncertain which tables to occupy, a ball appeared from the other side of the hill and landed in the thick bushes beside them. Adam strolled over and disappeared into the undergrowth. One minute later the ball was seen flying back over the bushes again and delighted shrieks could be heard from the far side.

Returning from the loos at this point, I see Adam emerging from the bushes, his hair standing up in spiky lumps. Sticky burrs cover his head, jumper and trousers. He turns to look back as Imogen, clucking softly, trots up behind him and reaches out. He flinches and lifts an arm to ward her off, but she shakes her head and he submits, childlike, as she begins picking off the twisted, clinging balls of dry seed.

She beckons the others, 'Someone help, or we'll be here all day.'

I see Ben, Anita, Bedrich, Vicky and Lindsay shuffling forward like nervous cattle and Adam standing there like a scarecrow, covered in burrs and wearing his least inviting expression. Imogen suddenly pops out from behind him and snaps, 'Come on, he won't bite.'

It's so absurd that I call out, laughing: 'Let's all roll on the ground together and share them out?' I surprise half a smile out of Adam, which pleases me, and everyone joins in. Not rolling on the ground but de-burring Adam in a spontaneous group activity. He seems almost human for a few minutes.

This evening Daniel produces twelve packs of cards and we have a noisy game of Racing Demon in the hotel lobby. Ben's eyes and hands move with astonishing speed. He empties his pile while the rest of us are trying to lift the top card. He's either cheating or he does this for a living. He's the runaway winner; his nearest rival is Anita who comes second most rounds, with Kip next. I'm invariably last.

I duck one round to go to the loo and when I come back sit watching the others. Lindsay, who spent the first few days with her shoulders round her ears, twitching at every word addressed to her, seems like a convalescent, looking out on the world instead of hiding from it. Vicky is laughing so much at the chaos of flying hands and cards that there are tears on her cheeks. Leon is playing without being plugged into his iPod.

Adam, needless to say, has made the least visible progress, yet even he's stopped looking over his shoulder every ten minutes. I wish Daniel showed more signs of relaxing. The lines on his face are deeper than at the start. He watches each of us, and anticipates our fears and worries, but we don't seem to have a role in helping him. I can see that Kip deals with all the driving and itinerary work where possible, but there is little the rest of us seem able to contribute. I wonder if something is bugging him. I wish I knew how to make him feel more peaceful.

The day follows me into the night. I'm in a forest, but not in Slovenia because the horses – angry, hungry horses – speak English. I'm bruised, lost among tree trunks, with urgent horse voices and bumbling, outsized bodies slapping me about as they hurry past.

The shadow of the dream still hovers over me in the morning. At breakfast I sit down opposite Leon. He's so solidly human that I find myself smiling idiotically at him. He tilts his head like a question so I explain about my horse nightmare. He's lovely; he has nightmares too. He talks about the dirty fog they leave in your brain and your stomach afterwards. I always like his voice, but never before realised how kind his eyes are.

## Blindfolds – Day five

This is our fifth day and after breakfast Daniel leads us down into the hotel basement. He opens a door and we enter a bare room with high windows and no furniture. As we tread on the cream-coloured carpet he holds out a basket. 'Can you all take off your shoes and put them in here. Socks or bare feet are both fine.'

I look round and hear not a cheep of protest as even Bedrich is parted from his heavy brogues and Lindsay from her heels. Leon has holes in his socks and quickly takes them off. I've always been happier with bare feet.

'For this game I want you to think with your hands and feet only, so we're going to blindfold each other. Grace could you...?' he hands me a basket of scarves. 'Vicky, don't worry, I won't let you fall. I shall stay sighted. Everyone is going to move slowly. There's no furniture in this room, only people – none of them strangers. The carpet, if you happen to fall, is delicious.' Daniel kneels down and buries a hand in the deep pile. We all follow suit, then stay down, like toddlers maintaining safe contact with our base.

I hand out the blindfolds and watch as Daniel goes round raising each person and turning them to face the wall with their palms on it. As he comes towards me I tie my mask, but something spooks me. I squeak and pull it down again. Daniel grasps my shoulder, shakes his head and gives me one of his mini-smiles. He goes on holding me as he talks to the others.

'OK now, I want you to feel your way along the walls. To start with everyone go to your right... your *right*. Other way, Bedrich! Go slowly until your feet and hands understand that they're doing the work, not your eyes. Some of you will go faster than others so you are bound to touch each other. That's fine.'

Daniel's hand on my shoulder is growing lighter. 'Now Ben, I want you to start going the other way – to your left. When you touch Imogen, pat your way across her back, then onto the wall and then onto the next person. That's it. Fine, now Leon, will you start the reverse too?'

Daniel is pulling the blindfold over my eyes but continues to hold me. After a bit he walks me to the wall, 'OK Grace, start from here. I shall stay with you.' I start and he keeps his hand on my back for a while then says, 'Grace, Imogen is going to go past you, you'll be fine.' And I am.

After a few more minutes of this, he asks if anyone feels like letting go of the wall. I am surprised to hear Anita say, 'I'll go. I like this.'

'Well done. Go slowly, hands out.'

'Oh! Sorry!'

Daniel laughs. 'Don't worry about bumping into each other. I wouldn't bother with sorry each time, either. That's great Imogen, go freelance.'

I'm starting to enjoy the multiple soft bumps as I encounter unknown hands and limbs, when Daniel abruptly calls time. We unmask and see Leon still standing palms to the wall in one corner. Daniel has an arm round him; he's crying. A few days ago I guess most of us would have become absent at the sight of a man crying. Now we cluster round and collapse onto the carpet. Leon weeps there in front of us with his head on Daniel's shoulder and Lindsay close beside him.

Imogen passes her handkerchief (trust her to be supplied with such a thing) to Lindsay to give to Leon. I'm distracted by the contrast of Lindsay's perfect nylons laid alongside Leon's bare, rugged feet. Kip, behind Leon, is gently rubbing his shoulder. Vicky asks him if he wants to talk about what's making him sad, but he shakes his head. She looks like she will press him, but then she grips his hand instead. We fall into a patient silence while Leon mops his eyes and blows his nose.

Then Anita says slowly, 'I liked it. I like being blind and walking around. It reminded me of my dancing days; my body felt free.'

I can just imagine Anita, a comb in her curls, bangles rattling, samba-ing across the room. It's a bit more difficult to envisage Bedrich as her partner.

'Anyone else?' Daniel asks.

'It reminded me of my birthday party when I was... eight, I think,' Imogen says, 'you know the game Sardines? I remember hiding in this unlit cupboard, heart thumping, waiting for someone to come and squash in with me. Then my two brothers, my three cousins, and my best friend all cuddled up to me.' She nods.

I look round wondering whose blundering body had reminded Imogen of that security, that tangle of comfortable limbs like puppies in a basket. Whose breath and hands in those blind movements had reminded me of teenage heart-flutterings?

Lindsay, wide-eyed, asks, 'Why didn't I mind... I don't understand. I don't like being touched or surprised. Why should it feel better when I can't see who it is?'

Vicky laughs, 'Because it's only us? I found I was concentrating so much on staying upright, nothing else mattered. I'm getting sort of used to handling people.'

'Yes, but why don't we mind?'

Kip's eyes crinkle up, 'Lindsay, is it that no one here is scary?'

He has a most endearing smile. Lindsay can't help smiling back. She looks around. I see her eyes pause over Anita then she answers, 'Maybe, but even people who sometimes seem cross don't worry me now.'

Ben adds, 'No one here could be angry with *you*.'

As Lindsay relaxes, her arm settles against Kip's. I see him lean closer and then withdraw as though he's thought better of it. My skin prickles as if I'm the one he touched. I have an idea that another fifteen days of this will test stronger wills than his.

I realise that our new confidence is wafer thin. Like Leon, we could crumble in seconds as some unexpected arrow finds the gap in our armour. Only Daniel stands between us and emotional meltdown. He releases Leon, who gives a last hiccup as he plugs in his iPod like a baby settling with its comforter.

Ben stands up somewhat abruptly. 'Are we finished, Daniel? I missed breakfast and am in dire need of a coffee break.' Daniel nods. We scramble into our shoes and head out to the bridge café for coffee, pastries and ice creams.

## Small trains

We are finding seats at the café when Anita suddenly squeaks. 'Bedrich? Bedrich? He's gone.'

We all look round, but he's nowhere in sight. For a few minutes we watch the road by which we entered the square, then we start looking at each other and in all the other possible directions. There are many, many routes in and out of Preseren Trg.

Anita stares at us accusingly. 'He was there, with me. We looked into some shops on the way, but we were all there in a group. Do you think he was… snatched?'

It's difficult not to giggle. Daniel is calm. 'He can't be far away, we'd have noticed if he'd been missing for long. Could those of you with mobiles, go back the way we came and look down all the side streets. He may be lost. After ten minutes call in.'

Would we have noticed?

We go in pairs each with a phone between us: Ben and Imogen; Daniel and Adam; Leon and me; Vicky and Lindsay. Kip stays to comfort Anita who is hovering between anger and irrational hopes.

'Such a great *Stupid* to get lost in this little city! Perhaps he met with an old friend.'

Going back the way we came, we find no trace of Bedrich and twenty minutes later we're all back in the square comparing notes. Anita cannot be held back now and starts off in a new direction. Daniel follows her and the rest of us stare at each other until a waiter comes and asks for orders. Although we only had breakfast an hour or so ago, Ben asks for a bottle of wine and some glasses. This is beginning to feel surreal.

Vicky suggests that he's changed his mind about dying and has run away.

Ben adds, 'I've sometimes wondered how much he's a willing traveller with us. Anita keeps him in his place.'

'He's willing,' says Kip shortly. 'Daniel's careful.'

Kip sounds so convinced it's as if he's known Daniel for a long time. I see Adam nod in agreement.

'Well, I think we ought to ask Bedrich if he's totally happy – assuming we find him,' says Vicky.

'Of course we'll find him, Vicky.' Imogen sounds quite cross.

I'm feeling as though the walls of my safe house have just blown down. While we were all together, we could rely on Daniel, but once people start straying, he will have to run after them and abandon the rest of us. What if *he* disappears now? Adam checks his watch and we all simultaneously follow suit; it's almost funny. Daniel and Anita have now been gone for half an hour.

The wine arrives and we sit round and stare at it. Remembering the Racing Demon last night, I ask Ben if he plays cards for a living.

He laughs. 'You could say.'

'No seriously, Ben,' Vicky asks, 'what do you do?'

'A lot of things, but I can give you a mean game of poker if you like.'

Before we can probe further a voice over my head says, 'What do we celebrate today?'

And there is Bedrich. He has come from the other side of the river. It's over an hour since he went missing, yet he seems barely aware of having caused consternation.

When we question, he simply says, 'Engines.' Then he beams. 'There is a shop for engines,' as though this explains everything. We stare at him. 'Trains. Model trains.' He explains. 'You have to hold them in your hand to feel the weight of the metal, to see the engineering of all the small parts. I would have liked to buy one. The shopkeeper wanted to show me how it ran but...'

At this point we're distracted. Anita and Daniel, summoned by mobile, are advancing across the cobbles. Anita lets out a shriek and Bedrich, after a moment, wisely goes forward to meet her, both hands held out. We can't hear what he says, but her voice is carrying.

'Mother of God – a *train*! For this you give me a heart attack?'

After this, Anita apart, we're all on a high, like children let off punishment. Ben does get a laugh out of Anita when he makes choo choo noises in Bedrich's ear to recall him from some day-dream. Bedrich appears to be totally unrepentant; perhaps he's less submissive than he appears.

In this mood we contemplate the café menu and Imogen points out, 'It's wonderfully liberating not to worry about the future. You can eat ice cream all day without feeling guilty.'

'I still feel guilty,' I admit.

'Me too, look at me.' Vicky sucks in her stomach. Of the women only Vicky and Anita could be said to be the wrong side of the weight barrier and neither too critically to my eye. Vicky adds, 'You don't need to worry, Grace.'

Ben lifts an eyebrow, 'Of course she doesn't, but you can't eliminate the protestant upbringing. I used to suffer, but I grew out of guilt at an early age.'

Adam adds his usual brief and devastating contribution. 'I can tell.'

Ben simply grins and nods. He seems proud that Adam can see through him. As if to reinforce the raffish air he has adopted, he pours himself a glass of the wine he ordered, waving the bottle invitingly towards the rest of us. It's eleven forty in the morning.

Feeling defiant now, I share a glorious ice cream – fruit juice and luscious globes of smoky chocolate and mint cream – with Imogen. Eating this gives me the sensation of being in a time-warp; I could be seven or thirteen or thirty. Imogen giggles as she reaches a spoon into the strawberry syrup on my side of the dish. Even Lindsay, who has these weird fight or flight reactions to food, joins the group frenzy over the last few spoonfuls.

Leon's body size is another matter. He isn't exactly fat, but in these first few days he's been eating and drinking for three; now he seems to be slowing down. I suppose there are now so many important alternatives to eating filling every hour of our current lives. We're all behaving as though his recent tears, not to mention Bedrich's Houdini turn, are everyday events.

Adam sits apart, naturally, and has a cup of tea – even though tea is tricky to get hold of here. Does he ever indulge in anything? Unlike the rest of us he still looks as though he's permanently strapped into an ejector seat.

For myself I have a feeling, and I don't think I'm alone, of coming out of a deep freeze. This is not exactly comfortable; if I mind about these people then I have to accept that what I say or do may matter to them. They're no longer aliens who happen to be travelling the same route. Earlier this morning, blindfolded, with the soft carpet underfoot, brushed by someone's hands and hearing tremulous breathing, I felt something new, an excitement, a potential for… was it gladness or panic? This intimacy has vanished, yet some wisps of the sensation are still lingering.

I want someone to talk to or perhaps a share of the gaiety that clings around Ben. This doesn't seem as foolish an idea as it did a couple of days ago. Before we cross the border Lindsay will surely join up with either Ben or Kip. Maybe it will be easier when my 'confession' is over. Perhaps this will give me freedom to play – that is if anyone wants to play with me – for the next two weeks.

## Grace

As we finish our ice creams Daniel suddenly says 'Grace, do you want to go ahead now?'

I stare. I have never known anyone like Daniel. He seems to have a finger on the pulse of each one of us. I feel hideously unprepared. Why did I think that I wanted it over? I stumble to my feet.

'Or would you prefer to talk another time?'

'No, now, I think.'

Daniel rubs my shoulder and I lean gratefully into him. At the slightest signal I would abandon the lure of Ben's green eyes and walk straight to Daniel, but so would we all. My knees tell me that standing is dangerous. I sit down again and pull my chair into the table. I drop my chin on my hands, so that I can see the sun glinting through the rippled strands of my hair. There's nowhere to hide though, so I shake my hair back. Today there's also a nibbling wind and this adds to my sense of imminent disintegration. I try to secure my skirt under my legs and look up at Daniel.

'OK Grace?'

I nod. With five days to prepare and three examples before me, I ought to know how to set about the task. As always, whenever I try to grasp it, my life turns into a series of question marks.

I dive down the tunnel back to my childhood, then blurt out, 'Why are adults so insistent on punishing children for small misdeeds, but crumble at the idea of their guilt for real crimes? I was slapped for dropping my felt-tips by mistake on the new carpet, but cuddled for deliberately killing my brother.' I daren't look up to see the horror on their faces.

'I can't even pretend it was an accident. I wanted him to die. He was a pain from the beginning. And the beginning was the day he turned up at home. I didn't mind in the hospital, I had new trainers. They made squelchy noises as we walked down the corridor and Dad laughed too and squeezed my hand. Mum was in this high bed with wheels. She let me climb up beside her. My new brother Oscar was all bandaged up, even his head, and he lived in a plastic box. He had his eyes shut.

'Then Mum came back from hospital in our car, our own blue car that glittered when the sun touched it, not the black taxi that took her to hospital. She bent in the back seat and couldn't get out at first. She had the white shawl with the holey patterns against her chest. My shawl. Granny said she had crocheted it for me. She used to push all her fingers through the holes to make people in the snow. Mum sort of fell out of the car and stood on one corner of my shawl and it went all tight and stretchy like a sail.

'Granny shrieked and Dad said "Shit!" and Oscar, who was hiding in my shawl, made cat noises. Mum was cross because I asked if she had a cat in my shawl. That was the beginning. Oscar made cat noises for the next five years.'

'Ouf!' Imogen stands up. 'I can't sit on that stool any longer. How old were you Grace, when you brother was born?'

'Four.'

'And were you and he the only ones?'

'Mmm, yes, but not exactly. There'd been another baby before me, a boy, but he was stillborn. I never knew about him until much later, when I was in my teens. But that must have made it even worse for them when I killed Oscar.'

Lindsay is shivering. Vicky says, 'You're talking as though you were a grown-up who committed premeditated murder.'

Ben scrapes his chair back and snorts. Vicky turns on him. 'I mean it's absurd for Grace to be talking this way. You must've been a little kid when all this happened. Children don't know what they are doing. They don't plan in a cold-blooded way; they're prey to their emotions. You would naturally have been jealous.'

Ben opens his mouth but Daniel stirs and he shuts it again. I only wish they would have an argument. I continue. 'Sure, I was jealous. Sure I was four, but I pretty much decided then and there, when those cat noises started, that he would have to go. I planned it whenever I was bored. I thought everyone would be grateful and look up to me as a kind of saviour when I finally succeeded. Have you ever heard a baby crying non-stop? The poor brat never had a hope in hell. I'd have got him one way or another.'

There's a clinking from Anita's bangles and I wait, thinking she'll speak, but she's watching a small boy licking ice-cream out of a cone. He's holding it above his head to stop the chocolate dripping onto his clean, blue shirt. We all watch knowing the shirt is doomed.

'Go on.' As Adam's drawl breaks the pause, Ben actually jumps and so do I.

I blink at Adam in amazement. 'Do *you* believe me?'

'Possibly. Anyway, go on.'

'You mean you know what it's like to want to murder someone?'

'Yes, and to do it.' Everyone swivels round to stare and then to look away again. Lindsay's mouth drops open and Kip raises an eyebrow, but the others look much like people who have had their worst suspicions confirmed. Adam lifts his chin in a resigned half smile. 'That's for another day. Go on.' His voice is not unkind.

The irritating wind plucks at the cloths on the table and lifts my skirt. I tuck the fabric under again and look round. 'Where was I? Yes, I had these fantasies.'

I look over at Daniel; he nods gently. 'Go on.'

I breathe deeply, 'My best bet seemed to be poison. I made tea with foxglove leaves, because my friend at school, Charlene, said that foxgloves were poisonous. Oscar spat it out and cried some *more*. I tried it myself thinking perhaps I could get sick and gain some sympathy. Nothing happened. It's the story of my life. I make a pig's breakfast out of every scheme and Oscar cried and *cried*.

'The worst thing is, he never got the message. He...' I can feel my lips trembling out of control, '...whatever I did to him, the poor brat would hold out his arms to me for a cuddle.'

Ben, his head angled in silent query, waves a wine glass at me. Up to now I've avoided drinking except during the evenings, it makes me so sleepy, but this time I nod. 'Thanks,' I croak, then get my voice back, 'yes, I'll have that drink after all. You wouldn't think something that happened more than twenty years ago could still get to you. Anyway, by the time he was five and I was nine I'd got used to the idea that he was armour-plated and I was the world's most incompetent murderer – incompetent human, full stop.'

Ben has filled several glasses of wine; he holds one out to me and gives my shoulder a comforting little rub as he sits down again.

'I thought I'd made a success once. I won a cup for high jumping and got as far as the morning of the prize-giving. Then I quarrelled with the girl who came second, pushed her and she fell over a chair. She ended up with a cut, a plaster, tons of sympathy and my prize. She was small and cute, with a neat ponytail; I was tall and knobbly with crazy hair. I think everyone was pleased with the exchange, even my parents.'

I take a good gulp of wine. 'Anyway, even at nine, I still thought there was a lot of mileage in fairy stories. Sleeping Beauty quitting for a hundred years seemed like a good idea, especially since she got the prince out of it.' My eyes flick, in spite of myself, to Ben's. 'I tried pricking my finger, but never seemed to get the spell quite right, so I thought I'd practise on Oscar. Maybe I'd succeed in finishing him off if I were just researching my own long sleep.'

'We were on holiday in Somerset, on a farm. One of those holidays when the grown-ups forget you because you're quiet. Oscar and I spent most of the days in the barn playing with the farm kittens and jumping from the half loft onto a pile of hay. The days were warm, soft and prickly, with straw up our noses and in our hair, and kitten fur and needle claws on our bare limbs. We got plenty of scratches from them, but I thought the wicked fairy had something a whole lot deeper than a kitten scratch in mind. I found these funny old tools on the wall in the barn.'

Anita who has been to the loo and been filled in *sotto voce* by Vicky, gasps, 'Oh no!' She looks disgusted.

I glare at her. 'You want me to say it was an accident? Well it wasn't. I was the Prince and Oscar was Sleeping Beauty – that's the way round we always did it because he was so much smaller. I found a tool with a long knobbly point, like a rough bradawl, that looked most like the picture of a spindle in the book. I told him to prick his finger, but he was scared. I pricked my finger on some barbed wire to make it fair. He held out his hand and shut his eyes. He was astonishingly compliant. I pricked him, the blood came and needless to say he cried; it must've hurt a lot. I wrapped it in a tissue and gave him all the jellybeans we'd been saving for tea.

'That night it was still hurting, so I washed it and let him sleep with my snuggly if he promised not to tell mum.' I take another swig of wine. 'Sometime in the middle of the night I hear him crying and he's in Mum and Dad's room. I can hear Mum get up and go to the bathroom and then I hear my name and I know what's coming. She comes in and yanks me out of bed to look at Oscar's finger and it's really red. She starts quietly enough, "Look what you did! You did that!". Then she gets louder and Dad comes. They give Oscar Calpol and take him back to bed with them. Then the next morning it doesn't look so bad, and Oscar says he's OK. He doesn't like the doctor.

'Anyway, he gets plenty of attention for a few days and I think it's going to be all right. Then he gets sick with a fever. He's often sick, so they feed him more Calpol. Then he starts to make funny jerks and gets really bad and Dad takes him to Accident and Emergency in the night because he's all stiff and he won't wake up. They think he has meningitis and it's really serious. Then when Dad comes to swap with Mum, he tells her that it's maybe tetanus, because of the finger prick, which is better than meningitis, because he must have been vaccinated. Mum says to me, "You realise that if Oscar dies from that wound it'll be your fault". And yes, before you say anything, I know that she was only trying to frighten me.

'They never sorted out about the vaccination. He died three days later of a heart attack due to generalised tetanus.'

Vicky is shaking her head, 'Listen Grace, I'm a biologist. People have this idea that you get tetanus from rusty metal. You don't, you get it from the microbes in the old faeces of animals. Almost anything in a barn could have infected your brother.'

'The hospital thought the most probable entry point was the puncture wound in Oscar's forefinger. And there's no way I can delude myself into thinking that was an accident. In fact if he had survived, no doubt I'd have found another way to finish him off.'

Silence. I don't look up. I've done it now. No-one will want to talk to me again.

Vicky is still shaking her head. 'But you didn't mean to kill him, did you?'

'I don't know. I don't know exactly what I expected in the moment that I pricked him. I half expected him to fall asleep. For the next few years I still wondered if they had got it wrong and buried him when he was only asleep, only I couldn't explain that to Mum or Dad. I certainly didn't expect what happened. I was so used to failure. But however I look at it. I. Killed. Oscar.'

Anita leans over the table, moves a glass of wine away from Bedrich and says, 'Grace, this was more a tragedy for your parents than for you. I think you're over-dramatising your role with an episode of childish fantasy.'

I duck under my hair. I can feel the tide of red burning its way from my neck upwards.

Daniel lifts a hand. 'Anita we're not here to judge, we cannot know the weight that presses inside each of our individual minds. This isn't the easy route for anyone here.'

'No, but think of her parents.' Anita jangles with intensity as she stands up. 'They lose a baby, then a young child and now Grace proposes to take her own life. If she feels so guilty she should be trying to bring them joy not giving them further anguish.'

'We know nothing of Grace's parents. Hold always in mind how little we know of each other's lives.'

I lift my head. 'My father died two years ago. Mother phoned me once last year. I phoned her before I left to come here "on holiday". I even asked if she'd mind if I stayed abroad. She didn't seem to care either way.' I can feel the colour receding from my skin at last. 'Anyway, I have caused my parents such anguish, I can only imagine that my death will come as a genuine relief to my mother.'

Lindsay falters, 'But grandchildren? Surely your mother wants grandchildren.'

'If I had children, what on earth do you think would happen to the poor bastards?' I leap up and walk over to the bottle to refill my glass. 'Knowing my luck I'd kill them by mistake while trying not to. I tell you, I can't organise the proverbial piss-up... .' I tip the wine bottle and of course slop it over the table as well as into my glass. 'See!' I lift the glass, but my throat is so tight I'm not sure I can swallow the wine.

Ben leans over and clinks glasses. 'Bottoms-up! Don't let the buggers grind you down.'

To my amazement Adam walks over, casually mops the spilled liquid, removes the glass from my shaking hand and puts it back on the table. 'Tell me how your parents reacted at the time.'

Once more the group is rustling at his involvement. No one speaks and being too astonished to protest, I continue. 'At first they were angry with me for playing with dangerous stuff. As time went on Mum got crosser and Dad got kinder. I heard them arguing. Dad saying: "She's only nine years old, Jessica. Nine! It's our fault for not looking after them properly, for not double checking the vaccinations." And Mum saying: "She knew perfectly well what she was doing was wrong..." Then Dad: "Don't say it, don't even think it. She's a child, she's nine for Christ sake" and so on and so on. But I knew that Mum knew.'

Imogen stirs, 'Have you ever talked to your mother about it?'

'No. What could I possibly say? Very sorry, I meant to kill Oscar, but I never expected to succeed? What *could* I say to her? She's never once talked to me about Oscar, but she knows; she *must* hate me.'

'What about therapists? You could explain to them. I mean you assume your mother hates you, but maybe she feels as guilty as you do. Maybe she thinks you hate her.'

'No... I don't know. I think there was someone, a doctor – a psychiatrist perhaps – who came to the house afterwards. He talked to me a lot; there were tests with paper and crayons and puzzles; nothing to do with Oscar. Dad didn't like the man who came. I never really understood, maybe the man told them I was sick or even mad... I have this memory of a fight between Mum and Dad, and Dad shouting "What if they take her away too?". He told me to avoid people who wanted to delve into my mind, so I have. We moved house soon after Oscar's death. I thought it was to hide from this man who might take me away. I'm not so sure about this now. Dad was in the Civil Service. They moved him around every few years.'

I have to sit down again before I disintegrate. I can't cope with the wind or the wine. I want to put my head in my arms and howl, or better still, go to sleep. I look at Daniel, hoping he will stop it for me. Instead he asks, 'What about after your brother died? How did you feel then?'

'Well, the thing I remember most was confusion. I expected his death to be final in some way. When you're little nobody tells you about the consequences of things. I mean being dead is returning to the earth or, if you think that way, going to heaven. It should stop there, but it doesn't. I always had this worry about him being asleep really, even now I dream about this. I didn't realise that Oscar *not* being there would be as bad as him being there. I could see it was bad for Mum and Dad. I guess in my fantasies I never thought about what they'd feel. I thought most people found Oscar as much of a pain as I did. Poor Mum and Dad; it didn't matter that it was too late, they still argued and argued about what they ought to have done. Then they cuddled each other. Once in a while they cuddled me too, but I felt so guilty I would wriggle out. They thought that unless I cried I was happy and didn't mind. Adults don't have a monopoly on grief, they don't feel more simply because they're bigger.'

'So you still miss him?' Lindsay sounds sympathetic.

'No, of course I... yes, I suppose... I can't define it. I only know that the world has been a mess for me ever since then. I keep trying, but I can't get it right. If he'd been here as an adult, maybe it would've been different. I can imagine almost anything, but I can't imagine Oscar grown up. He's stuck where I left him – a snot-nosed five-year-old, who was moronic enough to trail round after his murderous sister being a pain in the arse, until she finally finished him off.' I pull on my jacket hoping this will wrap things up, but I struggle in the wind. Leon helps me and as he holds my arm, I suddenly remember something.

'After he'd gone, do you know what I missed most about Oscar? Him clinging round my ankles. It used to send me crackers. He'd be sitting somewhere and I'd walk by and he'd grab me with his cool skinny arms and hold on, a sort of mini rugby tackle. That's what I missed, the contact, that cool flesh on flesh pressure. He didn't smile much, but he seemed to need me. He... Have I done enough?'

Lindsay looks troubled, 'Can I ask one more thing?'

'Sure.'

'Why now? I mean all this happened a long time ago. You're young and attractive and... sorry, I just want to understand.'

All round me there are eyes; busy eyes full of questions, anxiety and concern. I look up and high above us a silver bullet is drawing a white line across the bluest of skies. I have no answer. In a way the decision to leave life has followed on inevitably from the decision to end Oscar's life. It's just taken a long, long time. I look down; they're still waiting. 'There isn't a 'single' reason, more an accumulation. I can't make a go of anything. Each time I think it through I arrive back with my brother. He... he hangs out permanently in my mind.'

The jet stream above has spread into a woolly banner. The square is full of quiet buildings and noisy tourists. Why is there so little correspondence between people and buildings? Yet in a concert hall or an airport, say, the buildings are in charge of people's behaviour.

'Grace? Is that it?'

'Sorry. I don't know. Until I was nine years old, I had a purpose in life, however reprehensible. Since then I've felt dislocated, unintegrated, ungelled. I'm a collection of useless, aimless desires – no I don't even have desires – I'm a collection of left-over jigsaw pieces. I've become a watcher not a participator. I once heard this piece on the radio, it ended, "and he will never come again. Never, never, never, never, never.". That was it. I cannot undo what I did. Oscar will never come back. Never, never, never, never, never.'

'King Lear,' mutters Imogen.

There's a long silence, then Daniel lifts a hand. 'Enough. I think we order food.'

I grab a menu and bury my head in it. I've done it. It's over.

## Shopping and swimming

This afternoon we are free to explore Ljubljana. We finish lunch and Imogen sits back with a grin, 'Well I'm going to read and snooze; old ladies' privilege.'

Vicky says. 'I need to buy some clothes. Grace, I was wondering... would you mind helping me?'

I stare at her. 'Sure, but...' My limbs are still vibrating from the effects of making what I can only think of as a confession of murder. The last half hour has been a battle to swallow my lunch. I don't know what I'd expected: ostracism, disgust, criticism, certainly not an invitation to look at fashions.

I look up to find Vicky waiting, badger-striped head to one side, handbag ready over her shoulder.

'Sorry! Yes of course…' Apart from the timing, I am a little taken aback to be asked at all. I don't remember successfully advising anyone, certainly not about clothes. '…but wouldn't you rather have someone more expert than me. What about Lindsay?'

Vicky laughs, looking down at her customary jogging bottoms, 'Better not, she looks as though she eats Vogue for breakfast, which wouldn't suit me.'

I can see that there's too much of a stretch between Vicky's grey pyjama-style trousers and Lindsay's pink blouses, narrow skirts and heels. 'Imogen has lovely clothes.' I suggest.

She shakes her head. 'Well, if you really think I can help…'

'Oh thank you. That's such a relief. Your clothes look comfortable without heels or bows or anything, but they look pretty too and… D'you know, I'm tired of being so sensible. I'd like to splash out just once before we go.'

I can't possibly refuse and, as we set off, Leon comes trundling after us. 'Can I join in? I want to look up concerts. Maybe Vicky could do with a man's canny eye before she dolls herself up.'

I can't help laughing at Leon, who has barely changed his shirt since Trieste. He shrugs and laughs too. We set off in an upbeat mood. It is only an hour since I told the whole truth about Oscar – out loud – for the first time in my life.

Half an hour later we're standing in a shop with Vicky in a pale green flared skirt and a cream T-shirt. She has a better figure than I'd realised and the clothes hang prettily. As Leon says, she looks a treat, but she seems unable to actually buy anything.

Leon is watching, head on one side. 'How old are you, Vicky?'

She looks glum, 'Nearly forty.'

I summon a vague grin, hoping my surprise is masked.

Leon simply nods. 'It's your hair, pet. When did you last have it cut?'

Apparently never – her mother used to cut it, and now she always cuts it herself. Within minutes Leon has persuaded her into a salon and by wild sign language is telling the hairdresser how to cut it. An hour later Vicky's white stripe looks more like a feather in a dark hat. It frames a still sensible face, but with so much more appeal to it.

We smile, but Vicky stares back at herself, tears starting. The hairdresser's face falls. 'But that's someone else,' Vicky whimpers. 'I look like… I'm not… Do you know, they called me Badger at school.' She glances in the mirror at my scarlet face. 'It's all right Grace, I don't mind, I'm used to it, it feels almost friendly. But…'

Her lip is still trembling and I'm thinking we've made a terrible mistake and there's no way back. How can we convince her that she looks prettier now. The hairdresser leans over and strokes a hair into place. At last a wavering smile crosses Vicky's face. 'I didn't know I could look like this.'

Leon puts his hands on her shoulders. 'Well, now you do and we need to find some stunning gear to go with it. Come on, pet, let's get spending.'

We return to the clothes shop where Vicky, like someone released by wearing a mask, actually spends money. I don't know why she came, but my guess is that she'll return home at the end of this trip. I let myself weave a harmless fantasy about Vicky and Leon.

When we rejoin the others, Vicky's new hairdo provokes a party atmosphere. We all feel like making the most of the city, but can't agree on an outing that suits everyone. In the end we split up; Daniel, Vicky, Leon, Anita and Bedrich go to a concert. Kip fancies a swim and so do I along with Lindsay, Ben, Imogen and, unexpectedly, Adam – probably because the alternative is Bartok or Stravinsky or similar. This music is Leon's choice; he keeps surprising me.

I fetch swimming gear, feeling relieved that Imogen will be joining us. The strange atmosphere in which we now live has reduced us, or perhaps only me, to the uncertainties of our teen years. Imogen represents the token adult who will see fair play.

The play that troubles me is the undercurrent of rivalry between Kip and Ben over Lindsay. It seems obvious to me that Kip and Lindsay are attracted to each other. I suppose that doesn't necessarily put another man off. Ben might be planning to outsmart Kip, who will surely be no match for him. Also, looking on, I'm not at all sure that Kip will bother to make a stand. It worries me that I care enough to even think about it.

I change swiftly and reach the pool in time to see Adam dive in, a long curving arc that covers a third of the distance into that small pool. What little flesh he carries turns out to be muscle. When he turns, I dive in with similar bravado; swimming is that rare thing – something I can do. The cold jolt drives the breath from my lungs and I swim hard to justify my heavy breathing and to keep the circulation going.

Kip and Ben arrive together and sit dangling their legs in the water. I have to laugh; they look so like teenagers at a bus stop being cool. They do make a stunning picture, the dark, slight, almost teenage-smooth body against the bulkier, but well-shaped blond one. They're talking, but the damp air swallows their words. I climb onto the small springboard to watch them. Lindsay, arriving, slips quickly into the water, surprising me by her unexpected courage. Kip follows fast and Ben is still hesitating on the edge when Imogen arrives.

The boys splash around for a bit, looking frankly amateur beside Adam who is pure delight to watch as he slices the water with clean glittering strokes. Then Ben takes to the springboard where he looks good – and he knows it. He starts a diving competition – the bigger the splash the greater the kudos.

As we acclimatise to the temperature and leap haphazardly off the springboard, the bursts of laughter would lead anyone to see us as a holiday group. Imogen watches and smiles but Adam continues to plough up and down at speed. Ben, out of sheer devilment, yells out a challenge to Adam to dive. Adam hoists himself smoothly out of the pool, immediately runs along the springboard and with one bounce, leaps higher than any of us and splits the water like a blade. We're still clapping when he comes up. He even smiles, but he won't repeat the performance.

As we all leave the pool I notice an area of scarring on Ben's back, a snail-track of rough dots disappearing into the waistband of his trunks. They are neither operation-neat nor totally haphazard: a mapmaker's puzzle. I want to ask but I'm too slow. Then, when we are dressed Ben suggests that we all go for a coffee, thus frustrating any move by Kip and Lindsay to disappear into the night together. Adam has vanished and Imogen turns down the invitation to join us. I feel as though our chaperone has gone missing.

In the café I ask Ben about the scars on his back.

'A serious error of judgement.'

'An accident?'

'Something like that. Certainly a lesson learnt.'

I don't quite like to pry further. Ben keeps us all laughing and sprays compliments randomly. Kip is almost silent and I begin to wonder, maybe he is gay. Then as we walk home Lindsay trips on a paving slab and Kip's hand is instantly at her elbow. She leans against him, laughing as she pushes her foot back into her shoe.

He lets go almost at once, but I'm sure he cares. Then Ben reaches a casual arm around both me and Lindsay, kissing first one then the other. I let it happen, knowing myself for a weak fool, who is simply next in line if Lindsay is not available.

## Predjama Castle – Day six

I climb the familiar steps into the little blue coach and sit on my usual single seat. This is only the sixth day, but it seems like another world. I can't remember being this… not exactly happy so much as settled, as if I'm at last an adult instead of an overgrown child. Oblivion this instant would be good, *or* to live like this forever. I'm used to thinking two opposing things at once – what's unexpected is that one of them's so positive.

The new Vicky boards – new hairdo that is – she hasn't quite made it into her new clothes today. I have a little rush of pride. I don't ever remember feeling so genuinely useful as I did yesterday, zipping Vicky into flattering trousers while Leon made us laugh with his, 'Bonny, right bonny!'.

Today we're heading south-west of Ljubljana again. Not having bothered with a holiday for years, I find this whole tourist thing rather odd. I think Adam feels the same, but the others, especially Imogen, clearly enjoy it. We arrive at Predjama Castle – a great white building jammed into the side of a mountain, a sort of cross between a stately home and a cave. The most notorious of its previous owners was both a robber and a philanthropist. He was betrayed and ended his days hit by a cannonball while sitting on the privy. I don't see how you achieve a quirkier death than that.

Once inside, the building turns out to be a giant, eerie den gouged out of the rock. I climb up the iron steps to the roof of a cave section and get left behind by the main party. This decides me; I've had enough communal gawping in chilly caverns and sneak out for some warm, fresh air.

The sun has now reached the corner of the castle and is creeping at a microscopic pace across the courtyard as I slide onto a bench with my coffee and my map notebook. I'm careful not to attract attention from Adam who sits poring over his newspaper. The others are still inside. Did Adam skip the tour altogether, or did he march blindly through all that prehistoric drama determined only on coffee and the – by now surely irrelevant – English news?

76

I wonder if Daniel's bothered by Adam's resistance to change. Everyone else is making small or even large shifts – witness Vicky's bravery. Adam's reserve has barely eased since day one. Unseen, I study him. He's looking less intimidating than usual. Perhaps the remoteness is only for when he has to face people. Now, with his lashes veiling his expression and his mouth relaxed out of its habitual line, he looks to me pleasant, even attractive. There are deep creases round his mouth; he must have smiled at some time in his life. Perhaps he prefers animals to people.

I daydream a puppy gambolling up to him and then picture him transformed, pulling at the creature's soft ears, exchanging pleasantries with the owner – an owner I endow for maximum contrast with zig-zag-patterned trousers and a pink angora top. I grin at my little scene. In that moment Adam's eyelashes lift and he stares blankly at me. I laugh out loud at the contrast with my inner image. One of his eyebrows rises.

'Adam, do you own a smile, or have you foresworn charm until death?'

Even as the sun reaches his face to highlight the creases around his mouth, they deepen. The other eyebrow rises and I watch his lips curve in a smile. It might be a trick of the morning sun, but I think warmth is sparkling in his eyes. His voice even holds a suggestion of a laugh, 'I won't have to keep it up for much longer then, will I?'

I gasp. 'You fraud! You glower at us for six days, as if you've never known the word happiness, and now you… switch on.'

He shrugs, the smile dies and he returns silently to the paper. I might as well have imagined the transformation along with the puppy. I begin to wonder who and what he is. There seems to be a sense of humour lurking somewhere under the layers.

As we leave the castle and travel back towards Ljubljana on by-roads, the sun thins; this is our first day here with a greying sky. When we stop beside a river to eat the picnic lunch brought from the hotel there's a cool dampness in the air. I unpack my sandwiches, feeling genuinely hungry for once. This must be because I now belong to the club of those whose stories are out there. I can afford pity for those still to tell. Like others in my position I look around in curiosity for the next victim. As we finish Daniel lifts his head, but he doesn't have to ask.

# Adam

Adam looks into the distance for a moment, then says, 'OK Daniel, shall I... is everyone ready?'

Ready? We're alert, fascinated; we can't wait. Adam's face, once he starts speaking becomes expressive. The others have seen so little of this because he's habitually silent or extremely brief. His eyes, the darkest of grey, seem to deepen yet further. His mouth appears to be shaped by what he is talking about as though he can hardly control it. Perhaps that's the reason he keeps it clamped shut so much of the time. He doesn't stand or anything, simply talks from where he sits cross-legged on the ground, his hands moving softly among the blades of grass.

'Like Grace, I planned to kill. It took me a long time but I managed to go through with it in the end. My dad was loving and generous to me...' He has been looking at us, now he concentrates on his fingers, 'but I killed him. I did it with an axe as he lay with his ear to the tarmac on the old road through the forest by our workshop. He was showing me how to listen to vibrations to detect an oncoming horse or vehicle.'

No one moves, but an invisible drawing-in of skirts takes place; the distance between Adam and each figure in the circle of onlookers increases. No one else has admitted to using violence. I'm taken aback by his fluency. Never hearing more than one sentence out of him has led me, at least, to imagine him barely capable of coherent speech.

He looks up again. 'It gets worse. I was fifteen and slight, but tough and used to splitting logs. I got him across the neck – an execution. He died at the first stroke. My uncle Derek, his brother, came flying up the road moments later. He started cussing and swearing. He had this white shirt on and he turned my Dad over. The blood spurted up on his arm and chest. I'd dropped the axe, so he grabbed it and took a swing at me as he knelt on the ground. He got my leg before I scarpered. It was easy after that. I told the police he'd done it.'

Adam doesn't pause, but his glance flickers over Anita who gasps, hand over mouth. The rest of us have our mouths open too, but no one else makes a sound. 'Derek, my uncle, had been quarrelling with my dad over Grandpa's land. No secret. He could be rough, and I'd never laid a finger on anyone. I'd none of Dad's blood on me; he was drenched in it. He'd got me with the axe, quite a deep gouge, clearly not self-inflicted. His DNA was all over the handle. Open and shut. He got life. He came out this summer; he's looking for me.'

Imogen breaks the silence. 'Why, Adam, why?'

'Why kill my dad? Why blame my uncle? That's another reason the jury believed me. Why should I kill my father? Everyone knew we got on. To kill him I'd have to be mad or have a reason and we were one perfect family, my mother, my sister, my father and me.'

Alerted by the very lightness of his tone, I ask fiercely. 'But you weren't, were you?'

'No.' Adam, who is still sitting cross-legged, leans over, presses his hands on the grass and looks up at the mountains. 'Not exactly and not even a family.'

'What d'you mean?'

Adam hesitates. 'I told my mother the truth last year, when she was dying. Though it turns out she knew all along. I thought…' He looks round our circle of avid, appalled faces. 'Do I need to go on? I'm a murderer and a coward. That's what you expected, isn't it? It's enough of a reason to cop out.'

Leon stands up to put on his anorak. 'A bloody good reason. I should think you also had a bloody good reason for doing it, and I could stand to know what it was.' He sits down again. 'You'd have needed some guts to kill your dad with an axe when you were fifteen.'

Adam lifts his eyes to Daniel and waits. His mouth is clamped shut again.

Daniel half smiles. 'You don't have to tell us anything you don't want to. Of course we'd like to be given reasons for your actions. We're all hoping to feel better about what we've done or feel a fellow feeling with someone who has made decisions we too have wrestled with. Or even, you're quite right, to enjoy feeling less wicked than you. Telling us would be doing *us* a kindness.' Adam shakes his head but he doesn't speak.

I lean forward. 'Can you tell us why you weren't even a family?'

He looks up as if to check what I am asking, then down at the grass again. He surprises me by answering. 'My dad and my uncle were related to me, but my younger sister was adopted from a relative of Mum's. Mum only told me that much after the trial, when I changed my name by deed poll. Mum died nearly a year ago now.

I've changed my name again since then.' Adam gets abruptly to his feet. 'I'm going for a walk.'

Adam's taut figure sets off at speed along the riverside path. He is so thin that he appears almost as tall as Ben, but when they stand together Ben tops him easily. Everything about him is wound up like a spring. Even when he's sitting reading, he looks ready to run. The way his dark hair, which is cropped evenly short, stands straight up at the front only adds to his startled air.

Vicky, watching him, sighs. 'God, I didn't know how vulgarly curious I was until now. I feel cheated.'

Imogen says, 'I have a feeling that may be the first occasion he has told this story out loud. Give him time. He needs to digest his own words. I also detect a fastidious mind. He may feel that even if he had his reasons, no excuse can honestly justify such actions and who would disagree?'

We're silent. It is not easy to imagine a sufficient reason for killing a loving father – even if he turns out not to be your sister's father. How big a moral stretch from there is it to accommodate the shuffling of blame for this murder onto an uncle? Never mind the cowardice of running away from the justified revenge of his uncle. Adam has certainly made no effort to poll the sympathy vote. I look at Ben to see if he's enjoying a bit of *shadenfreude*, but he's talking to Lindsay. Daniel and Kip go to check the oil or something in the coach engine.

'Adam was a teenager at the time, do you think he was into drugs?' Vicky suggests. She looks around for an expert and fastens on Leon. 'He has that famished look about him.'

Leon shakes his head. 'I doubt it, not the type. Druggies are weak, like me, not resolute. Anyway his skin's healthy and his eyes clear.'

Ben lifts his glass. 'He said his dad was kind and loving but he refrained from saying he loved him back. My bet is that he hated him for some reason. Perhaps he had his pet dog put to sleep when he was little, like my Mum did. I never forgave her.'

Anita shivers. 'Maybe he's mad or perhaps he was temporarily possessed.'

Imogen snorts, 'He's saner than most of us and I detect nothing more evil in him than an understandable desire to keep the rest of us at arm's length.'

I feel impelled to add, 'I think he's sane too. I think he must have discovered something really bad about his dad, something in his past life, like... like, I don't know, say he was once on a life raft and pushed someone overboard, or something you can never forgive.'

I look up to find Leon shaking his head at me. 'That's some imagination, Grace. Bet it gets you into trouble.'

I begin to blush, but Vicky saves me from having to answer. She suggests, 'How about bigamy?'

Imogen gets up. 'Well, I don't like this speculation, especially behind his back.'

Ben grins. 'Our moral authority. Well done Imogen!' He picks up a Frisbee and shies it at Leon. 'Catch!'

## Singing in the city

This evening we wander round the city as a group. Outside a bar in a side street a local band is playing. After a while we realise that the music is a free for all. Audience members are taking turns. Daniel returns to the hotel to deal with some paperwork and Adam peels off and disappears in his usual way.

Imogen, Vicky and Leon have their heads together and call me over. They're worried about Daniel. Vicky is sure he's lost weight.

Leon is nodding. 'Well, I couldn't sleep the night before last and went down to the lobby at 5 am to get a drink from the machine and he was there, working on his laptop. He had a pile of papers. He joked with me and said he'd always been a night owl... but I agree, I think he's overstretched.'

'Did you get any sense of what's troubling him?' Imogen asks. 'It's not, for instance, money worries, is it?'

'Could be, but I didn't get that impression.'

We all agree to try and take over some of Daniel tasks and Imogen goes over to the others to fill them in. We stand about for a bit listening to the music and Vicky asks me what I make of Adam's story. I realise that I've been thinking quite hard about it, but feel baffled. 'He must have had a reason. But however you look at it, murder's never justified is it?'

Vicky makes a face. 'I don't know about that. I think Ben may be near the truth with his thing about a dog being put to sleep. Maybe he's seen his father having it off with a sheep, or something. Rural people get up to all sorts.'

81

Slightly uncomfortable with this idea, I'm glad, at first, that Lindsay interrupts, 'There was that guy who murdered mares, don't you remember? A fetishist or Satanist or something. Yuk!'

Leon turns round. 'What's that?'

Vicky laughs, 'We're trying to think of any reason why Adam should hate his father enough to kill him.'

'He'll tell us when he's ready. Hey!' Leon turns, distracted by seeing the dais momentarily free of singers. 'Come on, there must be something we can sing for this lot here.'

He's already oiled by a few pints, and climbs firmly into centre stage. We all shuffle back ready to dive for cover. He starts singing *Bridge Over Troubled Water* in a confident baritone and we relax.

Leon follows this with *Hey Jude* and another guy joins him on electric guitar; come the chorus we all join in. I can't believe it. Here I am in Ljubljana taking part in a karaoke session with a biologist (at least I think that's Vicky's job), an ex soldier, a retired university don, a recovering anorexic, an ambulance driver and Ben. I've no idea what Ben does for a living, unless he's the undercover reporter I keep imagining. He only jokes if you ask him directly.

After Leon's third song, a couple of German teenagers with guitars take over. They start with an Abba song in English. Imogen and Ben are chatting like old friends, though, as always, his gaze is on Lindsay, who's standing, eyes shining, between Vicky and Kip. All three are singing an enthusiastic chorus to *Dancing Queen*.

I turn, sensing people in the shadows behind me. It's Anita and Bedrich doing some kind of old-fashioned dance together. They looked absorbed, serious and totally detached from the rest of us. Bedrich leans over and says something in Anita's ear, she giggles and looks over at me watching and shrugs in a friendly way. So I give them the thumbs up. I'm glad they are having a good time too.

This is all way out of my normal reality. Later, as I mark up my maps with our wanderings today, I toy with the idea that I've died already and that there's an afterlife after all. No. Even purgatory wouldn't feature a sing-along bar in Ljubljana.

## Volcji Potok – Day seven

The rain sounded all last night; yet standing by the bus this morning I see that the sky is end-to-end blue. Vicky is approaching rather self-consciously in the trousers and the trainers we bought the other day. She's always going to appear singular, but she looks more stylish in her new clothes than she did in her sagging track-suits. Ben sweeps off his cap in an elaborate mock bow and we gather her up into the coach. Our mood, perceptibly lifted by this effort on her part, we drive off into a wet, bright world.

We're heading North out of Ljubljana, our objective the arboretum at Volcji Potok. Bedrich and Anita try unsuccessfully to opt out. I also struggle to get excited about trees, but by now I'm prepared to wander down any path of Daniel's choosing.

We leave the coach in a gaggle and Imogen mutters, 'Damn! Shit!' As she inspects her sleeve where it caught on the door. I didn't even know she could swear.

This place keeps on surprising me. In the park there are trees of all colours, as you might expect, but at home by this time of year, the leaves are limp and dusty, here they're vibrant and shimmering fresh. Most strange to an English person is the juxtaposition of different styles; Serious Landscape, Dainty Cottage, Plantsman's Heaven – all co-exist. There are also novelty areas, where people with fun ideas have had their way, an Alice world with a giant chair and a quarter-sized Eiffel Tower, miniature lighthouses on lakes. There are areas of bedding, both beautiful and zany, on a scale that would shame the roundabouts of Milton Keynes; elephants made of sedums, peacocks out of hillsides, all of this spread out like a banquet at the foot of the mountains.

We wander and gaze, darting this way and that like children at a beach, followed by the gentle drone of bees. The cheek-by-jowl contrast of the natural and the artificially tailored areas feel a bit like coming across a Parisian catwalk on Mount Everest.

'It's not my kind of garden,' Imogen admits, 'I like my plants on an empty crag, but for some reason the Slovenes can pull this off.'

Adam nods towards the wilder sections, 'I settle for this.'

A spontaneous remark! Perhaps telling his story, even in truncated form, means that he'll start to relax at last.

For those greedy to see the whole show, a track with a small train runs in and out of the exhibits. Ben persuades Lindsay onto this miniature transport and Kip, Vicky, Bedrich and Anita all join in. We wave them off and Ben sings out "Good-byee, Good-byee, wipe the tear, baby dear, from your eyee," as they tootle away.

I feel a sudden forlorn prickling at the sight of them receding. I don't understand. What can it possibly matter that in two weeks time we'll be saying goodbye for real? I'll be beyond caring within hours anyway. I watch them as the little train veers left and disappears behind a bank of scarlet Canna Lilies. Who is it I mind about? Perhaps I've grown to depend too much on Daniel, who will, presumably, return home at the last border. Even our Darby and Joan – Bedrich and Anita – little though I have in common with them, I'd rather not send them to their personal hell-fires.

I feel a hand on my arm and look up to see Daniel. 'Grace? What is it?'

'Nothing, I... What actually happens at the border Daniel? I mean in two weeks time? I know you can't tell us exactly where we're going, but what actually happens?'

He puts an arm round me and we follow after the others. 'Do you mean after we've crossed or are you worried about how we will separate if some people return?'

'Both. What happens if some people don't stay to the end? And on the other side…?'

'It depends, but we'll probably take our bus and I'll arrange transport for those going home. If only a few choose to cross the border, we might take a taxi. There's no need to decide for a while. Where we're going you will be comfortable, safe and not alone.'

It sounds as though Daniel is going to stay with us to the end. This is a relief, though I now have a new anxiety that he might get into trouble for being with us when we die.

'Please let me do the worrying, Grace. Concentrate on feeling the world around you minute by minute while you make your choice.'

'I made my decision years ago.' I mutter.

'That's fine. I meant don't worry about the arrangements, or the other people.' He smiles, 'I'll take care that everyone is able to carry out his or her wishes.'

We meet up with the others in an empty area of the park and gather round a bench for a light-hearted telepathy numbers game. Daniel says 'one', then, without conferring, someone has to say 'two' and so forth. The trick is to communicate silently so that there's no duplication. We quickly get the hang of this. Then Daniel makes us do it with our eyes shut and the results are pretty chaotic.

Afterwards Anita seems a bit miffed, 'Daniel, what was the point of all that?'

'Body language,' Ben supplies, 'that's what it was about.'

Vicky puts her head on one side. 'I suppose so. I had to watch everyone at once. But what about when we had our eyes shut, what then?'

Daniel smiles. 'Well you found other ways of communicating, like touching, when you were close together.'

Leon says slowly, 'I needed to be aware of everyone equally; not only the people I usually talk to, but everyone.'

'Wonderful. What is it Grace?'

'Daniel, I think it made me super-alert for a moment.'

Ben flicks my hair saying, 'There's a first time for everything.' Everyone laughs.

I don't mind. 'You know what I mean,' I protest, 'I don't think I've ever listened so carefully to people's breathing.' I feel chuffed to see Daniel's eyes crease warmly.

He says simply, 'Well done. I hope it was fun, too.'

We eat our picnic lunch in the arboretum. Then, in what has begun to feel like a pattern, we home in on a bench. Imogen, Anita and Bedrich sit down; the rest of us spread ourselves on the grass. I see Bedrich whisper to Anita who shakes her head.


## Leon

Suddenly Leon squares his shoulders. He has big shoulders, like a boxer or an athlete who lost fitness many years ago. His face is well lived-in, but not unpleasant, with sad, understanding eyes below heavy brows and a balding head. There are some brown curls at the back and sides. I relax, ready to be soothed by his warm tones.

He takes a resigned breath. 'I guess it's my turn.' He hitches himself up onto a small cast iron table beside the bench and starts talking before we've settled. 'Well, you've probably all sussed me by now. I'm a wreck. I have nightmares – every night, and that's when I am lucky enough to fall asleep. Insomnia's my middle name and...' He glances at us from under his brows, purses his lips in a grimace, shrugs and then laughs, '... I have – I think this is the first time I've admitted it, come to think of it this may be the first time I've spoken the words out loud – a bit of a drink problem. I'm unemployed; I live on benefits.'

Bedrich opens his eyes and Anita twitches. Leon responds instantly, 'It's OK Bedrich, I'm not a freeloader. I've paid my fees, or rather a friend paid for me, and he gets my cello.'

Bedrich lifts a lazy palm. 'I didn't say anything.'

Leon grins. 'I have long since lost track of whether I have any excuses for all this incompetence. I was OK until the age of twenty. At least I think so. Though I never quite belonged anywhere. Something my primary school teacher said gave my parents ambitions. I guess they thought I would be their ticket up the social scale but I failed to get into the local grammar school. They were so disappointed I finally agreed to have music lessons on my ma's old cello. Not that she or anyone in the family had ever played it – or any other musical instrument that I know of. Ma boarded some refugees in the last war and they left it behind. I fell in love with my cello, but it was uncool to play classical music where I grew up, so until I was sixteen, I keep it a secret. Then it was OK because I could play jazz. I practised during the night. How my parents or sister ever slept, I can't imagine. I failed half my GCSEs and ended up in the Army. In 1982 I found myself, age twenty, on a troopship in the South Atlantic, heading for the Falklands.' He looks into the distance, puts a hand in his pocket then pulls it out empty.

'My parents and my sister are still waiting for the boy they say they remember to come back from that war. They blame all my failures on that campaign. They tell me what a fine member of the human race I was until I went to war, but I don't trust my memory or their version of events. In fact I don't trust anything much. Yes, I've seen psychiatrists and had therapy, nothing seems to work for very long. I guess I just don't have the guts to live with my past. I'm so tired, I want out now.'

I look at Leon and try to imagine him fresh and young, playing cello in some dive in Liverpool or out on the tiles with his buddies.

'And in case you're wondering, I am not the kind of war veteran you should admire or feel sorry for. I did my bit, but I wasn't injured once. I was stretched sometimes. We marched long distances; I was tired, cold, wet, sore-footed and of course scared shitless – I'd done this stuff in training, so no surprises there – but I was never in pain. I had no impossible decisions to make; my best friends weren't killed. You might say I had a cushy war.'

Leon stops. We can see he has not come to the end, but it's as if he has run slap into a wall – some great, bruising barrier between this point in his life and everything that comes after. It's clear he can't jump over it. He pulls out the iPod that lives in his pocket and begins rolling the flex between his finger and thumb. He half lifts an earplug then seems to recall that he's in the middle of something. He doesn't put the little white box away, but his hands drop to his lap. He is rocking backwards and forwards muttering something; "Jesus", I think. We all remain attentive and silent.

'OK. There was stuff that happened in the Falklands that I couldn't – still can't – handle. It didn't happen to me or my friends, but the images got blasted into my retina, into my eardrums and into my taste buds and they're there to this day. No doctor can undo brain changes; drugs or alcohol can dampen them, but there they wait ready to grab you again whenever you sober up. Perhaps it was the same for everyone, and I'm the only wimp who can't handle it, but there we go. Music helps, but it's a transparent blanket, you can see what is waiting for you on the other side when you switch off.'

He pauses, lifting the iPod and putting it down again. Finally, taking an almighty breath he starts again. 'East Falklands, Galahad and Tristram, remember?' Imogen nods, several of us make uhuh noises. Kip and Lindsay look at each other with questioning shrugs, but no one is going to interrupt.

'We had crossed from San Carlos to Fitzroy. We were feeling cocky; things were going well. We soon got to Bluff Cove and started to receive the landing force. The two RFAs – Royal Fleet Auxiliaries – Galahad and Tristram were anchored in the bay, full daylight. The Argentines simply rolled up in Skyhawks and bombed them – sitting ducks. The ships were full of ordnance and, of course, men – Welsh Guards, poor devils. The ships went up like firework factories: orange fireballs, freezing blue sky and black smoke, like some kid's picture of a naval battle. We were on the beach. These guys were jumping overboard into the burning oil. You couldn't escape the fire into the water; the fire was *in* the water. The smell…'

Leon stops and looks round at our faces. He knows he can't do it; convey to us his experience. He bends his head and I can see that tears are not far off. I look at Daniel, but he's simply waiting.

We will Leon on. 'The smell filled your lungs and eyes. After a bit we could see nothing. People who knew what to do were running around like crazy. They did everything they could. I'm told it would have been much worse without them. But for units like mine, we had no role, we were just spare, ready, but almost in the way, with nothing we could do. Have you seen the guys who survived? We saw the guys who didn't.' Leon twists away from us, eyes closed, mouth distorted in disgust.

He opens his eyes again, but only to stare at the ground as he continues, 'Later we had to march inland. I think it was that same day, but it may've been the next – or even two days after. There was chaos; we were given three different orders in one hour. Whatever. We arrive in this godforsaken hole at dawn – another stunning, cold day. Seconds before we reach the site, the ground judders. A small ammo dump has blown up in the face of the advance party.' He stops again and looks up at us hopelessly. We probably look like kids in a playground to him.

He sighs. 'You've seen pictures in papers after a suicide bomber…' he leans forward hands spread out, 'sweet Jesus! they don't tell you a thing. Nothing. There's no smell of burning guts in newsprint; no whimpering and screeching; no taste of singeing hair in your mouth. No faces with the eyes missing.' He rubs the back of one hand across his forehead then down over his mouth. Suddenly he is speaking fast.

'One lad, same age as me, his intestines hanging in front of him, on fire, his legs wrecked. He sounds like a cat being raped. I'm damn sure I see the sergeant shoot him in the head. I don't know if anyone else sees it. That's a crime. Maybe I hallucinated it. If it happened, it was the kindest, bravest act I saw in the whole campaign. He made nothing of it. Just set about checking for mines and clearing up the mess, like he was tidying a house.'

Leon shudders, puts in his earplugs and switches on his iPod. We all wriggle a bit feeling there should be some further discussion. Suddenly he pulls his earplugs out again and says with a shrug, 'I didn't *do* anything. Now it's too late, I can't go back.' He replaces his earplugs and without any drama allows the tears to roll down his face. He abandons us without moving an inch.

Vicky goes and sits beside him on the table, shoulder to shoulder. He doesn't look up or move. Usually if she helps she does so at arm's length, purposefully, efficiently but coolly. Now in her stylish trousers, with her striking hair eased out of its new cut by the wind, she seems to have acquired another persona. The woman beside Leon seems easier, more accessible. I feel sad that she didn't discover this other self years ago.

I guess this thought is presumptuous. She didn't sound happy about her earlier life when we shopped. Her parents seemed to have both controlled and disapproved of her. Working in a biology lab does not, apparently, count as a suitable occupation for a woman, at least not their daughter.

Nobody says much as the minutes pass, then Leon removes his earplugs and sips his beer and Imogen asks, 'I want to understand, Leon. Does the world seem trivial to you now after the scale of events you witnessed in The Falklands?'

'Not trivial, unsafe; like living in a giant sieve and knowing you could fall through the holes any time. I thought I could walk away from that fear.'

Ben says, 'What about…'

But Leon interrupts, 'And before you ask, I've tried veteran's groups. I've tried digging roads and stacking shelves, but I don't last long. I even started an Open University music course. I've tried and, god knows, my family and others have tried to help me. I see other vets regain their self-respect and return to work leaving me still on square one. Being here works up to a point. You lot…' He rubs his shoulder against Vicky, still perched on the table beside him. 'It's crazy, the only thing I miss is my cello. You'd think I could cope for these last three weeks of my life without it.' He touches his iPod. 'I have to have a cello fix every day.' He shrugs. 'I told you I have an addictive personality. I cannot…' He looks round as if surprised to find us all still there, '… I cannot survive without music. That's weird now I come to think of it.' He looks down at his hands, blinking. He doesn't see Vicky reach out and not quite touch his hand.

Instead she says, 'Leon, can I listen to some of your music. I used to play violin.'

'Vicky! Of course.'

She laughs. 'I never got beyond grade six. It took up so much time and my parents insisted I give it up when I was thirteen. I was never going to be good enough to be a professional musician. For them it was always all or nothing. They wanted me to concentrate on getting into the best university.'

As she talks, Leon is fiddling with his iPod. He looks round for a moment, untucks his shirt and carefully polishes the earplugs on one corner. He leans over to put them in Vicky's ears. She blushes as his hands touch her hair and her hand half rises to take them from him, but then she submits. I look round, suddenly realising that it's the same for all of us. Every day we are trying, tasting, testing things we have never experienced in our lives. We have no tomorrow; no raft of censorious relatives to tell us what we should and shouldn't do. The route we've all chosen means that now is our last, our only, opportunity to try certain things.

'Listen. Listen to this.' The ugliness of the last twenty minutes slips from Leon's face as he sets the music going.

We all sit in silence as Vicky listens, her solid round face intent and open as a child's. Her expression doesn't change. I feel a moment's frustration; surely an exchange between the listener and the music should be visible on her face. After four minutes Leon presses a button and she removes the earplugs. We all wait.

'Bach?' she asks.

Leon grins. 'Yup. The St John Passion.' That's my favourite piece of all time, 'Mein Teurer Heiland – My Dearest Saviour – cello and voice, my two instruments.'

Vicky has a slightly lost look. I'm unable to work out if she hates it and doesn't know what to say, or is completely knocked out by it. Luckily Leon has no doubts. 'Again? I listen several times to a new piece – then it works its way into my bloodstream.' She nods happily, and we all sigh. She pushes her face forward, lifting her chin like a child, for him to put the earphones in again. This time it's Leon who blushes.

Ben mutters, 'Vulcan and Aphrodite, well I never.'

Imogen supresses a laugh. I feel that happy, vicarious tingle of witnessing a flicker of warmth between two people; two people who in another life I might have ignored.

## Journey to Ptuj – Day eight

We stand round the coach ready to set off east from Ljubljana for the Roman town of Ptuj, all of us trying to pronounce this impossible conjunction of syllables. I get the giggles as ten adults, like a Greek chorus, chant variously Patuj, Putwee, Tuwee to the hotel owner, who answers all our attempts with Puhtooey – or something similar. He is still dissatisfied with our version as he waves us off. After all this I expect to land up in Wizard of Oz country.

I'm not sure if Daniel engineers it by sitting next to Vicky, but there's a shift in our usual seating positions in the coach. Ignoring empty places, Lindsay chooses to come and sit beside me although this leaves Ben to find a new companion.

This is a real surprise. Lindsay seems so much the victim of fate, the straw dropped into the whirlpool, that I expect her to wait passively while Ben and Kip continue their curiously polite dance over her. She's reacted minimally to both Ben's blatant admiration and Kip's almost reluctant kindnesses. Perhaps by sitting next to me she is taking control.

Lindsay turns to me. 'Grace?'

'Uhuh.'

'Grace, do you mind if I ask you something?'

'Of course not.'

'It's about telling my story. I don't think I can do it.'

I change gear. 'Um, well, I'm sure Daniel will let you off. In fact there's nothing to stop you saying no. Why don't you talk to him? He must know your story, he'll understand.'

'He doesn't know it all. I wondered if you could tell it for me.'

I am open-mouthed. 'You've not told him? You want *me* to?'

'Yes, you're more like me than anyone else here.' I continue to gape, unable at first to think of a single common factor. Lindsay, like Kip is in her early twenties, at thirty-five I'm the next in age, I think, but that's about it - unless she, too, has killed a sibling.

'Is it because your story is like mine?'

'No…' she shakes her head vigorously, 'no. I'm not… it's my own fault… but I haven't done anything.'

I push my fingers through my hair. 'Lindsay, you need to ask Daniel. If he thinks this is a good idea, we'll talk again, but I can't agree to anything without him. Have you tried asking anyone else?'

Lindsay's glance lifts to the figure behind the wheel. He is out of earshot. 'Yes I told Kip I was scared. He said to talk to Daniel too. He thinks my courage will grow, but I can't do it, not in front of everybody.'

'I'm sure Daniel won't force you into anything. Could you do it if someone helped you?' Seeing her eyelids droop with disappointment, I add hastily, 'I'm not saying I won't do it, I'm only thinking of different ways to help. Can you tell me why you think I'd be the right person?'

'Well, Vicky said how kind you were about her clothes… and you're not as old as the others and you're a woman.' Lindsay is clasping her hands as if in prayer, 'You understand about how I feel about…' she stops, head bent, but her eyes fly towards Kip's shoulders behind the wheel.

I don't have any subtle ploys to hand. 'It's Kip that matters, isn't it? I think you should ask him again, not me.'

'But he's not a woman.'

I've lost the thread somewhere. 'Does that matter? Why do you need a woman?'

She looks at me and tears start running down her cheeks. Seeing her face I feel an unexpected urgency. 'Ask him, Lindsay, ask him. He's an ambulance driver, he's trained to help people. He'll know how to advise you. This is your only chance.' Lindsay puts both hands over her face. She seems suddenly a child. I put an arm round her. 'You don't want to cross the border do you?'

'I did. I do. Only now I can't bear the idea that other people will die... that Kip will die. Before we came we were only deciding about ourselves.' This is an echo of the thought I had yesterday; a complication that I would never have dreamt of prior to this journey. The tears trickle through her hands. Glancing up I can see Kip's eyes in his mirror. Ever watchful of his passengers, he is aware of Lindsay's distress. So too is Imogen who suddenly appears beside us.

Through her sobs Lindsay goes on, 'I want to hold him back anyway I can. His dad will mind, I know he will. So much kindness, so much... beauty to be ended deliberately. It can't be right. But how can I stop him.'

Over her head Imogen says to me, 'Kip?'

I nod. To my astonishment Imogen then walks up the coach and stands talking to Kip as he's driving. A few minutes later he steers into a motorway parking area. Daniel has joined us by this time. He leans over Lindsay and, with a flicker of a smile, he pulls her head against his chest and kisses the top. Then he walks to the front and slips behind the wheel. I move out of my seat as Imogen escorts Kip to Lindsay.

Kip stands looking down at her bent head for a moment as the tears continue to spill between her fingers. He takes an enormous breath and, as the coach starts moving again, sits down beside her.

All these moves happen so neatly and quickly that they feel almost choreographed. I haven't imagined them though, because Imogen is now sitting beside me nodding. 'Sorry if I startled you, Grace, but I think those two needed their heads knocking together and I've never been very patient when I feel sure about something. They're far too lovely to call it quits at this stage in their lives.'

'No, I'm thankful you came. I agree with you but I didn't know what to do.'

Lindsay talked about beauty, Imogen called them lovely. Should we find the loss of beauty so disturbing, so heart-wrenching? I'm trying to think of a more appropriate thing to be regretting. Ever since the arboretum visit, I've been imagining some members of the group going home. Lindsay and Kip and the yearning that so evidently exists between them are top of my list. I can hear the murmur of Kip's voice, soothing, continuous. The calm acceptance of death I felt at the start of this journey has evaporated, not with regard to myself, but to certain others.

What was Daniel's moment of emotion all about? Perhaps, like Bedrich's sculptor, he loves us because he knows us so well. I am still mulling over these thoughts when we arrive midmorning at Ptuj. We cross the great Drava river at the point where it spreads into the Ptujsko Lake and I have this sensation of entering another country, another era. The lake looks almost like a coastal estuary. This miniature city not only feels, but actually is, half Roman.

While we have coffee, Kip tucks Lindsay into his arm and disappears. I check Ben out, but he appears indifferent. I pray that he doesn't interfere. After this we wander through the town.

We're in a sort of art gallery craft shop, when I look up and see Imogen with tears in her eyes. She's standing looking out of the shop window and blinking. 'Imogen? What is it?'

She sighs and shakes her head. 'Nothing.'

'No, tell me.'

'It's so trivial. I crave this scarf,' she laughs. 'See, your sympathy is wasted.'

'Well, buy it.'

'I can't; that would be irrational.' Her fingers caress the silk, which has a delicate watercolour painting on it in peaches and greens. 'Stewart would have liked it. He used to buy me a scarf on each of our holidays and I would buy him a tie – men used to wear ties in those days – I have a lot of scarves.'

'So what, buy it.'

'I'll be dead in a fortnight.'

'Wear it for a fortnight.'

She shakes her head, pats the pile and leaves the shop. Leon comes over and says, 'What was all that about?' I explain and he says, 'I'd buy it for her, but look at the price!'

I look and my jaw drops. Then I think why on earth would I be worrying about my diminishing pounds now. 'OK, I'll buy it for her,' I say.

In the end Vicky, Leon and Adam help out. Adam, amazingly, contributes most.

Ten minutes later we catch up with the others outside the archaeological museum. We walk through the area of rough grass and untended shrubs strewn with Roman remains and hand the scarf to Imogen. She gives a little cry and sits down rather suddenly on a stone sarcophagus. Very slowly she unwraps the scarf then sits gently pulling it through her hands and grinning at each of us in turn. Now, in this moment, I know I'm happy. In festive spirit, we settle with our sandwiches on rustic benches overlooking the Drava.

Kip and Lindsay reappear then. He still has his arm around her, but it's clear from her swollen eyes that she's not long stopped crying and my chest tightens. Even as disappointment surges in me, I watched Kip drop a kiss on the back of her neck. Lindsay's pale mouth trembles into a smile. Looking round I see this smile echoed over other faces. I never thought I could be susceptible to other people's tenderness. If they cross the border at all, they will clearly go together. I look to see how Ben is taking this; he instantly winks at me and I turn quickly as I feel the heat surging into my face.

## Vicky

I'm still unwrapping my picnic when Vicky, our new, pretty Vicky, looks up from her seat. She starts without any fuss.

'I don't really have a story. I'm going to die anyway, but in a slow and to my mind unbearable fashion. I've decided I'd rather get it out of the way now. We don't have any children, only nephews and nieces. They're busy. I don't want their lives distracted by looking after me. I could wait a few more years, but I know I've got Huntington's. I know too much about it and I've chosen not to go through with it. This way my husband has a chance to start again. He could re-marry and even have children. I would never do that because of my genes. I decided to get it over with, because the decision's the difficult bit. I've felt better since I made it. That's it. The end.'

Lindsay leans across the table and clasps her hand. 'Vicky, oh Vicky, that's so unfair to you.'

She shrugs. 'Not really, it's just life. Only a fool genuinely expects life to be fair. I often wish my mother had thought it through before having me, but perhaps she really didn't know. We do know and yet both my brothers have children. We haven't learnt much.'

Leon pulls his hat off, rubs his forehead, puts it back on and clears his throat. 'Huntington's?'

Vicky looks out over the river. 'Huntington's Chorea. It's an inheritable degenerative brain disease. You've probably noticed, I'm not so good at physical tasks, I sometimes stumble and I can't always pick things up properly. This will only get worse; my bodily movement will become totally uncontrolled. I will eventually dement and need twenty-four hour care. I nursed my mother through it for sixteen years. My grandfather and my great aunt had it. I've got it and I'm pretty sure my older brother has it, but he won't take the tests. Two or three of my five nephews and nieces will have it.'

Bedrich, in a rare gesture, puts a hand on Vicky's arm. 'But you're married.' Vicky nods. 'He does not mind?' Anita snorts and he flinches. 'Sorry, I mean he accepts that you come with us?'

'He doesn't know.'

Anita's bangles clink and she raises her brows. 'You think he'll be grateful when he gets a letter from the British Embassy telling him of your noble sacrifice? I wouldn't bank on it.'

'I'm banking on not caring either way by the time he finds out.'

'True.'

'Don't you care what he feels?' Leon asks.

'Yes of course, but I *know* he'll be better off in the long run.'

'Why come with us? Wouldn't Dignitas take you?'

Vicky looks across the river, then blushes and twists the top on and off the water bottle in her hand. We wait. Eventually she looks up. 'OK, the truth? Daniel. Dignitas had no Daniel. Three weeks of his company is my reward for my sensible choice.'

Daniel bends his head and shakes it slightly. Imogen with her sweetest smile adds, 'There's no need to blush Daniel. I perfectly understand. I wanted some of the same magic. And I applaud the logic of your decision, Vicky. To my mind, yours is the most acceptable reason of all those so far given.'

This strikes me, too, as an unassailable reason to go early. I should have known, though, that it wouldn't get approval from all of us. We split, naturally, along religious lines: those of us who have no beliefs supporting Vicky's decision, Bedrich and Anita fiercely opposing it. Lindsay and Leon are sympathetic, but divided.

'Vicky, medical research is discovering stuff every day. Couldn't you give it a few more years? You're still well enough to enjoy things; to have a haircut, or buy clothes or, best of all, listen to music.'

'Thank you Leon, but I've thought of all of this. I know too much about the disease. I don't want to lose control of my choices. Even if the law allowed assisted dying, they'll never let someone like me, with a dementia, be helped.'

Lindsay is worried about the shock to Vicky's husband, happily at home thinking she's having a holiday. Kip, I'm afraid, looks as though he has something else on his mind. Of course, behind these decisions lie months, even years, of thought. Anyway Vicky appears unmoved by our comments, which dents my fantasy about her feelings for Leon. Poor Leon.

Lindsay asks tentatively, 'Does anyone else worry about people at home, how sad they will be and whether they will think it's their fault we did this?'

Ben says, 'Nope.' With such certainty that I laugh and get a shocked stare from Anita.

Imogen says, 'It's a valid question. Suicide is selfish; we shouldn't kid ourselves. I've done what I can to leave as little unhappiness behind me as possible.'

'Me too,' says Leon firmly.

'Me too,' Lindsay and I echo.

Leon distracts us from the discussion. He's been reading about a musical instruments collection and wants to walk up to the castle above us to find it. We start tramping up a steep, blind bend, roaring with passing traffic.

Is my suicide selfish? I still don't think anyone will care for more than a few minutes about me. Certainly no one will think it's his or her fault except... Last night Imogen asked if I was angry with my mother. I said no, it's the other way round. I suppose when Mum gets the news of my death she might think I did it because of her anger, but surely she won't think of it as revenge, as Imogen suggests. I wish I felt anything as strong as anger towards anybody.

I can imagine myself as an astronaut or even an ant, but I never could get into Mum's head – which is what Daniel advises. Anyway, what difference can it make now. The only way I could change my mind is if Oscar walked in whole and healthy and that will never happen. Never, never, never, never, never.

I start to cross the road to the castle gates, when Ben grabs my arm and a car whooshes past our noses.

'Steady on, Gracie, I'd like the pleasure of your company for another few days.'

I mutter embarrassed thanks – that's the second time he's saved me from a premature end. With some relief we enter a bright colonnaded courtyard edged on three sides by the castle building. There's the usual jewel-green grass, boxes of flowers and an ice cream café. In our short time in this city it seems to me that every other entrance in Ptuj is an ice cream parlour.

Leon's instinct is spot on. The main castle, mediaeval to seventeenth century, has its furniture and layout so well preserved, so efficiently captioned that it's a pleasure to view. There are further delights: first a ballroom filling a whole wing. The floor is empty but for a grand piano, the walls lined with forty or more giant paintings of Turkish, Persian, African, Armenian, Greek, Tartar, Russian and Cossack men and women in full exotic dress. These run like a frieze around the white walls with light pouring between them from floor-to-ceiling windows on both sides. Standing in this great space, flooded with dusty sunshine and edged with colour, I feel the world standing still. Vicky and Leon stand by the piano running their fingers over the lid.

In another wing, an upper floor is swarming with school children and devoted to the weird local Kurent ceremonies – all rustic animal/monster costumes and implements – very unsettling. Far below this, on the ground floor, is an armoury.

I have never been so close to real weaponry before. The hall smells of cold metal: stacks of dented lances, battered pistols, tired swords and the odd cannon. The men sniff around the hardware like dogs in a familiar field. There's no question about the thuggish, functionality of these items. Everything is well used; men have been spitted on *this* lance, horses have been torn apart by *this* cannon. Lindsay is shivering.

From here we cross the courtyard to the ultimate contrast, a vast collection of musical instruments. A violin workshop sends Leon into ecstasies. He has hold of Vicky's elbow, I'm not sure he has given up hope there. One room houses perhaps thirty polished pianos, clavichords, virginals and organs. There are buttons to press to hear the different instruments. These prove a temptation too far for Ben, who presses one after the other making Leon growl.

By the time we return to the sunlight and settle in the tiny bar, my head is spinning. Leon is talking to Vicky about her disease; Ben, Adam and Bedrich have been lured back to the armoury. I can't see Lindsay and Kip. I sit staring at the bright patch of lawn, trying to penetrate the dangerous, foggy space that has opened in my mind. Does my mother think I hate her? Do I hate her?

'Grace? *Gra-ace*, what do *you* want to do?'

'What, sorry?'

Daniel lifts a calming hand to balance Anita's impatient gesture as she asks, 'Grace, do you want to swim today or tomorrow?'

I open my mouth, just as the men rejoin us and Daniel clarifies, 'Grace, we were discussing whether to travel on first thing tomorrow to get to the Terme, the spa swimming complex at Moravske Toplice. There's a smaller spa here, but the waters in Moravske are hotter and bubbling and have special properties.'

Ben's hand makes a brief warm touch on my back, 'You bet she'll swim. She's an ace.'

'Yes, I'd like to swim. I like the idea of bubbling underground water. The real swimming ace is Adam, you know.' He looks mildly shocked, so I persist, 'Have you ever swum competitively, Adam?'

'Uhuh.'

Ben presses, 'And...? Like where for who?'

'School etc; it's ancient history now.'

'Which school? Which University?'

'It doesn't matter.'

Imogen grins. 'Leave it Ben, we don't all need to wear our trophies on our sleeves.'

He waves his coffee cup. 'OK, OK, just curious.' He quizzes Imogen with his eyes. 'Want to know about my trophies instead?' He has our full attention. 'Not a one! Unless you count the children's cake prize in the local Conservative Fundraiser, aged seven.' We all, including Adam, relax into laughter.

I feel a little guilty at having exposed Adam to intrusive questions, but his reticence makes no sense in the context in which we're now living. What's the point of hiding anything? What can it possibly matter to say he came first in the hundred-metre freestyle at dot University?

# Mothers

Later that afternoon we walk over a footbridge across the Drava and down a path with the river on our right and rippling maize on our left. I think I smell the sea from the river. I can certainly smell the dust of harvesting as cobs are being cut in a distant field. We don't talk much as we wander; it feels like a sun-soaking-up day.

Daniel leads us down a strip of field and through a gate into a large flat meadow. This has been recently cleared, tractor lines march up and down and cut strands of longer grass flick against our legs in the sharp wind. The city is a distant picture and the only buildings in sight are farm outhouses.

Daniel is surveying the land with a look of satisfaction. 'This is perfect. We need a big empty space; I want you to make a lot of noise for this game. This is about letting go. First, for practice and to get into the mood we will all run a circuit of the field together shouting "help, fire". Keep running until you reach full volume. OK? Follow me, here goes.' Our embarrassment soon turns to hilarity and when we are all out of breath, Daniel makes us hug each other enthusiastically. With the wind nipping at us this is very comforting.

'Now we come to the real exercise. Think about your mother, really bring her into your head, start a conversation with her.'

Dammit, how does he do that? He wanders round my mind at will.

'If you have no mother now, you can remember or imagine her. I want each of you to run alone in a circle around the field. As you go, I want you to call out Mum, Mummy, or whatever is natural to you. You can start in a whisper and end in a scream if you feel like it, but you *must* reach full volume. You will get a big hug from the women. Please can you give everything, run your fastest, shout your loudest. Does anyone want to go first or shall I demonstrate?'

I hold my hair against the wind. 'I want to go early, but not first.'

'OK Grace, that's fine, I'll start. One of the things I find helpful is to think of a time when I really needed my mother. So I imagine waking from a nightmare when I was little. Or walking home from school and meeting someone frightening, or seeing an accident. All I want is Mum – *now*! I want big motherly hugs from all of you women when I reach you.'

Suddenly solemn, Daniel stands for a moment, then sets off running across the short grass to the far fence, 'Mum, Mum, Mum, Mum, MUM, MUM, MUM, *MUM, MUM* ... '

The jokiness vanishes; the wind and Daniel's desperate voice turn my body rigid. He turns and runs back bellowing, then falls on his knees for Imogen's hug. Anita is crying. She holds and pats him, murmuring, 'It's all right, it's all right.' When it comes to my turn, I cradle his head against my chest feeling greater fulfilment than at any other time of the whole trip. Vicky can hardly let go. In many of the games we've handled each other, but they've been either emotional or physical; this is definitely both.

When we've thoroughly hugged him, he turns. 'Grace? Ready?'

I stand in front of the others. I can feel trembling in all my limbs and put my hands over my face. Then I start running and only pull my hands away when I stumble and almost fall. I whisper at first, but as I fling myself into the wind, it isn't so difficult to yell. The adrenalin pumps through me and my breathing grows ragged. I land crying and laughing in Imogen's arms and it's wonderful. I find myself clinging tearfully to Vicky. For a moment I feel some profound safety, some flash of memory of something craved and never satisfied. Also, for a millisecond, recognition. Perhaps, just perhaps, my mother did once love me.

Eyes shining I urge the others on, 'It feels wonderful, brilliant, exciting!' They laugh at me, but I can feel our collective mood rising with my elation. Daniel grips my arm. 'Well done Grace.' My cup runs over.

Not everyone manages to let go. Of the women, both Vicky and Imogen do short circuits and never hit full volume. Lindsay overdoes it and can't stop crying. Kip takes her away for ten minutes while we chat. The men are a little more reluctant than the women. With Daniel's encouragement, they fall to their knees at the end, which helps the sense of a mother/son relationship. Ben yells all right, but treats it a bit as a joke and does as much hugging as being hugged; it doesn't feel quite right. Of course he never knew his biological mother. He does a good job of hiding his feelings; I'm beginning wonder if he has any.

Leon and, unpredictably, Bedrich are full on, passionate, lost children. Adam is brilliant going out, but gets stage fright at the far end of the field. In the end Imogen goes and hugs him, brings him back, and he drops on his knees and passively receives the rest of our hugs. He feels to me, as I hold him, like a very small and lonely boy. Kip, having spent time soothing Lindsay, goes last and suddenly has us all in tears, so passionate and desperate is his call to his mother. I don't think I've ever heard him raise his voice before this moment.

After holding Kip, I feel stupid for thinking that Daniel had me in mind when he set up this exercise. I'd forgotten, Kip's mother died when his brother was so ill, so Kip's feelings are much more important. I wonder what happened to her.

For the remainder of the day we are all rather gentle with each other. I feel protected among these strangers that I now know more intimately than any other humans. Has this level of warmth been available all my life?

Before supper I leave the hotel for a breather. I'm sitting on the edge of a concrete flower planter, when Ben creeps up behind and puts his hands over my eyes. I jump uncontrollably and he catches me in his arms. 'Hey Grace, calm down, it's only me.' He is patting me and I gradually relax. He sits beside me with his arm casually round my shoulders. I almost panic, thinking I'm committing myself before I'm ready. Then I see Bedrich and Anita walking up the hill towards us. I get up and walk towards them. Ben doesn't seem to mind.

After supper I watch Kip and Lindsay walking and sitting together, each one always inclined slightly towards the other. I begin to crave the tenderness that hangs about them like perfume. As he gives me coffee, Ben leans over and runs a finger lightly down my arm and whispers, 'Want to make hay while we can?' Something about the way he nods towards Kip and Lindsay makes his offer quite clear.

I try to smile lightly. 'Not tonight, Ben.' As soon as the words are out in the air, I realise that they imply that another night, for instance tomorrow, I'll be willing. Perhaps I will, perhaps I will. I don't even know myself why I've ducked his offer tonight. I wonder at my resolution. Especially given the sight of Kip and Lindsay clearly counting the minutes. It is almost, but not quite, funny. Lindsay has his hand in her lap and is drawing lines on it. He keeps on closing his eyes, his breathing shallow. He laces his fingers through hers, but you can see this only makes it worse. When Daniel suggests we all go for a walk before we retire, Kip is the first on his feet.

I get up slowly, then catch Vicky glancing from me to Ben, she says something to Leon. I look around and note that Adam also has us under observation from behind his paper. Perhaps this is why I turned Ben down, simply a strong resistance to fulfilling expectations. If I go ahead with this fling with Ben I'll do it uninfluenced by the Hollywood glamour and seductiveness of the Kip/Lindsay pairing. I remember, too, that getting what I want is certain to make me miserable.

As we drift off towards bed Daniel reminds us that tomorrow there will be no story and no games, only water, mountains and relaxation. I feel curiously unsettled by this. I have found it easy to go passively along while every hour of every day is catered for. Freedom to reflect is not a gift, more like an open hole through which I might fall.

## Moravske Toplice Spa – Day nine

The sun is barely up and still making long shadows of the hay-frames as Kip drives us cross-country to join the main road from Maribor towards the Hungarian border. The scale of Slovenia is confusing; you can set off in any direction and hit a border in a couple of hours – a squash court of a country. An hour and a half later we're parking and entering the giant Thermal Spa complex at Moravske Toplice. We wander through, eyes stretched at the scale of the flumes and skyscraper diving platforms.

As we assemble in our bathing costumes, there's an air of bashfulness amongst those who haven't swum before. This vanishes as we plunge into the hot-water pool, bubbles surging around us as we bob and clutch each other to stay upright. Music and happy shrieks echo thoughout the park.

After a while Imogen says wistfully, 'I suppose I'm too old to go down one of those flumes. Just a short one.'

Adam leans over and says, 'Will you trust me? I'll take you.'

She looks like a child offered candyfloss. 'Yes. Oh yes *please.*'

Ben calls out, 'Come on Grace.'

I accept Ben in the role of brave protector and Adam (who never voluntarily touches anyone outside a game) scoops up Imogen. We start on the easiest ones, then, with Ben's encouragement, we go in pairs and tackle a monstrous descending snake. Yesterday I thought nothing would make me happier than seeing Kip and Lindsay hand in hand; now Imogen's beaming face as she and Adam splash down from the long flume kicks my heart into a realm it has not visited for a long time. Daniel takes Vicky who looks transfigured, but Leon declines, saying he's allergic to heights. Even Anita and Bedrich manage the short one. We are unravelling our lives and returning to childhood.

High from this experience, we go on to visit the famous diving pool and stare in awe at the twenty-two metre high platform. As we take turns to dive off the more accessible three-metre boards, I notice once again the odd dotted scars on Ben's back. Adam, no surprise now, proves superb in the water. Then Ben challenges me to dive from the fearsome Olympic height ten-metre platform. I look up and think what the heck and set off with Ben and Adam behind me.

I hear muttering and Adam catches up with me. 'You don't have to do that, Grace.'

'I know, but what have I got to lose?' I see his face open up with momentary laughter. Ben and I dive well and enjoy the back patting admiration when we emerge. The next instant Ben and Adam are discussing the twenty-two-metre platform soaring above us. Ben shakes his head. 'Not for me, I'm not in that league at all.'

Without thinking I say, 'None of us are, except Adam.'

Adam looks up and then at me. 'You think I could do that?'

'I'm sure you could.' I say, intending a compliment, not a challenge. Then I see his face. 'No, Adam, no! You wouldn't do anything that crazy.'

He shrugs, his expression almost dreamy. 'What have *I* got to lose?' He's gone as he speaks and we watch, hearts beating, as he ascends. Divers from this platform are rare enough to cause a stir and as he climbs higher, heads turn. He appears on the top, walks to the end, rock steady, lifts his arms, jumps and dives. He slices the water like a shard of glass.

As he breaks the surface, clapping can be heard over the noises of the pool and the ubiquitous music. He swims quickly to the protection of our group, keeping his head down as we hug and pat him. The unthinkable seems to have quietly occurred. Adam, in spite of himself, belongs with us and we feel proud of him.

After four hours of soaking and a quick lunch, we pile back into the coach and leave the resort. I sleep as the coach speeds down the A1 and wake up as we appear to be driving across a gigantic lawn.

How this land stays so green even in September continues to baffle me, though the sporadic monsoon-like downpours may explain it.

The lawn quickly gives way to mountains and we gradually ascend, arriving at our guesthouse in a tiny village near Luce in mid afternoon. A Scotsman staying in the guesthouse spurs us to go and look at the dramatic scenery of Mount Rogatec nearby. Kip drives us up a scary winding road, the surface only made up in places. There's a strange noise from the back of the coach as we start up the hairpin bends. Anita has her head in Bedrich's jacket and is almost hysterical.

Daniel brings them up from the back of the coach, where the two always sit and puts them right behind the driver's cab, while he sits across the aisle. He gives Anita a weird little puzzle, almost like something from a Christmas cracker and tells her that she has to move it around gently so that all the balls drop into the little holes. Daniel leans across the gangway and keeps her attention glued to the task.

The small coach is remarkably nifty on these mountain roads, but this really tests the steering and, as we later discover, the engine thermostat. So obscure is the road, that we encounter only one car on the way up. Anita is still in one piece when we reach a high isolated alp where everyone disembarks. I decide to remember that trick with the puzzle for future reference then remember I have no future. How could I forget that?

With our muscles loosened from the morning's water treatment and the sunlight heavy on us, we move drowsily and in awe up the green gash in the mountains. We pause for tea at a tiny bar feeling as if we're the first tourists ever to venture this far. The sun lies hot and heavy in the open alps; in the shadow of the mountain it's almost cold.

Vicky collapses among the wild flowers. 'What next, Daniel? I'm all in.'

'Nothing. Study relaxation for an hour or two until our special meal tonight in Luce.' Everyone flops onto the hot grass and lies about basking.

I try stretching out in the sun, but after five minutes some inner urgency brings me to my feet. I ignore Ben's outstretched hand – he is, as so often, on his mobile – and move off. I need to experience something, not simply to exist for these last twelve days. I wander up the path past a wooden shrine and into the tumbled rocks. After ten minutes a great satisfying split in the earth opens up ahead of me, the ground beyond the edge falls away; the sky invades the landscape and seems to hang below my feet.

## Mount Rogatec

I climb more quickly now, glad of the time and space to myself after the undressed intimacy of the morning. At the time I felt undone by the hothouse atmosphere and unable to resist Ben's lightly possessive hands, and yet a terrible ambivalence prevents me committing myself. I have this sense with Ben of being very carefully handled, drawn in, let loose again, then drawn in closer, like a fish on a line. I wish he had not come on this trip. I wish it were next week. I wish it were over.

Breathing seems more refreshing up here, perhaps the difference in altitude. I scramble further up the path then hesitate as I spot Adam's lean silhouette ahead. He's standing at the lip of the chasm. Too late. He turns and seeing me jerks his head in invitation. I shrug and go to stand beside him, both of us silent, drinking the air, breathing lightly.

He nods towards the immense space. 'I think,' he steps the last pace to the edge, 'I could go now.'

'I'll come too.'

The grass tussock under his front foot bends slowly forward. He speaks conversationally, 'No. You should stay. I think you should live.'

I don't want to be left on my own and reach out for his hand. 'Adam?'

He flinches as he did the first time I saw Daniel touch him. For a second I think this movement is the first muscle contraction of the jump. Then he shifts his weight onto his back foot and looks down at our linked hands, then at my face. Until this moment I've been filled with a peaceful sensation, a calm born of certainty and exhilaration at the scale of the scene before us. Tacked on the rim of a thousand metres of rock, it seems of very little importance if we drop off it or stay put. I feel sufficiently small in the scheme of things to take my leave without disturbing the world.

In the ensuing microseconds as these sensations are working through my body, my whole being divides. My mind, or some department within it, soars gently into the space beneath me.

105

Finish. Freedom. Peace. Home. My physical being starts down a different route. My body becomes my hand in Adam's hand and the experience of the contact between a million cells. Under his gaze I have the sensation of being turned inside out – blood bolting unchecked, internal chaos revealed. My heartbeat drowns out all other sounds and my knees begin to give way. His grip on my hand increases, he takes my other hand and we both step one pace back from the cliff edge.

I open my mouth, but nothing comes out and Adam, his chest rising and falling as if he's run a mile, frowns in concentration. 'We could... jump or... we could...'

I release one hand and put two fingers over his mouth. We kiss as barely as if we're ghosts or as if the slightest movement might destabilise us and send us plummeting. Adam lifts his head. 'Grace?' I can't breathe enough to answer. His voice is hollowed out and fragile. 'Grace, do you want to jump?... I don't mind. Whatever you want.'

We help each other back to the path then walk on. His arm, as it lies across my back, scorches through my shirt. My arm around his waist feels his every bone and muscle shift as we descend. We bypass the little alp where the others are gathered and go straight to the empty coach. We lean against the far side kissing. There is no need of questions, no uncertainty, no possibility of misunderstanding, no inhibitions, we drown in each other. Tomorrow is, after all, all we have left. My cotton shirt and trousers feel like a winter coat. I struggle to breathe.

Adam says, 'Shall we walk?'

I look down at the narrow road, running in giddy loops between the trees, leading to our hostel in the valley. I don't know if my knees will carry me that far in their current state. I must look appalled because Adam's half grin appears.

'I could carry you.' He pulls me close, serious again. 'I don't think I can talk to everyone, or wait until tonight and... and you?'

I open my mouth, but I'm mute.

'Listen Grace, we have twelve days left, for all of the last nine I have ached for you, indulge me by a few hours. It's all we have now.'

He steps back, leaving me weak-kneed leaning against the bus. He waits, arms slightly spread, palms open, his body pinned to the sky and when I lean forward to touch his chest it seems to me that it vibrates like the strings of a plucked harp. I feel light as a husk, as if he's drawn my substance into his body. I fear I might never wholly recover.

'I'll walk, if it kills me.'

'Brave lass! Here, I've got a receipt from coffee, I'll write a note for Daniel.'

'But what will we tell him?'

'We don't need to tell him anything. Daniel knows.'

'But how does he know when we didn't?'

'Oh Grace!' We're in the middle of another unstoppable kiss when Lindsay's voice sings out. We separate. Adam scribbles his note and we set off down the hill.

Verbal communication has been suspended. Yet like magnets placed too close, we struggle to move independently and every physical contact delays us. We're only half way when, after yet another pause, I move back a pace and laugh out loud, 'Look at us. We're ridiculous.' Adam's face cracks into his first full smile this afternoon.' He simply nods. My face crumples, 'Such an amazing smile Adam, why have you given us all a cold shoulder until now?'

He looks beyond me at the steep mountain then back at my face, but shakes his head. We stumble on reaching the sanctuary of our hostel as the sun is setting.

## Luce

Much later on, in the restaurant in Luce, we sit still for the first time since our revelation on the mountain. I look at my hands still trembling in my lap. I can find nothing rational about my feelings or actions; I can only admit that something cataclysmic has happened. Adam says that he knew what he was feeling many days ago, whereas I've managed to ignore all the signals from my own body. The result is a physical landslide over which I have zero control.

When the others appear, Adam and I, without prior discussion, feign normality. We're helped by a non-stop pealing of the local church bells, which distracts the others. I do not, I have to admit, consciously spare a thought for Ben until much later that evening.

My excuse for this cruelty is minimal – that we are being fed an astonishing meal; first a "lollipop" of fried cheese on a stick, then some tiny squares of toast with delicate home-made paté, then onion soup, a small whole trout – perfectly cooked, some mouthfuls of tender goat and finally a mango syllabub; the food is probably the finest I've ever eaten. Combined with hours of soaking and swimming this morning, a mountain walk and descent with lovemaking this afternoon, it's as if someone has planned to give my body an inclusive package of sensual thrills in the shortest possible time. Daniel may have designed the meal to persuade us that there are things to live for, but he can't have anticipated the double assault.

I have a shock when, back at our hostel, alive to my fingertips with these new sensations, Ben snuggles up to me on the sofa. I plead a headache and go up to bed shaken by the meanness of my actions. Once again, I know myself to be supremely incompetent. I now add deserting Ben to the lumber room of my conscience.

Tonight I leave my door unlocked and sit in my pyjamas clutching the edge of the bed. Adam pushes open the door and stands waiting until I pat the bed beside me. We sit side by side.

'Adam, we need to talk.'

'Uhuh.'

'This afternoon I... we... I felt fine this afternoon, now it feels odd, because we pretended to the others all evening.'

Adam presses his palms together and looks at the ground, 'You want me to go back to my room?'

I lean against him quickly. 'No, no. It's just I'm not good at pretending. We don't seem to be doing things in the right order, do we? And now I don't know how to get things back on track. There isn't time, is there? We should get to know one another before we behave like we did this afternoon. I feel bad acting towards the others as if nothing's happened. I feel bad about Ben.'

'Did you and Ben...?'

'No.' I grip his arm to make him look directly at me. 'No, but he probably expects we will.'

I sit up again pressing my palms together. We must look like a pair of anxious children about to kneel and pray.

Adam runs a hand over his face. 'It's crazy isn't it? My body remembers how to act, but my brain's forgotten how to talk.' He picks up my hand. 'It's five years, you know, five years since I touched anyone, five years since anyone touched me.'

'Why, Adam, why?'

'Perversity, probably. I knew my uncle would be out of prison sometime and my life would be worthless. I didn't ever want kids in case... Jesus!' He gets abruptly to his feet, takes two steps towards the door. I don't know what's happened. I stand up and grab his hand. He freezes. 'I can't... I don't know how to talk about it.'

'Adam, whatever it is, it doesn't matter. We don't have to talk. You can tell me anything, or nothing.' I can still feel him tugging towards escape. We stand there. I murmur, 'Adam, I'm cold.' But he doesn't react.

His face has shut down again: his mouth a thin hard line. I have the feeling that if I move, or speak or even smile, he will run. I can hear Leon talking to someone in the corridor. There's a shower going on in the next-door room. The walls are pretty thin. I wonder if others heard us earlier in the evening.

Adam's eyes, which have been flickering with inward thoughts, suddenly engage with mine again. We're so close I can see his pupils widen and contract. He looks down at the cartoons on my pyjamas and his mouth relaxes. He takes my other hand and slides his hands up to my elbows, his thumbs pressing gently.

'Are you prepared to sleep with a liar and a killer...?'

I try a smile. 'Ditto?'

He doesn't smile, '...and the son of a... I can't say it.'

'Adam, whatever you are the son of, I'm prepared to sleep with you. I'm guilty too.'

He cries out as he pulls me to him, 'It's not the same. It's not the same at all. God, you *are* freezing.'

He does talk, but not until nearly dawn. I wonder the next day if either of us has slept for as much as an hour that night. My body burns, glows and yet feels beaten up. I've not been so thoroughly handled for years. Adam's not rough, far from it, merely starved. Both of us are aware of the dwindling hours ahead. Once he starts to talk, he and the birds go on for a couple of hours. Twice I drop off, and wake each time fearing he will be hurt, but he's tender and sorry to rouse me again. He needs to be heard. He does not know how to stop. He fears stopping.

## Slap Rinka – Day ten

This morning we set out early to the Logarksa Dolina – the Logar Valley. I'm barely functional though we both, Adam and I, try to go on as usual. We know we have to do this until I've had a meaningful conversation with Ben. The others keep asking if I'm all right.

The whole valley is a National Park and we pay to enter. We then drive across another mile of lawn lying between the forested mountain walls. The road gives out at a busy car park. Unlike yesterday afternoon, there are plenty of tourists here. We stop to drink coffee before starting the climb up to Slap Rinka. I love that the myriad waterfalls in this country are called Slaps, it suits my dazed mood. Adam hands me a full cup of coffee; I instantly spill it. He and others cope with the mess, while I stand feebly by.

Anita, in a kindlier tone than usual says, 'You're not yourself this morning, Grace. You know Daniel's taking Vicky back after coffee. Why don't you go with them? You look as though you'd be happier in your bed.' I am startled into looking up at Adam and he is startled into inappropriate laughter. I cannot believe that Adam's name is not branded on my forehead. The others must think we have both taken some personality-altering potion.

I stumble on. As we walk I have to keep my head down, I am aware at any moment of Adam's body and its distance from mine. If he speaks his voice resonates in my chest, if he moves, his limbs activate mine. I place each foot in front of the other, like a robot programmed to reach the waterfall. The path climbs through beeches crowding and stretching upwards to the light. The sun glitters in vertical shafts between the trees. I could be in a cathedral.

As I pant my way up, the others ask how I'm feeling. 'Fine.' I fib to anyone and everyone, 'fine.' I feel dazed, smashed open, I can barely function appropriately and conversation is impossible, otherwise I do indeed feel fine. Once, after I've made a particularly inane remark, Bedrich puts his hand on my head and gives me one of his sleepy smiles. Ben shows an inclination to help me over rough terrain and I cannot rebuff him.

Adam, too, attracts notice. He approaches Leon and chats to him, asks Imogen if she has slept better on the hostel mattress than the night before in Ptuj. He talks, he smiles, Vicky says later, as if he's been released from Siberia and is astonished to find the grass still green in the rest of the world.

The waterfall, when we reach it, is a delicate pencil-slim stream cascading from a cleft in the rock-face and dropping ninety metres to spill itself another fifteen metres over a conical rock at the base. Hot from our climb, I wander across the boulders to feel the spray on my face. I feel a tug on my arm as I get nearer. Ben has hold of me. 'Gently Grace, we don't want you to vanish in the stream.'

We return, exhausted, to the hostel. My stomach heaves at the sight of food, my interest in my fellow travellers, Adam apart, is minimal. I feel like a truant, endlessly waiting for a chance to slip away. Then, when the opportunity comes, we react in confusion.

Daniel gathers us. 'As you may know the bus thermostat has been giving us trouble, I've just heard from the garage that they can supply us with a spare one in Bled. We are going to set off and make a detour there. You can all go and relax and pack and we'll meet up here in an hour.' Adam's eyes lift to mine. His skin stains red, then pales, while I stare at him unable to look anywhere else.

Anita repeats her earlier advice: 'Why don't you take a nap Grace, I'm sure you'll feel better for it.'

I nod and slip away. Adam joins me in a few minutes. In the first moments behind our shut bedroom door, as we shed clothes, I cannot imagine how we've kept our bodies apart for the last few hours. It mystifies me that someone who's been no more than an unsettling presence in the corner of my eye for the last nine days can, in one split second, occupy the whole of my vision. Some sub-conscious part of me must have been craving this for some time.

Laughing, crying and making love as silently as possible in the middle of the day is not going to make me any more coherent during the rest of it. In a few hours I've become a teenage obsessive, ruled by my body, idolizing Adam's and completely identifying with what Adam wants.

## On the route to Bled

Far too soon we are back in the real world and I hit the problem I have so far blotted out. Ben follows me on board the coach and sits down beside me without so much as a glance of request. I look wildly round for Adam, but Daniel is talking to him. He sees my panicky face and laughs with a tiny shrug. I really regret having given Ben so much encouragement. I've no excuse. I must tell him... tell him what? Tell him that Adam and I have discovered each other? That's the best interpretation I can find.

I reckon Ben must be using the hotel's laundry; either that or he has a massive suitcase. He's in clean clothes and smells as fresh as if he's just showered. He turns his green eyes on me and asks tenderly if I've managed a rest. I stare at him. The effect of the last twenty-four hours is so seismic I cannot believe that the changes in me can still be hidden from anyone. Yet Ben clearly had no notion that I'm a new and different person

I duck the question. 'I have things on my mind.'

'Don't we all?' His eyes glint. 'Ideal time for a little distraction.' He leans over to pick up my hand.

I evade his move, pulling my hand through my tangled hair and breathe in deeply. 'Ben...? Yesterday I made a discovery. You know I went on up the mountain, up Rogatec, when you lot were sun-bathing?'

'Uhuh. This sounds important. Did you discover the wonders of the world and decide not to go ahead?'

'No. I almost jumped.'

'Seriously?'

'Yes, well, sort of. The thing that happened is that I got talking to Adam.' (My second evasion: we hardly spoke at all).

'Yes, he seems to have recently rediscovered speech.'

'Ben... Adam and I seem to get on... we have more *in common* than I guessed...' (We have very little in common, we have simply found something we need in each other).

'You and Adam?' He laughs and I glance round to see if Adam has heard. He has.

I grow braver. 'Yes. I know I've encouraged... given you the impression that I would enjoy a fling with you – I would have enjoyed one – but I'm going to spend the last days with Adam.'

He laughs again. 'No Grace, no, you're teasing. You must be teasing?' He looks at my unsmiling face. 'Don't do this to me. Who am I going to… talk to if you head off? Lindsay's well and truly occupied, Vicky? Imogen? Have a heart. Why Adam? He seems pretty self-sufficient to me. I need companionship.' He reaches over and touches my cheek lightly then he pulls out a strand of my hair to its full length. 'I really appreciate you.' It's impossible to tell from his voice, if he's hurt, genuinely resisting the information, or complaining out of social convention. His eyes plead. 'It would be wasteful to spend the last days of your life in heavy conversations with Mr Serious.'

'But Ben it isn't like that, we... I mean...' I look down knowing that my face has gone scarlet.'

'Well, well!' He says lightly. 'Looks like I should have been bolder. Brooding Heathcliff more your style? I put you down as preferring something more subtle.'

He's almost sneering and there's an uncomfortable edge to his voice. I remain silent as I try to decipher his feelings and find a disarming response. He's clearly read the situation as his miscalculation rather than my preference. My first instinct to correct his impression is overlaid by a sense of danger. I now only wish to placate him – by a lie if necessary. He must not think that Adam has outwitted him or has some quality that he lacks.

'Sorry, Ben. You're essentially right; I'm not a Heathcliff type. I don't think Adam is either.' I try a smile. 'Put it down to the scale of the scenery yesterday. In a couple of weeks it'll make no odds.'

'True. Well, if... you feel like a change,' he looks at me this time with a hint of mischief and I think, in disbelief, he is going to suggest a *menage à trois*, 'I won't be far away.'

I sit staring out of the windows baffled by how first impressions are so often reversed. I had thought of Adam as one of the more opaque specimens of the human race. A closed book, no way in and yet, after a bare twenty-four hours face to face with him I have an entirely new sensation of walking safely in and out of his mind. It's as if I have touched a secret catch and his personality has sprung open. Yet Ben, so open, transparent and straight, has turned out to be in camouflage kit. I should know by now that there is no rulebook for being human. Not much longer now.

We stop for tea in Kranj and Vicky, Imogen, Anita, Lindsay and I find ourselves at one table with the men on the other side of the Café. Briefly and rarely, the talk reaches outside our tiny navel-gazing world; prices in Slovenia, the Common Market, Climate Change, contraception in Africa, the grip of drug companies. Then a joint laugh from the men's table makes us all turn. A moment later we notice Lindsay still gazing that way.

'Penny for your thoughts,' says Vicky.

Lindsay shakes her head, a little smile on her lips.

'She watches Kip the whole time,' says Anita.

'Well…,' she giggles, 'I love to watch his mouth as he talks.'

'We know,' she laughs. 'We don't blame you.'

Vicky says, 'We shouldn't fool ourselves; we have a pre-programmed Darwinian response to mouths, they tell us about the health of possible mates.'

'In that case,' Imogen puts in, 'Ben, with that Grecian profile, should father the most children, but for my money Adam, if he relaxes for a second, wins on some indescribable come-hither factor.'

Heat is washing through me. 'I know what you mean. I'd better confess at this point that Adam and I have... have got together.'

'Adam?' Lindsay is amazed, 'but what about Ben?'

'I feel bad, but I don't think Ben is too bothered. Let's be honest, he would have preferred you, Lindsay.'

Imogen laughs. 'I wondered when you two would see the light.'

Anita looks across at the other table. 'Poor Ben.'

Vicky puts a hand on my arm. 'Tell us what happened, Grace.'

I open my hands as I try to rediscover my brain. 'I'm not sure... we both stood on the edge of Mount Rogatec yesterday and... it just happened.'

'Well it's wonderful to see you and Adam come to life. Did any of you expect this, I mean us making friends or even relationships?'

'No.' I am categorical. 'I couldn't have been less interested. I haven't bothered for some time. I think it's some magic that Daniel is working.'

Vicky says on a sigh, 'I've become fond of Leon, but Daniel is the only person I really care about.' There are emphatic nods and murmurs all round the table.

After a quick glance at the men's table, Lindsay says quietly, 'I did wonder if he was gay.'

Imogen, too, looks across the room. 'So did I. He has that quality of empathy you associate more with women, but I think it's mostly that he's a good therapist. He keeps a finger on everybody's pulse and a tiny distance apart from each of us. It must be very lonely.'

'I like myself better when I'm with Daniel,' I say, 'he acts like a fairy-tale mirror, reflecting back our better images.' The others nod.

When we return to the coach I sit with Adam. He takes my hand in both of his, turning it palm upwards and running his thumb over the palm and then between each finger.

'Jesus, Adam, this isn't good for me.'

Without looking up, I can hear the smile in his voice as he says, 'I wanted to do this in that hand exercise. I was in meltdown. You didn't know?'

'No... no. I'm sorry. I had no idea why I felt so unsettled. Stupid, huh?'

'Why should you look at the grim bastard I was then.' He lifts my hand to his lips.

'Adam, don't.' I try to withdraw my hand. 'There are limits to what we can do on a bus.'

'Want to test them?'

I laugh, 'The best thing we can do now is sleep.'

'Some hope.'

I can feel his mouth against my hair and sleep seems unattainably distant. Remembering the café conversation earlier, I try to visualise what so moves me about Adam's mouth, but listing features – the shadow under his lip, the turn of cheek to lip, of lip to chin – explains nothing. Something in his movements is so tentative, hopeful and expressive that he has only to turn and speak and I dissolve.

Unable to do anything else, we do eventually drop off and only wake up when we reach the garage in Bled. It turns out that the thermostat will not arrive until tomorrow, so we have to stay an unscheduled night here. When Daniel boards the coach to explain this, I am shocked at how drained he looks. Is he ill? He takes Ben, who speaks the language, with him but turns down further offers of help, and disappears.

After half an hour Vicky stops talking to Imogen and leans round her seat addressing us all. 'Did Daniel say where he was going or how long he would be?' We all shake our heads. 'I worry when he's away. What if anything happened to him, what would we do? I don't want to do it on my own.'

Leon says, 'He'd better come back. I've already tried and failed twice. You'd think a soldier could finish himself off.'

'What happened?' asks Vicky, never shy of the personal query.

'The rope was more elastic than I thought.'

'I cut my wrists,' says Lindsay, 'but not enough to work.' She looks up at Kip. 'An ambulance driver saved me… there must be something special about them.' We all laugh.

Kip says, 'I OD'd – overdosed – but my flatmate guessed and dragged me into A & E.'

'I tried the gas oven,' I admit, 'but I was drunk and fell asleep and there was a vent open *and* it turns out natural gas doesn't kill you – I'm that incompetent. If Daniel doesn't reappear, someone will have to help me.' Adam's arm tightens round me, whether in support of, or against, the idea, I can't work out.

Adam doesn't say whether he's tried. I can't imagine him trying and failing, so I guess he probably hasn't.

115

The others are talking about what happens over the border, but Daniel told us from the beginning that we have to leave that in his hands. He said we're booked into a self-catering chalet somewhere in another country, he promised that we will not be alone, and that someone will alert the right authorities the next day so no one has an unpleasant shock, but he cannot tell us more.

I remember that Saturday when I tried by myself, two months after I found Daniel. I remember starting crying, about nothing, around teatime. It was May with the birds outside going mad, feeding, fighting, nesting, singing, and me inside a useless wet heap. By 2am I was still at it, walking round in circles, dripping and intent on making an end that night. Deciding made me feel better. I found some cans of cider, shut the windows and put the sofa cushions on the slate kitchen floor. I downed the cider as I made preparations. I curled up on the cushions and wrote a note, so no one would get into trouble, turned on the gas and fell asleep. Job done. Three hours later I woke up, cold, stupid and alive.

When I tune into the conversation again, Imogen is organising us. 'When Daniel does get back,' says Imogen, 'we must make sure that we give him every stitch of help we can.'

It is more than an hour before Daniel and Ben return. They have fixed accommodation for all of us in a hostel in a nearby village.


## Bedrich and Anita

Supper is over and we're lounging in low chairs in the coffee room of the hostel. Anita and Bedrich are sitting stiffly side-by-side on the only sofa. In fact they both look as though they're in court or sitting at The Right Hand... I still struggle to like Anita; she has an alarmingly busy air and I always feel I am not quite up to standard when she's about. She also jangles with her buckles, bracelets and operatic gypsy-style handbag. She makes me feel underdressed.

Bedrich on the other hand is big, comfortable and so laid back he's almost absent at times. This evening he's definitely awake. In fact he looks positively startled. These two have remained on the periphery of the group by virtue of their closeness to each other, their reticence about their personal lives and, perhaps, some un-acknowledged cultural barrier. Their faint accents tell of another country in another time.

Bedrich starts in a low voice, 'We only ever had the one child. We tried for another...'

'Bedrich, we can't hear you.' Imogen speaks gently.

Bedrich clears his throat, but Anita gets there first, her voice packed tight and hard. 'We wanted children, lots of children, but we only ever had Jacob.' With an anxious movement Bedrich takes a breath to interrupt, but Anita overrides him. 'When he was born he was beautiful. He was full term. He had masses of glossy, black hair. Then, when he was two days old he got jaundice. His poor skin went all yellow. It happens to babies and no one seemed very bothered at the time, but he began to curl up in a funny way, like a sea anemone when you touch it. Then the doctors started to take him away for tests and investigations.

'It was like the tap dripping. A curious look here, an odd word there, the nurse giving my beautiful boy a pitying glance. The days passed and Jacob was never quite well enough to go home. Other babies were born and went home. We were told he might have a slight problem with muscle tone, then a bigger problem with the way his brain controlled his muscles. Then one day a really cheerful consultant sat us down and said, as if it were good news, "Well, there's no doubt that young Jacob has a form of Cerebral Palsy."

'Since that day there's been nothing else in our lives. We took our baby home to the room we had prepared for him. I laid him in his crib and he looked so much as I'd imagined he would in my dreams, but it was an illusion. Someone else had come to occupy my son's cradle.

'The life we had planned, the things we did up until then – everything went. You wouldn't think it, but we used to do competitive ballroom dancing.' She looks at her husband as if she expects him to disbelieve her too. 'Bedrich used to have these toy train club meetings...'

A small spasm crosses Bedrich's face, he mutters, '0 gauge model railway club.'

'OK "0 gauge...", you know,' she gestures in the air, '*little* trains. There wasn't ever room to set them up after that. These things went first, then everything else – even my working clothes. I had an old flamenco dress... old, old, from the 1930s... green with tiny bells.'

Anita waits for a couple of teenagers to move their half-clad bodies out of the area where we are sitting. 'At first Jacob was helpless because he was a baby. Only the doctors knew he was sick.

When we were out, people would look in the pram. They thought... they said he was beautiful. He even learnt to smile – months after other babies did, of course. Still we knew when he felt happy. In his bath, he squealed, kicked and laughed. Sometimes we thought the doctors had got it wrong and he would catch up and grow up like any other little boy. Then one Sunday when Jacob was nearly two, we were in the supermarket...' Anita stops and looks at Bedrich.

He speaks very quietly, but no one interrupts, we all lean forward instead. 'This woman held out the monkey Jacob dropped. He wanted to grasp it, but couldn't. She knelt down really close holding out the toy and Jacob's hands only pushed it. He fell sideways. Then she put her hand over her mouth and tears came. She kept saying, "I'm so sorry, so sorry". The hope left us that day.'

Anita purses her lips and takes over again. 'We didn't know the half of it. With each year the doctors found another problem. They stopped telling us about the many children with Cerebral Palsy who go to ordinary school, even to University. Not Jacob... he had little movement control and his mental function was poor. Then there were the fits... He was what you call profoundly disabled.'

Anita shakes her head as if belief in this chain of disasters still eludes her. 'I was twenty-three. We had no money. We stopped seeing friends, we don't either of us have any living relatives in England. When Jacob was born we had not long moved to Watford from Birmingham; we didn't know our neighbours. We still don't and it's thirty years on. From that day we never went out to eat a meal or go to the cinema. For the next thirty years, we talked only to doctors, neurologists, care workers, social workers, physiotherapists, health visitors, community nurses, disabled equipment manufacturers, delivery drivers...' Anita's eyes narrow, challenging us. 'I don't suppose any of you can imagine living in this world day after day.'

Kip stirs. 'Anita, I had it different but... I can imagine.'

Anita looks at him, momentarily at a loss, then remembers his brother's long illness.

'Sorry, Kip, of course, yes it was a bit like that for you.' She reties the little silk scarf around her neck as she gathers up the threads of her resentment again. 'Bedrich was able to go away to his office most days, but I stayed in day after day, year after year to look after our son.' She throws out another fierce look. 'Don't get me wrong – *I* loved him.'

Bedrich lifts a surprised hand, and she corrects herself. 'We *both* loved him, but he could do nothing, *nothing*, for himself.'

Vicky leans forward. 'But Anita, if he was that… disabled, did you not get any respite, any day care?'

'Day care? Of course. It started when he was four and stopped when he was sixteen. Do you know what I did when the carers came? I slept. Bedrich had to work every day so I did the night shifts. From the age of five Jacob would be taken to a special school, but he was often too unwell to go. Day care in our area lasts from 8.30 to 4.30 five days a week. Someone still has to do the shopping, the cooking, the washing – and there's plenty of that – the collection of medication, the filling of forms: different forms for every penny we received and every single thing that we needed. So that's what I did when I wasn't asleep.

'Respite? We got some of that too. I think we got a week when he was seven years old so we could move house to a bungalow. In the last thirty years, we've had perhaps six weeks out of the house. You need money to go on holiday. You need to have the energy to organise yourself. The NHS contributes; it doesn't cover all the costs of this kind of care.'

Bedrich reaches for her hand, but she avoids him.

Imogen asks, 'What happened after he was sixteen?'

Bedrich answers, 'Well, it's different now, but back then once a child had passed school age, the state was no longer obligated to educate him further. You are handed back to the health service. We tried to find day care for adults, but there aren't many NHS places for younger adults. The ones that became available were too far away or…'

Anita jumps in. 'Grim. That's what they were, grim.' Bedrich opens his mouth again, but Anita shushes him with a raised hand. 'None of that matters now. When Jacob was twenty-five Bedrich was sick for a fortnight. He had his gall bladder out and he couldn't lift for a few weeks after that. I couldn't cope. Jacob didn't understand. He couldn't help at all. He fell when I was trying to put him in the hoist. The Social Services asked us if we were coping. So I said, no, we weren't coping. Then they got funny and started watching, investigating us.'

'When Bedrich got better, we began to think about things. What if we died suddenly? Jacob would have to go to a new place to be looked after by strangers. We tried to find him somewhere permanent he could get used to. But the places available were hundreds of miles away or full of senile people. Because we turned these down, the Services decided we didn't really want help.

'Then this new doctor changed Jacob's medication for his muscles… no, sorry, for the epilepsy. Bedrich thought... By mistake Bedrich gave him the same dose of the new medicine. Jacob went into a coma. They took him into hospital for two weeks. During the second week we went off to the coast for four days.'

Anita falls silent and this time she lets Bedrich take her hand. Eventually she looks up again and takes up the story in a less aggressive tone. 'We sat on a bench in the rain and we faced the sea. We watched the tide pulling out, the mud stretching in front of us and plopping with tiny living things. We never saw it turn, only the water climbing so slowly back up the beach. Then we talked. We talked about the hour when we thought Jacob had died. I'm not going to pretend otherwise; that was by far the best whole hour for both of us since that consultant first gave us the diagnosis. It's not that there were no good times with him alive, but for one hour that perpetual uncontrollable motion in our lives stopped. For one hour the darkness – the *fear* of him dying – was no longer a shadow over our heads.' She looks at us hopelessly. 'Nobody understands.'

Once again Kip holds up his hand. Bedrich looks at him slowly, then nods. 'Maybe you do, maybe you do.'

Anita goes on, 'I felt God in my soul again. I thought how much better off Jacob would be with God than with us.' She bends forward, fierce again. 'You must understand. He – Jacob – looked so well in that coma, so normal, simply asleep. He looked... right.'

She looks up, almost smiling. 'It is strange that I am telling you all this, because that's not why we have come. Something else happened on that beach. With God in my soul, I understood finally why we had been picked.' The smile fades and she takes hold of the beads hanging down her front. Twice she looks as though she will go on, but nothing comes out.

Bedrich whispers in her ear 'Shall I? Dearest?' and she nods. He says, 'When we were young, we… our faith was weaker.' Anita nods. 'We had a problem with money, so we shared living in Birmingham. We had a room – a studio room – in Selly Oak. I am looking for a job and Anita is teaching ballroom dancing. We… Anita… we found we were going to have a baby. We were not then married. We… we chose not to have this child.'

Behind me I hear Kip whisper, 'Abortion,' to Lindsay.

Anita takes over again. 'On that beach I received enlightenment. I understood why we had been given Jacob and what we should do next. God will gather him in when we have atoned fully. Jacob was never as well after the coma as before and the Social Services did find a place for him. He is settled now in a home where they are good to him. We said goodbye; we are not necessary any more.

'We have taken a life, we have committed a mortal sin. Jacob's pain is our punishment; he will not be able to rest until we've paid for it.'

'But surely,' Imogen says, 'it is also a mortal sin to take your own lives.'

'Yes, and we will be punished, but we think this is what God planned for us. We also think the fires will be less severe if we have paid for... our baby's life with our own. God will judge us fairly.'

In disbelief I ask, 'Do you really believe in hell and fires and angels and suchlike?'

'Yes,' Anita answers.

Bedrich echoes, 'Yes.'

I look round. Mine's not the only mouth hanging open. There is a hiatus then Adam says, 'I may not go along with the fires of hell, but I understand the bargain with the gods. A life for a life.'

'But,' Leon asks, 'what about God's great forgiveness? All your devotion and work looking after your son, wouldn't God forgive you because of all you did for him.'

To our surprise Daniel asks a question. 'You said you would talk to your priest again, how did that go?'

Bedrich and Anita look at each other. Anita shuts her mouth. Bedrich says, 'He... he didn't understand. He said that we had borne our cross and the Lord understood our burdens and forgave us our sins. He gave us penances – passages of the Bible to read every night – they were all about mercy.'

Anita looks suddenly forlorn. She shakes her head and Bedrich mutters, 'Mercy cannot be ours until we have paid the price.'

Ben suddenly explodes, 'Jesus, this is such twisted logic. I can't believe you buy into it...'

Daniel makes another of his surprise interventions. 'In this instance it doesn't matter what you believe, Ben, only what Anita and Bedrich believe. I'd like to hear a little bit more about Jacob.'

Anita looks round at our concerned faces. 'You think we are unfeeling? That for us Jacob was only a burden? How to tell you about the good times. These were real but lasted perhaps two minutes out of every twenty-four hours. As I was washing him he would giggle when I squeezed out the sponge and the drops fell on his chest. We made these moments last; we talked about them for days. Before he went into the coma, Jacob liked wildlife programmes, especially with the animals moving: lions stalking, sharks hunting.

'He squealed when he enjoyed things. No one else liked the noise, but it made my spirits rise.' She looks sadly at Bedrich, 'We should have bought that cat for him. I was too tired for an animal as well, but we should have bought the cat.'

'We bought all the National Geographic videos and DVDs.' Bedrich reminds her.

The talking goes on and I shut my eyes to imagine Bedrich, Anita and their boy. And there in my mind is Oscar: Oscar squealing as we squirted water pistols at each other; Oscar laughing at a Marx Brothers film, not because he understood, but because I laughed; Oscar nearly drowning, because he jumped into the swimming pool to follow me. I killed what Anita and Bedrich could only dream of – a healthy child.

Adam nudges me awake and I am amazed to find that everyone else has gone to bed. I wish I'd said something kind to Anita and Bedrich. I feel ashamed now about my thoughts; I had assumed that their story would fit my prejudices, that they would confess to fraud or something un-Christian. Although for them abortion is a crime, in legal terms it's not and their situation must have limited their choices. Anita's supressed anger and Bedrich's frequent mental absences make sense now. Their tragedy looks even more pitiful through the glow of my new happiness.

Before we fall asleep that night, Adam says, 'That's it. We're all desperately ordinary, aren't we? I was expecting a gang of criminals, but I'm the only one who's actually committed a crime...' I open my mouth, but Adam corrects himself, 'a legally recognised crime.'

'You've forgotten Lindsay.'

'Good God, so I have, but I doubt she's a criminal.'

He's right; we're a surprisingly mundane crew. 'Lindsay might duck her turn,' I tell Adam, 'but I know what you mean. I was expecting to meet certifiable cases, I guess we're the people who don't feature in the papers, except as stats, and there are millions of us.

No one as far as I can tell is more than a little mad or bad. Daniel was probably spoilt for choice.'

'People think I'm bad. I *am* bad.'

'No you're not. And I don't think they do anymore, Adam, but you must tell them the rest of the story.' He shudders and pulls up the covers. I wish I hadn't reminded him. I backtrack. 'Do you think Daniel chooses similar people every year?'

'I imagine so. There must be an awful lot like us. I'm never surprised about people wanting to die. I have my doubts about Ben though, I think he's laughing at us.' As Adam talks, he is re-arranging my hair, lifting each strand away from my face. He says, 'There's no way to measure guilt.'

I close my eyes to answer, my concentration distracted by the soft movements of his hand against my face. 'Is that why I feel so unattached to life? I am this loose cloud of guilt. I can't parcel it up and throw it away. It disintegrates like mist whenever I try to grasp it, but never ceases to surround me cutting me off from reality and feeling.'

Adam's hand drifts down my back. 'We're real enough, aren't we?'

I laugh. 'Up to a point. I half expect to find this bed is just a magic carpet and I'll wake up soon.'

'This…' his mouth covers mine, 'is the most real event in my whole life... here... now.'

## Adam, Lake Bled – Day eleven

This morning we wake and the sun is missing behind high greyish clouds. I feel chilly as we collect outside the hostel. The plan is to drive down into Bled and visit the picture-book lake there. Adam is marching ahead, his jacket slung over his shoulder, he climbs two steps up into the coach, then turns abruptly.

'Grace seems to think I should tell you about what drove me to kill my father. I'm not sure it alters my guilt, but it's true I didn't tell you the whole.'

He has caught me – in fact all of us – by surprise. My chest begins to thud and I look desperately at Daniel. The lines of strain around his eyes are visibly marked today. With all of us standing around, I can see the car park is not an ideal story venue. I pray he won't put it off. I'm six feet away from Adam. No one moves.

Adam stares at his feet, 'My dad was a great father to me. He spent time with me. He taught me all he knew about woodcraft, all he'd learnt about the behaviour of animals. He really understood them. We'd walk the hills together. The smell of dawn on a June morning, watching the mist lifting, searching out the heart-shaped prints of a deer or the pigeon-toed spoor of a badger; these things I owe him. He let me handle grown-up tools, taught me to use guns. He protected me from Mum when I got my clothes torn or mucked up or we missed dinner. I loved him.'

He lifts his eyes to mine and gropes with one hand for the door-frame of the coach. 'I loved my mum too, but the way you do when you take someone for granted. She never got it quite right with Dad, and being a coward I decided early on I wanted to be on the winning side. My sister also seemed to be on the wrong side of Dad. I couldn't understand this; she and I were so alike. We played together and I would pass on to her what he taught me; but he never spent time with her.'

'I grew up thinking maybe there was some difference between men and women, and I'd understand it when I was older. Dad's patience with me vanished in all his dealings with Mum and Amanda. It was my job to protect my little sister from getting into trouble. I never thought to help my Mum.' Adam stops. His forehead creases. He puts his jacket on. 'We were simply two halves – male and female. I thought women must be cleverer than men, Dad seemed to expect so much more from them than from me.

'Then one day...' Adam stops, takes another half a step up into the coach, then turns back. 'I must've been thirteen, it was a weekend and I was helping out on a neighbouring farm. I gashed my arm on the cutter bar...' I watch his hand move automatically to the scar I stroked last night. '... and was sent home to get it bandaged up. The blood kept dripping and I didn't feel so good. I came up the lane to the back of the house and there was this shed where we kept old tools and overflow machinery. We didn't use it that much, but I wondered for a moment if I should just sit down in it until I felt stronger. I reached about a car's length from the door when I heard noises. They were odd... not quite human. I thought... I thought maybe one of the dogs is trapped in there.'

Adam's narrative is growing slower and slower and I fear he may dry up. He takes a big breath and I see Daniel nod to him. His voice drops to a quiet conversational pitch as though he's forgotten us.

'Then I heard Amanda. She was begging, "please Dad, please don't, please don't, oh please, it hurts...". I didn't understand. I thought she was being smacked for something. I looked through the little window, thinking I could distract him perhaps... I couldn't really understand what I was looking at, but it scared the hell out of me and I ran the rest of the way to the house bellowing for Mum and they all came running. I fainted. My gory arm looked like a good enough reason for my panicky behaviour.'

Adam shakes his head, lips pressed in disgust. 'I was such a coward; I did nothing about Amanda immediately. I started to notice things; how hollow she looked. One day I heard her crying and she was on her own in her room. I told her I knew – though it turned out I didn't know the half of it. She told me things I could never have imagined. My father *and* my uncle... both of them... whenever Mum and I were out of the way. They threatened her with being thrown out on the street if she told Mum. Amanda begged me desperately not to tell her. She implored me not to let Dad know that I knew or he'd kill her. She really believed it. She was eleven years old. It was then that I started plotting my father's death.

'The confusing thing is... ' Adam shakes his head again, his face is contorted and I want to go and hold him, but I daren't move a muscle. Now he has hold of both sides of the coach doorframe. '... the really weird thing is that my relationship with my father stayed the same. When I talked to Amanda I loathed him, but when I was with him, we went on as usual, as if he was the person I had always loved. I am living proof that you can think and feel two opposing emotions about the same person.' He presses one hand to his mouth and I start forward thinking he is going to be sick, but he reaches for the frame again. 'It took two years for me to get the courage – and the opportunity – to deal with him. I'm ashamed of that. All that time my sister suffered. I didn't dare tell anyone, I thought they wouldn't believe me. I couldn't think of any other way to solve the problem except to kill him and...' he hangs his head, 'I couldn't face him knowing I had betrayed him.'

Adam suddenly looks up. I suppose our faces bring him up short.

Imogen murmurs, 'Your mother...?'

'Mum didn't know, she really didn't know. Amanda told her after my uncle was convicted. I'd turned sixteen and left home by then. I thought... I thought, when Mum was ill later she was so bad because she was missing Dad. I didn't know what to say to her. It was only when she was dying – nearly two years ago now – I managed to talk to her, to tell I'd killed Dad, that I found she was ill because of what Amanda told her. She forgave me; she never forgave herself. She couldn't bear that Amanda would have been safe if she'd never adopted her.' Adam's shoulders drop. He mutters hurriedly, 'That's it. I think that's everything. I didn't plan to incriminate my uncle; that seemed, at the time, like some kind of divine justice. The rest you know.'

He sits down abruptly on the coach step, sweat pouring off him and Daniel says, 'Well done.'

I hug him and then to my surprise all the others come too. Nobody says anything much, they simply hug him.

Then, as we climb into the coach Anita says, 'I hope you don't mind me asking, but what happened to your sister? Is she safe?'

'She's fine, she's doing fine. In fact she's married and she's... she's not in England any more.'

As we travel the short journey to Lake Bled Adam's hand trembles in mine. There's a weal across his palm where he clutched the coach door. On arrival we face a choice of water expeditions and opt for a double-seater canoe, rather than join in the bigger boat trip. As soon as we are out of earshot of the others, Adam says, 'Can we go somewhere? Even if we can't... I just want to hold you.'

We cross the lake swiftly, avoiding the island, and let the canoe drift under a group of trees. There's no landing stage and I slip as we scramble out of the canoe. Adam hangs onto my arm and manages to haul me up the bank still clinging to the canoe's painter. We attach this to one of the trees and drag ourselves, dripping and shivering, to the top of the bank. As soon as we find level ground, we hang on to each other. Adam rubs me down. 'Sorry, I'm sorry, Grace, that was stupid.' He laughs. 'We need to find somewhere to get you dry. Coffee wouldn't hurt.'

'What about the canoe?'

'We'll come back for that later.'

As we walk, the sun appears and grows swiftly hot, so that by the time we find a hostel with a bar we feel almost comfortable. There is a little sports gear shop and Adam insists on looking at the clothes. He's like a kid, pulling out all the most garish items. We have other shoppers besides ourselves giggling as he holds blue shorts and purple tops against me. In high delight he buys me a bright green T-shirt and white shorts.

'That's the first time I've bought clothes for someone I love.'

'Surely not, Adam, that must be nonsense. I'm not your first relationship.'

'No, but I ended up with someone who sewed for a living. It doesn't matter, I only meant it was fun. I'd like to do it again.'

'But Adam...'

We stand there by the till, surrounded by fishing tackle and sporty clothes looking at each other. Adam stares at me in disbelief. 'I was forgetting.' He runs a hand over his face. 'I was *forgetting?* I can't think how... I've not done that before.'

'Well...' I start.

He puts out a hand to stop me. 'No, don't say it. I'm not changing my mind. It wouldn't be safe. It wouldn't be right.'

We walk slowly back towards the canoe, sober, silent. We drag the canoe to a better boarding spot and manage to get back in without capsizing it. This small success cheers us for a moment. By the time we reach the others they've nearly finished lunch.

Imogen calls out, 'What a relief, I thought you might have lost your paddles and be spinning in circles in the middle of the lake.'

Ben halloos us, 'Hey, why the new wardrobe?'

'I had an unplanned swim; we had to shop. Sorry we're late.'

'Like the shorts, let's see those legs more often, Grace.'

I slide quickly into place behind the table.

## Lindsay

Lindsay is more agitated than usual. In the last week her complexion has gained a bloom, but today she looks pinched again. Her amazing hazel eyes are too big for her face. As Adam and I start our late meal, she pushes away her barely touched plate. Kip leaves his chair and stands behind her, putting his hands on her shoulders.

Without looking up, she says, 'Adam was so brave this morning. I'll do mine now.'

She remains sitting and Kip, who has barely left her side except to drive in the last three days, keeps his hands on her shoulders all the way through as if to keep her from flying off.

'I had anorexia. You may think I'm thin now, but truly I'm well. You should have seen me three years ago. My mother didn't ever understand. She thought... she seemed to think I was perfect – except for anything to do with food.'

Kip's fingers lift and he brushes her neck with the back of his hand then lets it settle back on her shoulder. Lindsay leans into the caress with the barest smile. I glance at Adam. His eyes warm, he puts a hand to his mouth and my heart flips. A week ago a tiger could have come crashing through the undergrowth and I would have barely raised a sweat, now I can almost hear butterflies breathing and the air seems to be thick with silent human communications.

Lindsay goes on in a stronger voice, 'I don't understand where it went wrong. I did love my mother once. I remember sitting on a rug. We were having a picnic in our own garden and there were flowers humming with bees and I was frightened, but she made me see that bees were different from wasps. She put her hands in the flowers, carefully, and the bees took no notice, they were only interested in the blooms. Later she let a wasp walk all the way up her arm.

'I know I loved her then, but by the time I was about thirteen I knew I hated my mother. I didn't – I still don't – know why. She wasn't unkind to me; she kept trying to understand. Whenever she was around me, I felt sick. She seemed gigantic and... and bouncing. She was a cook – I mean a real cook, she cooked for a police conference centre. She concentrated on food. Whatever I did around food, even when I was little, I got it wrong: too much milk in my cereal, not enough salt in the vegetable water. Meals took forever. I decided she must have been someone else's mother. The grimmer I became, the louder she became. After a while I couldn't swallow in the same room as her, so I ate less and less. The more I begged her to leave me alone, the more she hovered, bellowing encouragement. So I stopped eating.

'I couldn't tell her I hated her; I did tell her to go away, but she said she had to stick by me. Every single meal, until I was sixteen and had to go into hospital, was a nightmare...'

She stops and Kip's hand slips down her arm.

Imogen asks, 'Lindsay, where was your father while all this was going on?'

Lindsay looks bewildered. 'Father? I haven't got a father. It was just me and Mum.'

Leon says, 'Lindsay, everyone has a father. Didn't you ask.'

'Some people come out of a test tube these days. Mum really didn't have the faintest idea who he was. Anyway, I was never very interested when I was little. There'd always been just me and Mum. She didn't have any other relatives.'

'Sorry, go on.'

'When they took me into hospital the first time, they made Mum see a psychiatrist. I don't really know what went on there, but after several visits to this man Mum got really angry. Then, about three years ago, I had to be hospitalised again and this time Mum saw a different therapist and when she came to see me she kept saying sorry. I didn't know why she said sorry and I couldn't change the way I felt about her just like that. I said sorry too but I still felt sick when she came. The hospital worked out that I always relapsed after her visits. Someone decided I would be better off not being visited. Mum took an overdose. She meant it. She took a week off work and told colleagues she was going away.'

Lindsay half rises from her chair. Kip lifts his hands as if to say you are free if you want to go. No one moves. She sinks back and Kip drops a kiss on the top of her head. '

'A guy came to read the meter and he got a "funny feeling" about her flat and called the police. They got her to hospital still alive.' Lindsay looks down at the table.

The group stay motionless. Very slowly and carefully Kip lifts one hand and rubs the back of it softly up and down Lindsay's neck. It is as if he is calling her back to the present. After thirty seconds, she looks up again.

'She was in the same hospital as me for four weeks.'

Imogen, speaking very softly asks, 'Lindsay, did you see your mother?' Lindsay only nods. 'Did she... could she explain? Had she left a note or anything?'

Lindsay frowns. 'Yes. There was almost a court case. The social services were very angry. Something the therapist said made Mum think it was all her fault – my illness, I mean. Then, when the hospital wouldn't let her visit me because it made me worse, she decided that if she died I would get better.

'They said Mum might not recover, but she did; we sort of got better at the same time. Later, when we were both back home, she said that the only thing she wanted in life was to see me healthy with my own children. She was the end of a line and had gone to great trouble to keep her genes alive in me, but if I died that would be the end of them. She believed that she was the one thing that prevented my survival.'

Leon says, 'But Lindsay, by coming here you are making her worst fears come true. Surely you are guaranteeing that your mother will die?'

'Yes, I know.' Lindsay's head is hanging down. 'But you see, after Mum's attempt I tried so hard. I finished my exams, did a holiday job with the police, and started a training course with them, but then I found out...'

She slumps and breathes out despairingly, 'I can never have children. The anorexia bought on a premature menopause. You see I am not a whole person any more. I'm what my mother would call damaged goods – a woman no man would ever want and...' she looks up, face flushed, 'there will be no grandchildren. How can I tell my mother that?'

'You have told us very bravely,' Imogen says, 'I think now you could go home and tell your mother.'

Leon says, 'Lindsay, this isn't a reason to commit suicide.'

Vicky leans over. 'No, Leon, you don't understand. Women are still pressurised to feel incomplete without children. It's incredibly bad luck, Lindsay, but you've been ill. It's not your fault and I do think you could have a good life even without having children.'

'Thank you, Vicky. You once said there's no one on this trip with a mental illness, but that's not true. I understand this now. I have one and it's a bit like an obsessive-compulsive disorder. I fix on quite small things and magnify and distort them. As a child everything appeared outsized to me and it blitzed my brain. If I showed you a picture of my mother you wouldn't think her big, if you ever met her she might seem quite quiet to you.'

Lindsay sounds astonishingly serene and when we stop commenting, she continues, 'I'm not sure I want to die anymore, but I can't think how to tell my mother or make it up to her. But now Kip thinks there might be a better way to manage our guilt at home. He's so brave.'

I look round. Eleven days ago all these faces looked dull, sickened by life, aching for the quick exit. Now we're wearing silly grins, Lindsay is lit up from inside and the ice has melted out of Kip's expression.

Lindsay goes on, 'I guess you may feel that I'm a fraud coming on this trip and wasting Daniel's time. I really did mean it and I used all my money to come. If we go home, Kip and I, we'll have to start from scratch, but that's fair enough.' Lindsay's shoulders have relaxed, her voice is firm; she looks us in the eye. 'Don't laugh, but I feel bad about Jez, my cat. I know she's not a person, but I don't want to abandon her too. I want my workmates to meet Kip, I want to meet Kip's dad. We may make an unholy mess, but together we think we'd like to give it a go.'

This is the first open suggestion of returning anyone has made. Looking at Daniel, I see him close his eyes for a long moment, he looks as though someone has given him a good night's sleep at last. I have a split second vision of giving Daniel a similar gift then push it aside. Adam is going to cross that border for a lot of better reasons than most of the rest of us and there is no way I will go home without him. No, we have ten more days of bliss, but that's it.

## Awake at night

This evening, I sense the group changing focus. Until now we have been slowly knitting together, today's near decision causes us to start unravelling. I feel almost resentful towards Lindsay and Kip. When we all had a common purpose, it was easy to focus without pain on our end, to feel a certain pride in our resolution, now that they have broken rank it calls into question all our decisions.

We go to bed straight after supper, supposedly to pack for an early start the next day. As we lie exhausted, Adam, his head buried in my shoulder, murmurs, 'We must talk,' and promptly falls into a deep sleep. I too succumb, without even switching off the bedside light. A couple of hours later he stirs, rolls on his back and repeats, 'We must talk.' Then speaks urgently as if there's been no interval.

'Grace, I know I'm not good at explaining, but I need to tell you why I have to go ahead.' He is running two fingers up and down my arm as he speaks. 'You say you feel untethered. I'm the opposite. My "deed" has handcuffed me to the dark side of life. Never mind Derek coming to get me,' his hand pauses, '– and I am turned to jelly by that thought – I am also tied to the foulest, the grimiest of human behaviour.' I catch his restless hand. He reacts as though I have interrupted. 'No, let me say it. You once said religion is sticky stuff; believe me, child abuse, and I'll bet that's just as ancient, clings like tar.' Adam pulls his hand away to rub it on the sheet. I grab it and hold it to my face.

I wonder if there's anything I can say to release him from this dark bond. Not that I've ever said or done anything of the least use to anyone. I wish Daniel could be here to answer Adam. A description of the beautiful world he might inhabit sounds idiotic coming from me. Daniel talked about life as like building a wall, if you put in a duff brick, it's best not to waste time trying to extract and replace it because you can't undo the past, but better to accept the mistake, and keep building with better bricks.

Adam is frowning and shaking his head. Letting go of my hand, he slips off the bed and walks over to the window, pulling the curtain aside and peering through. I can see a glaring almost circular moon above us. My hand lies abandoned, cold against the sheet. I feel on the edge of a possibility. He wouldn't be talking through these ideas if his decision is irrevocable.

I love him and don't want him to die, but on past record, what are the chances of me making a go of anything? Though perhaps with Adam... 'Adam? Couldn't we...?'

He stands across the room staring at me. Neither of us moves for some time. I don't even remember how it ends – at least I do in the sense that we finish up back on the bed – we make no decisions, I think we agree without speech to let the idea of living take root or simply dissipate, then we drift back into sleep.

I've been lying in the dark trying to work out which day we've reached. I creep out of bed to hold my watch up to the streetlamp outside the window. It is not yet five o'clock. Not wanting to wake Adam, I drag on my jeans and a jumper by feel, grab a map notebook and go downstairs.

There, before dawn, in the hostel lounge, I find Daniel on the computer. He has a pile of forms beside him. No wonder he looks as though he never sleeps, he really doesn't.

'Daniel! Have you been up all night?'

'No of course not.' He speaks lightly, 'I bet I've had more sleep than you.'

I laugh, 'Probably. But why are you working at this hour?'

'I need to sort out some paperwork. It's easier when it's all quiet.'

*Some* paperwork? He has a box file full of documents, as well as some loose papers. He's fully dressed, including the brown jacket. He drags a hand through his already roughed-up hair.

I want to help him, but can't imagine how. 'Is it to do with where we will go at the end?'

'Some of it. With Kip going home, there are changes. The self-catering chalet that we had hired in… where we are going… was in his name. It's not a problem, but there are rules and we must abide by them.'

'It's not illegal, though, to commit suicide, is it?'

'No. It's not illegal in England either.'

'It's the assisted bit that's illegal, isn't it? You could be in trouble for helping us.'

'You will be in charge of what you take and when you take it, so I won't be helping you in that sense.'

'But you'll be there?'

'I'll be there.'

I wander over to the drinks machine glowing on the other side of the room. It's humming gently. That combined with Daniel's voice is making me feel sleepy at last. There's something I don't like, though. I think it's the smell – old peaches? Probably an air-freshener.

'Why do you do all this, Daniel? I mean take us lot and work so hard? You make us all feel better, but what do you get out of it?'

'Oh I do it mostly for selfish reasons. As for rewards, don't you think Kip and Lindsay's faces are rewards enough? Not to mention the kick I get out of seeing you and Adam together.'

I drift over to the sofa and curl up on it. 'Daniel?'

'Uhuh?'

'I'm not sure about us.' Then seeing his puzzlement, 'Oh no. I'm sure about us *together*. I would love to make you happy by going home, but I'm not sure about us changing our minds. Adam can't go back ever. He…'

'Grace this decision is for you and Adam alone. You must not try and please anyone but yourselves. I can't say that emphatically enough. My wishes, even if they were as you imagine, are less important than the Man in the Moon's.'

He's bending over his work again, so I pull out my notebook to look at Lake Bled on the map. I cannot concentrate for worrying about Daniel, yet his profile is serene with a complete absence of irritation in his gaze. How rare is that? Is he good-looking? I can't assess him impartially; his physical presence and his emotional responses are a gigantic safety net on which we all depend. Kindness makes its own magnetism.

'Daniel, have you got a girlfriend?'

He doesn't look up, but I can see his smile. 'No.' I wait hoping that he will qualify that statement if I am patient. He turns to me still smiling – it looks to me like a contented smile. 'I said goodbye to my last girlfriend before I left on this journey.'

Does he mean he broke up with her? Why should saying goodbye make him happy? I can't think of a way to ask more. He doesn't look sad. Baffling.

He's already turning back to the screen, though not in a dismissive way, so I ask, 'Do you have to keep making arrangements all through the journey? I thought it was all booked and planned beforehand.'

'Yes, it is mostly, but there are always things to deal with, especially with the transport. The coach, for instance, was a gift to me and I need to make sure that it's in more than one name.'

There's a sound; Adam is in the doorway, in boxers and a t-shirt. His hair, already growing out of its short crop and now crumpled with sleep, makes his face that of a child. I want to eat him.

'Grace, thank God, I thought... Morning, Daniel... at least, is it morning? What's the time?'

'Five twenty am. Go back to bed, both of you.'

'Good idea.'

'Remember you have to be packed, breakfasted and at the coach by eight forty-five. Some of us are climbing a mountain today.'

Adam, in the act of scooping me up, pauses, eyes widening. 'Jesus, Mount Triglav. It's the one thing I planned to do on this trip. Oh God, I'll never stay awake.'

'It's all right. No one's actually climbing; we're doing the hike to Viševnik, which is close to Triglav. The mountain itself is a two-day hike for fit people, we're only going to sample the nearby hills, get the feel of it.'

## Hike up Viševnik – Day twelve

Four hours later we drive up to the end of the road west from Bled. The mountains open and close before us; now hidden by soaring conifers, now spread out beyond open meadows with the rocks pushing through. We park near a barracks and in minutes Imogen, Bedrich, Anita, Lindsay and Kip are waving us off. Imogen is miserable at being left behind; she twisted her ankle yesterday. Ben has promised to photograph stuff on his mobile for her. Vicky, whose health has improved every day, has decided to come. She now reveals that she and her husband David used to holiday in Scotland, before her mother became so ill. They would climb several Munros each year. I've not walked any distance for years and my knees are not in the best shape after so little sleep. Still, I crave the space and air of the mountains.

We follow a signboard to a ski lift and take it to the halfway station. At least we get to sit down for a bit. Then we walk – and walk. I worry about Leon, who is dripping with sweat in minutes. Ben looks astonishingly cool and alert. He has a pair of binoculars today; I've not seen these before.

He scans the horizon and pauses over some distant figures: 'You'd think this was the back of beyond. I mean, in this country the locals are thin enough on the ground to say hello to tourists, but look, here we are up a mountain and I can see at least four other clusters of people. If I wanted to hide, I think a busy city would be safer than this.'

'And do you want to hide?' Adam asks casually.

Ben chuckles, 'I don't think my particular past is likely to be hiking in green fields. How about you?'

'My past might well be found in mountains, but in England.'

Vicky is crouching by a rock on one side of the track. She beckons. 'Imogen would love this. Look at these scarlet flowers, any idea what they might be?'

Ben looks down. 'I haven't the faintest. I'll take some for Imogen to identify.'

'No, no don't, Ben, we're specifically asked not to pick anything.'

Ben shrugs and desists. I doubt he worries about the prohibition, but he isn't interested enough to argue. I'm beginning to wonder if there's anything Ben does care much about.

A couple of hours out, the land spreads into a sudden high green plateau and we stop for a ten-minute break. Adam and I wander to one side sharing a bottle of water. There's no one in sight, no sound, not even birdsong. Adam's face crumples. 'Why can't we stop right here?'

I don't have an answer and lean against him, silent. He laughs, 'I'm dripping; you'll get wet. It's amazing how unfit I've become.'

I run a hand down his arm – all sinew. 'Nonsense. Hey, we forgot to put sun cream on, we're really high here, we could burn.'

On cue, Daniel calls out, 'Anyone not protected from the sun? It's quite important up here.'

Ben makes a wry face. 'I'm beginning to think we're all faking it. What's the point of worrying about cancer if we're going to be dead in a week?'

Leon says, 'Well I've had real sunburn and I don't fancy even one hour of it. By the time you realize you're burnt, it's too late.'

We return to the group and paint up. I notice that Leon seems to have got into his stride. Of course, in his past he must have done a lot of this. He's found a stick for Vicky and is carrying her kit too. Ben looks a little weary and is not talking so much. I'm just about coping. I wonder if it is possible to walk and sleep simultaneously. Daniel and Adam look to me like they're out for a stroll.

Our next stop is the peak of Viševnik. I pull out my map; we have reached 2050 metres above sea level! Of course we have only climbed 700 of them today and some of that was by ski lift. I still feel we have climbed to the top of the world, but there is Triglav towering another 700 metres above and to the West of us. I have never climbed a mountain before, so although it only counts as a gentle hike, for me it's a new world, an unanticipated achievement. I stand on top grinning and almost wagging my tail. Energy flushes through me. Vicky is sniffing, beaming and wiping her eyes. Leon looks about ten years younger.

On the route back we all seem to be wrapped in bubbles of calm, or in my case fatigue. With lead in my limbs I climb onto the coach and fall instantly asleep only waking up when Adam shakes me, whispering, 'We've stopped for a game.'

I groan.

Daniel wants us to play at being very hungry lions and anxious deer. The deer are clustered in an inner circle and the lions get to prowl around an outer one. They can invade the deer space and snatch and drag one into the lion space. The Lions are allowed to touch but not speak, the deer can talk, but not touch. In one of the rounds Ben, Leon and Adam are alarmingly successful predators.

Afterwards Vicky flops down on the meadow. She is collecting starry white flowers for Lindsay who is weaving a daisy chain. 'If that was about co-operation, we didn't do very well, did we?'

Daniel hands her some daisies. 'As well as anyone does. It isn't easy. You need all your senses to communicate and in this case you were deprived of either touch, as deer, or speech, as lions.'

Ben says, 'It was as good a way of getting exercise as any other. I enjoyed being a lion, but it all seemed a bit of a joke.'

Anita gives Ben a look. 'And what wouldn't be a joke to you?'

'Ah, that would be telling.' He answers with a disarming smile. 'I meant it seriously.'

'OK. I have a problem with these games, they're too remote from everyday life. It's a jungle out there in the real world, real human lions and jackals and vultures. These exercises feel like kid's party games – no disrespect, Dan.'

All eyes swivel to Daniel. He smiles, looking, I'm relieved to say, wholly relaxed. This is the nearest thing to criticism anyone has voiced or, I assume, felt.

'You're quite right Ben, these games and exercises have nothing to do with real life. The framework I'm using, such as pretending to be lions or deer, *is* more like the games children play. When they play, children are serious, concentrated, committed and open-minded. They play for the game itself.

'I'm trying to make something special happen for you – for us all – when we play these games. Even though we're adults, we can sometimes recover that same state of mind and freedom from major life goals that children have. We may be able to live 'in the moment' the way they do – that is without any concerns or thoughts about yesterday, tomorrow or even this evening. With this kind of focus, it is possible to gain new insights into what you enjoy, how others behave, how that affects you and how you feel about them.' Daniel grins at our furrowed brows. 'OK, lecture over, but I hope that makes some sense to you Ben.'

Ben shrugs, lips pressed in a half grin. 'Yup. Though I can't stop myself from seeing the comical side.'

Lindsay, frowning, pauses in her daisy work to look at Ben. 'I'm not sure it was that funny. I didn't like it at all when you and Adam and Leon were lions. You looked so big and… and *ravenous*. It reminded me that I'm a woman and of that feeling in your stomach as you walk down an empty street at night and hear footsteps behind you.' She shivers.

'It happened to me once,' Imogen admits. 'He was up to no good, but someone opened a front door at the moment he caught up with me. I ran in and he ran away. I was very lucky.'

'Me too,' says Vicky. 'I guess I was very lucky too. He did grab me and his trousers were undone, with his bits dangling out, but he was very young and scared and I had on a big winter coat all buttoned up. I just kept walking and in the end he gave up. I feel bad that I never went to the police, but I would have felt bad if I *had* gone. He was more like a sick person than a bad person. I have sometimes worried about how dangerous he might have become when he grew older.'

'Did it help at all, Vicky,' Daniel asks, 'to know that you were part of a group and could call out warnings if necessary.'

'Ye-es, it did in a way. It's always comforting being with friends.'

Again, most of us nod and the ripple of anxiety passes.

## Night at Kranska Gora

We arrive for the night in Kranska Gora, a mountain pass away from both Austria and Italy. We find a hotel designed for skiers, with luxurious heating and spanking swimming facilities. Remembering Daniel up and working in the early hours, Imogen, Vicky and I have an impromptu meeting and decide to buy him a massage that evening. Imogen wants to pay for it all, but allows us to chip in a bit.

Daniel is honestly delighted. I just hope it helps him relax a bit. For the rest of us, after our hike, wallowing in the Olympic-sized pool and swimming our over-taxed muscles back to health is pleasure enough. I float on my back, watching glittering lights and savouring something intangible; a sense of rightness, a fusion of mind and body. I'm dazzled and can hardly bear to leave the pool. Is this happiness? Perhaps it only feels so good because it's transient.

In bed tonight we make lazy, carefree love and talk about nothings. I look at Adam's body beside me. All his limbs are so finely and lightly drawn, every bone is visible at the surface, softened only by resting muscles. I wonder how I come to be there beside him. It all still feels unreal. This isn't me in this drama, it's as though I am being auditioned for someone else's role. There's naturally been some mistake. Any minute now Adam will turn round and say, sorry, I thought you were someone else.

'What is it, Grace?'

I jump. 'I'm only looking at your... your bones. I...'

'Is that what made you frown?'

'No, I... Why me, Adam, why me? I can see why anyone might want to touch you, but what have I got?'

He gives a small crack of laughter. *'Had we but world enough and time...* You're the nearest thing to a wood nymph I could find.'

'No Adam, I mean it honestly. I think I need to know.'

His smile fades as he scans my face. 'Grace, you must believe me. When I set out on this trip, the last thing in my mind was women, sex or any distraction at all. Only something as potent, as inescapable as... as you, could have got past my defences.' The lamp behind my shoulder shows the clear grey of his irises, they have a darker outer ring with little irregularities. He blinks at last. 'You want to know what it is that you have? I'm not sure I can describe it. You're like a wild creature, sure in some moments, uncertain in others; aware of your surroundings, rarely aware of yourself. You sometimes escape to places no one can follow. And your eyes... your whole face... it's like sun and storm clouds: far away, aware, fierce, calm, ... I'm not doing this very well, am I? I'm trying, I really am trying.'

I open and shut my mouth.

He reaches over and pulls out a strand of my hair then takes a whole handful and gives it a tug. 'I love this stuff and...' He shrugs, 'I think perhaps you were a cat in a previous life. I see it when you fold your body onto the grass for our exercises.'

I find speech again. 'Don't you mean a goat? I'm so awkward.'

'Goats are very elegant, sure-footed creatures.' Adam looks away across the room, 'I don't know if I dare ask you the same question. My constant panic is that I have captured a wild thing and you will escape at the first opportunity.'

'Adam. You idiot, how can you doubt me? For the first time in as long as I can remember, an image – your image – haunts me more frequently than Oscar's.'

'Really? Then perhaps I've done some good in my life.'

'You have, though I'm now so incompetent I can't cope when you're away from me. I hate it when you leave a room. I feel sort of... chilly?'

He starts shaking with laughter. 'OK, so I'm a good draught excluder.'

'Don't laugh. I have a teenager problem; when you speak unexpectedly my heart speeds up like I just said something really stupid in public. Then there's your bones... which is where we started...'

As he is lying on his side I reach out and lay my hand on the wing of his hipbone where it shades the hollow curve beneath.

Midnight, three am, or dawn? I can feel Adam breathing on my bare arm. The sensation is incredibly faint; shades of warmer and cooler. If I stop concentrating I stop feeling. The light behind the curtain looks more morning-grey than yellow lamplight, though it's too dark to see Adam and I daren't move for fear of waking him. Four days now since Adam and I... discovered each other? We subsist in an increasingly fragile balance: on one side the new strength between us, on the other our waning physical and mental reserves.

I should wake up feeling deadbeat, but my limbs are taut with the thrill of being alive. I want to climb another mountain today, or swim in a wild sea. Sometimes, when I was little I would feel like this just before a race, as if a bolt of power had detonated my heart and flung me towards the finishing line. I *knew* I would win.

I lie now, relishing my stillness, feet and fingertips buzzing with energy. I close my attention down to the pinpoint on my arm where Adam's breath is stroking my skin. This is the most physical sense of joy I've ever known. The fates, enigmatic as always, have given me more than I dreamt of, but only for another nine days.

I have no fear of the death ahead. I have everything in the world here and now, I'm aware that I have it and I know there is no possibility that time will destroy my love. This once I'm lucky. Maybe this is what Adam meant yesterday on the mountain top – he wanted to die at the instant of perfection.

Adam sighs, shifts and looks towards me in the half light. He puts his hands over his face and says, as if in the middle of a conversation, 'I daren't do it. Derek might find us. I'd be putting you in his path. I can't risk that.'

'Can't do what?'

'Live with you.' He opens his hands to look at me, 'He promised torture. He might hurt you, to get at me. Even if he only kills me, you'll be back where you started. You'll have gone through all of this for nothing. I can't bear that responsibility.'

'Adam, I'm not your little sister. If I cared about living I wouldn't be here. If we went home and then something happened to you – you died – I would get in a car and gas myself. Easy.'

He laughs and groans, 'But Grace, my darling, you'd get the hoses mixed up... God, I shouldn't joke. I don't know what to do.'

'Hey, Adam, just for once let someone else take responsibility. I think I want to live, but only on condition that you do too. So long as we don't have any kids we'll be fine. We can change our minds.

Neither of us fear death – only being alone with our consciences.'

'I don't know, I don't know.' He falls asleep as abruptly as he has woken up. When I wake him two hours later, I'm uncertain if he remembers our conversation.

## Vršič Pass – Day thirteen

Before we leave the hotel at Kranska Gora, we gather in the spare breakfast room for an exercise like grandmother's footsteps, but crossed with musical chairs. I fail to bag a chair when it's my turn. Adam goes last and walks in circles for nearly all of his five minutes. He stumbles and the others laugh thinking it's a ruse, then he stands still and covers his face. It's only when Daniel puts an arm round him and signals that game over that we see the tears spilling between his fingers. My knees tremble. I've never seen Adam cry.

Daniel says softly, 'More sleep, less thinking, for you over the next twenty-four hours.'

I put both arms round Adam and Imogen and Lindsay come and hug him too.

Struggling to speak, Adam asks, 'Daniel, can we talk?'

Daniel gestures the rest of us onto the coach, while he and Adam sit down on a bench. I stop half way and perch on a bollard.

Adam turns his wallet over and over in his hands. He speaks as though I'm not there. 'Daniel I've thought and thought. I want Grace to live, I'd like to live with her, but I can't. Yet if I cross the border to die I can't prevent her coming too.'

Daniel turns Adam by the shoulder and looks at him for a moment, then says, 'Adam, first, Grace came along with her mind made up. She would have crossed the border anyway. Second, however complicated it might prove to be, I believe it must be possible, if you both want to live, to find somewhere safe from your uncle. That doesn't mean I think you *should*, only that you *could* – if you wanted to. He may take a year or two to adjust to modern technology, presuming he has the capacity for a start.'

Adam is silent, his hands still rolling the wallet.

Daniel asks, 'What else is troubling you?'

Adam looks up. 'I promised I would pay for my father's life and my lie about my uncle with my own life. I had to wait until my sister was safe. Now I must pay my debt.'

'Debt to whom?'

'... my conscience... society... justice... I've never articulated it.'

'Try and work out who will benefit from your sacrifice. You're not religious are you?' Adam shakes his head. 'So the balance is between you and yourself. Have you thought that with Grace's appearance your moral equation might need re-balancing? Perhaps giving her a reason to live could be set in the scales against your moral debt – the killing of your father.'

Adam stands up and registers me nearby. 'I don't know, I don't know. I'm not certain of anything any more. I've never had trouble making decisions before, now I'm lost. It's as if aliens have scrambled my brain.' He puts both hands on his head as if it might be in danger of mutiny. He's almost laughing and calls out, 'Grace, you haven't by some magical property infiltrated my mind have you?'

Daniel laughs outright. 'I fear you should be blaming me, Adam. Part of the work I've been doing with you is intended, not so much to destabilize you – the lack of sleep is to blame for that – but to expand your vision. Where once decisions were easy, because you didn't look beyond your own established arguments, I've tried to help you view other possibilities.'

Adam looks from Daniel to me then back again. 'If staying alive means Grace lives even one more week, then I'll try to think of a way… of somewhere I can work.'

I'm so surprised I stand suddenly and then feel dizzy. Daniel and Adam both look like people who find the pan they're holding hotter than they expected.

'Go slowly,' Daniel says, 'sleep on the thought, talk to each other. There's time.'

To complete my sense of destabilisation, we set off up the dizzying road through the Vršič pass, built by Russian prisoners in the First World War. Poor Anita suffers again from her terror of heights and Daniel produces another fiendish little puzzle for her to concentrate on. Now the road is full of traffic, including pedal bikes. We proceed very gingerly round almost circular bends, our attention alternating between the ancient cobbles surfacing at intervals between the stretches of tarmac and the breathtaking vistas.

At the summit viewing area we pause the coach. Rocky peaks etraces of snow surround us, with here and there swathes of conifers and deciduous trees and the usual bright green grass. We wander about, drinking it in. Adam and I, on another planet, stand handfast, filling our eyes with the panorama. We don't talk. The enormity of his suggestion earlier has silenced us. My mind has gone into sleep mode and is avoiding all conscious activity.

We drive on to the Alpinum Julianum Gardens. Here you need a magnifying glass to spot the colour among the rocks and thin grasses. Once again Ben is using his binoculars, but to watch other tourists as far as I can see. He's quieter than usual, is that my fault?

When I next look round Ben has disappeared; so has Anita. Vicky and Bedrich are scrambling up some rocks. Imogen, with her nose to the ground, is beaming, though she says the flora would have been a lot more rewarding in spring. This is one of the places she and Stewart planned to visit. When she sees an interesting plant, she looks round as if she expects him to come and share her discovery. Adam goes straight over to her and stays beside her.

I walk on through the gardens in a daze. Going home? Good idea? Bad idea? I imagine some isolated suburb in Australia, where Adam's skills have no relevance and he feels I've imprisoned him there; or the two of us stuck in a cabin in the backwoods of Canada, with no friends and few jobs; or making do in a city in South America, with Adam struggling to learn the language and no work.

Apart from being with Adam, there's nothing attractive about these options. They all involve being somewhere strange, not knowing how to earn a living and worrying about whether this passion will fade into my usual indifference. My instinct is that of course it won't, but my rational mind begs to differ. My past is not a good augury for the future. If I get something I want I can guarantee it will turn bad. Poor Adam, taking me on is like being lumbered with an albatross.

I continue to slide towards despondency, while Adam wanders with Imogen. I'm not going to be much use in any life ahead if I can't manage twenty minutes solo or become jealous of the likes of Imogen. Back on the coach, Daniel takes over the driving. I sit with Adam's shoulder solid against my own and slowly recover the euphoria of an hour ago. We reach the family hotel in Kobarid in time for a late supper. Tonight our group are the only guests.

## Vicky and Dancing

As we sit over the remains of the meal, Ben looks casually around and raises his glass. 'Well fellow travellers in guilt, I don't know about the rest of you, but I'm enjoying myself in spite of all.'

Daniel asks, 'Is that what you feel connects everyone – guilt?'

'Yes, well in most cases, Vicky excepted, someone has died or been hurt and we feel guilty about it.'

Vicky sighs. 'I'm not really the odd one out. You lot all seem to think you've committed some kind of a crime – except perhaps Imogen – but you probably think I haven't. Well I have.'

Imogen looks as if she might speak, but Vicky shakes her head. 'No, let me finish. When we got married my husband didn't know about the Huntington's disease in my family and I very carefully failed to tell him. I didn't lie; I avoided the truth. I told myself I had as much right to fall in love with David as anyone else. Other people will get Alzheimer's or any number of other diseases, why should I give him up, because of a gene I might not have? I fooled myself that we could have children. Even if I carried the gene, all I would need to do is have a test and terminate any foetus that carried the gene. It sounded fine in my head.'

Anita wants to know, 'When did he find out?'

'Well, one of my aunts at the wedding did mention a genetic disease in the family. He wasn't too worried immediately, but my mother's symptoms, only a few mild twitchings at our wedding, became painfully evident within a year or two of our marriage and he began to ask questions.'

'What on earth did you tell him?' I ask.

'A half-truth. I said it was like cancer, some people have genes more likely to make them vulnerable to, say, breast cancer than others, but they don't necessarily get the disease. I might or might not have the Huntington gene, but I couldn't live my whole life anticipating it. He was amazingly sanguine about it. I still felt guilty though; in my heart of hearts I knew I had deliberately deceived him. He wanted kids. The only sane thing I did was insist on being tested before getting pregnant. I tested positive. That was the moment I realised the extent of my crime.'

Vicky starts rearranging the mats on the table in front of her. 'Since then we've watched and nursed my mother as she descended into dementia. She died a year ago and David is stuck married to me. Even if we went ahead and had a selected child who did not have the gene, both he and the child would be faced with me to look after – and it can last for many, many years. I can't do it. David keeps pressing me to get pregnant and I really wanted children – my biological clock is at its limits now.'

She is stacking the little beer mats in a pile. 'I'm forty today.'

Lindsay jumps up, 'Vicky! You should have said. Happy Birthday!' The words sound horrendously inappropriate. We all try to echo them without sounding stupid.

Vicky waves our efforts away. 'No don't. I can't celebrate, can I? Let me finish. I need to be honest now. I want to say that if you lot are all guilty, then so am I. What's more, I can't live with my crime – see! I'm no different from any of the rest of you – except that my death really will absolve me. In my opinion some of you would gain better absolution by living and making reparation for what you think you've done. That's up to you, of course. I hope my death will set David free to marry, have children and not have to spend ten or more years caring for me.'

Kip picks up a couple of mats adds them to her pile and says, 'Vicky, what if he feels he's caused your death? What if he never marries again, never has children and… grieves the rest of his life.'

'Of course, that's possible. More likely he will be sad, then rebuild his life and start again. He's a couple of years younger than me. He's a nice guy.'

Her face crumples and a few tears trickle out. This is so unlike the Vicky we thought had been sharing our travels, we are devastated. She bends over and dabs her face with a napkin.

'I did leave him a letter, but it says all the wrong things. It's like a list of household chores. I told him to remember to make the bed every day. I couldn't bear the idea of him going upstairs to sleep and finding a cold uninviting mess – but I didn't tell him that was why. He would have stopped me, he wouldn't have believed I prefer to die now, but I do, so I had to come without telling him.' She ends on a wail of distress and we all crowd round, petting her.

Between sobs she gulps out, 'I want to have children. I want a normal life, but I can't have that. I hate my parents… for giving birth to me. The only thing I can do… is not pass on this hatred and these brutal genes.'

Vicky's cruel choices turn most of our decisions into almost comfortable dilemmas. I feel grateful relief for my good health, which should be irrelevant if I am going to die in a week's time. Does that mean I want to live? I know I don't want to be a mother.

As we leave the table and go into the big hotel lounge, Leon and Lindsay, who had both slipped out, suddenly reappear with a prettily wrapped parcel and give it to Vicky. They've given her some really good hand cream – and I've heard Vicky complaining about her dry skin – so it's exactly what she would like.

Now I'm tearful too and sad for my mother. I don't want to be her, with me as a child. I don't want to have a child who might die.

Vicky holds Lindsay's hand and reaches out to Kip. 'I dream that you two will go home and I know that you can't have babies, but perhaps you can adopt – as I would have done if only I could have brought them up. Will you... Do you think you could one day go to Newcastle – I know it's a long way – and talk to David? Tell him what it was like? Tell him I cared?'

Lindsay, who tends to give Vicky a wide berth, lays a cheek against her hair. 'We'll do that. Don't worry, Vicky, we'll explain that the best thing he can do to remember you is to start a family.'

Newcastle. I had wiped the map of England from my mental images so I'm struggling to digest this link back to home. Vicky is blowing her nose and beginning to smile. Daniel starts pushing back the furniture.

'Party time,' he says.

Our mood flips. I assume at first that the dance idea is spontaneous, yet Daniel has a small player and a handful of CDs with different styles of dance music. Bedrich and Anita are the unlikely stars and have us all doing a vigorous Lindy Hop – or some wild equivalent. We Cha Cha, Twist, Waltz (Imogen) and wind in and out of an Eightsome Reel (magnificently managed by Adam). Leon performs a mean Rock and Roll, but none of us are really able to match him except Anita. Kip suddenly lets his hair down. He does a sort of Singing in the Rain tap dance style – very slick, quick and funny and he sings along. The transformation has me surfing on happiness. Then we all have a go.

When it comes to me, I can't decide on anything and protest that, ballet lessons apart, I can't remember any dances.

'Fine, give us a ballet lesson then,' Adam says.

We line up, all a little bit tiddly by now, holding onto the backs of chairs and I have them doing *pliés* and *jettées* like professionals. Vicky is reluctant, but as soon as she has the chair back to hold she's as steady as the others. In fact, her feet point correctly in the five ballet positions and she confesses to having passed Royal Academy of Dance exams up to grade four. We do a little demo of *port de bras* together. Ben's not bad, but the other men are hilarious and I almost wet myself watching Leon do *pliés* like a pantomime dame.

Ben's turn comes last. He stands there frowning. 'Hmm, I've never danced.'

Imogen says, 'I thought they taught that sort of thing in Public School.'

'Only as a special subject nowadays. I know – a Conga.'

He grabs me round the waist and steers me out into the September night. We all sing the rhythm and weave our way round the outside of the hotel, avoiding planters full of petunias and geraniums. Only the lights glowing through the windows show us the way. We shed a few dancers as we go and finish up in a breathless, laughing heap in the hotel reception.

So this is what living could be like.

## Kobarid Trail – Day fourteen

Some mornings, as a child, I would get up thinking Oscar was still alive, and all the nightmare that day in the barn and afterwards had been just that – a bad dream. I could be halfway through dressing before something in my head realigned with reality. The next few minutes were always very bad.

Today I'm in the shower, my body humming with a sense of wellbeing and the new possibility of planning a future with Adam. Then, without warning, I'm back in the past. I know I have fooled myself; Adam, Daniel, Slovenia – they're all a dream. My blood is thudding in my veins; my eyes are dimming. I head straight out of the shower, wet as a seal, and clutch poor Adam, who, barely awake, has to cope with a frantic mermaid. He does well and yet later, as I pull on my clothes, I find my hands are still trembling.

For the last few years, I've been emotionally cataleptic; now I feel as though I am wired to the central grid. I don't think I'm the only one in an altered state. I glow when I see Vicky no longer stumbling in the rear. I never dreamt I would care for Vicky, now I hurt when I think of her choices. Lindsay, too, is like some slight, shiny creature that has crept out of a dark place. Now she's drying her wings in the sunlight. Yesterday I watched Leon loping across a field with big bouncy strides, almost teenage-like in their urgency. I remember how, in that first week, his feet dragged, his body carrying all of its forty-four years on display. Ben remains an enigma. When not glued to his mobile screen, he's cheerful and totally unforthcoming. Curiously, I've never seen him actually make a call.

147

Adam and I are the odd ones out. We're hyper; on a high that might come crashing down at any moment. We've told no one yet that we are discussing – actually we haven't even got *that* far – the idea of going home. Yet the air around us is fizzing with expectation. The trouble is, although I've shed a skin and discovered a new body underneath, I know that my mind contains all the old mess.

Dressed at last, I look over to see how Adam is progressing. He has dropped off again, curled like a child with his fist against his mouth. Poor man, deep sleep is a fading memory. He needs sleep more than he needs breakfast; I leave silently.

Three quarters of an hour later I carry up a cup of coffee and a roll and find him still flat out. I wake him gently to tell him that we have half an hour before we have to be ready in the right gear for a long walk round the Kobarid Trail. He's warm and half asleep and I foolishly snuggle up. He regards being woken as an invitation and half an hour sounds plenty. He acts with the same trembling urgency to crowd in the minutes as always and I have to question how committed he is to planning a future. We end up scrambling into our clothes with seconds to spare.

The border area we visit today is one of those parcels of land that endlessly changed hands, fought over like a scrap of meat in the dog yard of Europe. We find the Museum at Kobarid a sobering place. It's full of the photographs and diaries of young men – boys really – Italian, Austro-Hungarian, Austrian, German and Silesian, who wanted to live and who ended up here, dead. They died fighting up, or down, a mountainside. They died by enemy fire, or of hypothermia or through climbing accidents or errors in handling their own explosives. I feel overwhelmed by the pointless mess of it all. I'm sure none of them, given the choice between going home and death, would have hesitated in choosing life. In the face of their lack of choice our expedition looks like a luxury.

When I come face to face with Leon, I see he's fighting tears again. The rest of us are looking at faded sepia photos of a Gustav, a Giovanni – boys with foreign-sounding names – he's looking into his own memory and seeing real individuals.

Ben's reaction is more surprising; he's fixated on one of the soldiers who committed suicide. I find it revealing that he identifies with a man who chose the exit route over the terror and degradation of scraping an existence in dugouts and caves. Perhaps Adam is wrong about Ben; perhaps he's sincere in his purpose after all.

Ben is coming on the long hike today with Adam, myself, Leon, Kip, Daniel and, to my surprise, Lindsay. The other four are spending the day in Kobarid and then travelling by taxi to reachable parts of the old front.

We set off with our guide, who looks about sixteen, but assures us he's been taking visitors to the old war zones for the last eight years – we learn later that he first accompanied his father aged eight. We start our walk up the steep zig-zags to the Italian Charnel House above Kobarid. Over seven thousand Italian soldiers are remembered here, nearly three thousand of them unidentified, their bones huddled in niches lining the central staircase. For the next four hours we walk. Mostly we walk along a mule track, stumbling every few metres across the remains of the hopeless defences of one army or another.

At one point I stop, out of breath, to see Kip crouching in one of the ivy-filled blast holes on a steep slope. His face is in his hands.

Leon turns back and goes to him saying, 'Those boys lived for weeks in places like this. Our campaign in the Falklands was almost cushy in comparison, we were never more than forty-eight hours without sufficient food, clothing and water.'

Kip looks up. 'I know, I know. And these guys wanted to live and had no say in the way they died.'

'There's never much choice for the ordinary soldier in war. I don't think you have to beat yourself up because someone else's suffering was greater than yours.'

Kip is on his feet now. 'No, but I didn't care about anybody, I shut myself in. Daniel's made me... I dunno... open the door? These guys went through hell; chased up and down mountains by guys who needed to kill them, for nothing but a pit-hole like this.'

Further up the track, Adam is listening. He is tracing something, perhaps a name carved in the rock, with his fingers. He's silent again today. When I get a chance to talk to him, he says in a troubled voice. 'I don't want that kind of life. I don't want to be hunted. I'm not a brave man.'

'Adam, anyone would be scared of being hunted. The thing is, your uncle can't be everywhere in the world, can he? These guys were stuck here; we can go anywhere. We only need to be where he isn't. Does he have money, or other relatives?'

'He has the house and land. That's what he and Dad were quarrelling over. Grandad left it to both of them, so it became his when

Dad died. There was some kind of deal with my mother, but I'm out of it. Mum hired workers to run the joinery business. It closed after she died. The house and land are rented out to some local farmer.'

'Relatives?'

'Only distant ones on my father's side. They've steered clear of us. I guess...' Adam half smiles, 'Derek might have his hands full for months sorting out a living.'

'Adam, I think those months could stretch to years.'

He shakes his head. 'You don't know how badly he wants revenge. Twice I changed address and jobs and he contacted me. I still don't know how.'

We catch up with the guide and continue clambering up the rocks on some invisible track. Several minutes later Adam suddenly adds, 'My uncle's not stupid, he decided to admit to the crime he never committed and be a perfect prisoner. That's why he's out so soon. It terrifies me to think he might find us... find you.'

'Adam, he doesn't know I exist.' I look round at twisted remnants of barbed wire and dugouts, in which boys died without the opportunity to choose. 'I'm prepared to take that chance. You were so young when all this blew up, perhaps your fear is bigger because you're thinking like a child?'

'Possibly, though I reckoned fifteen was grown up. And there are other fears...' He stops until the others are out of earshot then holds my eye. 'There's a whole package of them; I *did* commit a crime. The police will want me if... And what if it's genetic? What if I discover I'm like them?'

I grip him with both hands. 'You *must* trust me. You're *not* that kind of guy.'

He shakes his head. 'Thanks, Grace, but two weeks...? You can't know me for sure.' He lets go of my hand to take two handfuls of my hair and hold my face between them. 'Am I mad? Sometimes I kid myself it'll be all right. If he thinks I'm still alive somewhere, maybe Derek would be scared to ever do things to another child.'

He turns away from me as his face twists, muttering, 'But what if I'm like that too?'

'Adam, Adam, shush! I know that's not true.'

He shakes his head, but falls silent as Leon joins us.

One of the last places we visit is the church in Javorca, where the interior looks decorative, but is chillingly lined with wood from boxes of mines. On these are burned the names of the 2800 Austro-Hungarian men who fell on the Soča Front.

## Evening in Stara Fužina

Later we rejoin the other party and travel through lush meadow and woodland towards Lake Bohinj, but our sombre mood persists. About a kilometre east of the lake, we dive into the shadow of a mountain, leaving a green glass sky behind us, and climb the steep road to our night's lodging.

The day's sights linger in our conversations tonight. I think it's the letters from sweethearts and mothers found on bodies, or that arrived too late. We've avoided discussing death itself until now, but Imogen puts it to us. 'My husband died and I didn't. Several of us are here because of an encounter with death in one form or another. This has obviously had such a profound effect on us that we're planning to do the same, but we ought, at the very least, to acknowledge that we may be doing to others, what has been done to us. Vicky has accepted that, but what about the rest of us?'

Leon says hesitantly, 'I had a moment when I worked out that my being alive stressed my family so much they'd only be relieved if I topped myself. I dunno. It seemed a blindingly obvious and sane decision at the time.'

Imogen smiles sweetly at him. 'You have an astonishing sense of responsibility, which is at variance with the lifestyle you have clearly been leading. You must know that your parents – and I presume from what you've said, that they're still alive – would regard your suicide as a message to say that they failed you. Is that what you want?'

Leon's head is down. He lifts a hand defensively. 'They tried so hard – Ma, Da and my sister but I can't go home even if I want to; I left my cello to the friend who paid for this 'holiday'. I couldn't live without my cello and I can't pay any other way.'

Vicky puts a hand on his arm. 'Oh how I wish I had money and could buy back your cello.' Leon gives her a quick hug.

I glance away from them and notice Anita looking infinitely sad; does she have relatives after all? Borrowing some of Imogen's courage I ask, 'Anita, do you have someone who will miss you?'

'No. I don't think anyone will be troubled, except our priest. I am sad for a personal reason. I wished to go back to Poland one day. I had a dream that I would meet my distant relatives, but they probably do not know I exist. So it's a personal sadness.'

Daniel nods, 'I don't suppose anyone gets the balance quite right. Feeling sad and guilty doesn't do much good, does it? My personal antidote to guilt is trying to make someone else feel better.'

Ben laughs, 'You must feel very guilty then.'

We all laugh and look at Daniel, to us the personification of goodness, with affection. He smiles but also nods, looking keenly at Ben. I have half a mind to ask him what he thinks he's guilty of.

Kip says, 'That's real – the helping stuff, I mean. As a kid, I thought it a mean deal being shut in with Mark. After he'd gone, that's what I missed; making him comfy, finding his music, or watching films *he* liked. We never went fly-fishing, but he collected those fancy flies. Nothing made him happier than getting them out and trying to decide whether to use a caddis or an orange pupa or some weird fluffy beetle thing, when he got well. Little stuff, but it made me feel better about being able to kick a ball or eat a curry, when he couldn't. I guess that's why I became an ambulance driver.' He looks up at us rather defiantly. 'Dying's the coward's way out.'

'I am not a coward,' Anita states flatly.

Kip looks startled. 'No, no, I mean only me. I...'

Daniel lifts a hand. 'We can each of us only speak for ourselves. Some of you will change your minds, perhaps more than once, before the three weeks are up. Be gentle with yourselves and with each other.'

Lindsay asks, 'OK, Daniel, but it's all right to ask the others about things they say that we don't understand, isn't it?'

'Of course.'

'I mean, I worried about Kip's father and now I worry about Grace's mother.'

Even as I gasp in surprise, Imogen nods and Bedrich actually says, 'So do I.'

I look back at Adam but he, too, is waiting for me to respond. 'It's kind of you to worry, but my mum lives her own life. She never contacts me except at Christmas, especially since Dad died. Honestly, she hates me.'

'Hate and love are bedfellows,' says Imogen.

'She could also be sad, couldn't you do something about it?' I stare at Anita, who's making this suggestion. What on earth does she expect me to do at this stage?

She laughs, 'OK Grace, I am going to pretend to be your mother. You don't have to agree with me. I will imagine her situation. I give birth to a little boy, but God, in his wisdom takes him away again – the stillbirth your mother had. To comfort me, he sends next a little girl and I love her dearly. I'm still sad about my missing boy, so in his goodness and seeing my distress, God sends me another, healthy little boy. That's... What's your brother's name?'

'Oscar.'

'Oscar. Now because of the baby I lost, I love this new baby boy perhaps a little too much. Possibly I neglect my healthy little girl, but my husband gives her plenty of love. She's not always a nice little girl and gets into trouble at school. Then disaster strikes, my darling boy dies and I wasn't there. Who can I blame?'

'She knows who to blame,' I mutter, but Anita ignores me.

'As the years go by there is a chill in my heart. I feel guilty about my son who was born dead, my son who died because I failed to take care of him and my daughter who must hate me for her neglected childhood. It's too late to get close to her now. Besides I don't want to be a burden. She might think I'm only getting in touch because there is no one left since my husband died. She has her own life. I have no place in it.'

I gape at Anita. I don't really know what to say. I look at Adam and he puts an arm round me. Taking the God stuff out, it does make sense, but that doesn't mean it's true. Still, what if she's right? I must try and think of Mum from this point of view. 'I don't know, Anita. You might be sort of right, but she could genuinely hate me. I know she saw me do bad things to Oscar.'

Imogen nods again. 'I don't want to add to your uncertainties, Grace, but I think Anita has made a valid interpretation of the data. You wouldn't think perhaps of phoning her, seeing if you can have a conversation.'

I must look aghast, because Daniel says. 'Don't feel pressurised, Grace. No matter how good the advice, only follow it because you want to.'

Anita's not giving up. 'Well, she's still your mother. If someone depended on me I might feel justified in returning home.'

I see Bedrich's eyes widen for a moment. Surely their son – even if he doesn't recognise them – needs them. I don't like to say so. I look round hoping someone else will step into the limelight.

Adam turns to Ben. 'What about your parents?'

Ben who has barely entered the conversation, grins cheerfully. 'My parents will love me better dead. I reckon it's my life and I get to choose. I left a letter with the bank a couple of years ago for delivery in case of my death.'

I breathe out in relief. He's certainly grabbed attention. The others shy away from a certain callousness in his tone and our conversation turns to all the practical steps we've taken to make sure the right people are informed after we go. I notice that no one tells Ben to get in touch with *his* mother. Surely it is bedtime. Today has been full of so much sadness I want to sleep and start again.

Kip says slowly, 'I feel bad about those dead boys today. Different bad. Are we pathetic? There's tons of guys with really tough lives: like in India scavenging plastics off rubbish dumps, in Africa walking hundreds of miles for food. I don't understand, why don't *they* give up?'

I almost laugh because most of the faces round me are heavy with guilt. We know we're perverse and feel bad about it. I imagine swapping lives with a scavenging street child but I can see so many obstacles the image won't run.

Imogen adds, 'Some do give up, but many of those who fight impossible odds have either people who need them, such as children, or people who love them.'

'Well I think it comes back to guilt,' pronounces Leon. 'Guilt's a lead blanket.' There are nods all round.

'And it's impossible to share, so you end up lonely,' I add.

Imogen shakes her head. 'I don't honestly think I feel guilt. Stewart was in pain and ready to go. I was unhappy about surviving, but not guilty. I'm going because I've had enough of life. I think some of the people who battle to survive think it has to be better than this and are willing to live in that hope, however slim.'

'For me it's about guilt.' I say, foolishly entering the debate again. 'Back home living was pointless, no one needed me. I do feel differently now.' I daren't look at Adam, 'But you're right Kip, we *ought* to feel glad about what we have in life – but we don't.'

Daniel stirs. 'I don't have any wholly satisfying answers, Grace. I've noticed that feeling guilty *and* not being able to help others are a mean combination. The saddest people I've met are those who feel they have nothing to contribute. Being able to give another human – or for some people an animal – something they need makes me... us feel good.'

Bedrich speaks suddenly, 'This...*this*...is true. For us,' he takes Anita's hand, 'Jacob, he was the one person who needed us, now he doesn't.'

Lindsay asks Bedrich, 'Are you sure you aren't needed? Anyway can't you give things to each other now instead of to your son?'

Anita withdraws her hand from her husband's clasp to wave a bangled arm. 'It's not the same, Bedrich does not need me.'

Bedrich sits up sharply and opens his mouth, but Vicky and Imogen laughing together, get there first. 'Of course he does.'

He nods vehemently, but Anita shrugs it off. I look at Ben, who is covertly watching his mobile phone. He yawns elaborately.

Daniel yawns too. 'OK I'm for bed. We'll spend tomorrow on the lake – a good place for contemplation.'

As we close the bedroom door, I snuggle up to Adam, desperate to stop thinking. Anita's words and my mother hover over us. Adam, after starting a sentence, takes one look at my face and stops. 'It's all right, Grace.' He pulls me to him. 'Let's get some sleep.'

He slips his hands under my jumper and I feel yet again the amazing contact between the palm of his hand and the small of my back. I slip my hands into the identical place under his shirt, and hear his excited intake of breath. I laugh. 'Sleep? That would be a fine thing.'

## Lake Bohinj – Day fifteen

'What time is it? Adam? Are you crying?' I flick on the light. It is three am. Adam is leaning over me, his tears falling down my neck. I hold him, but I cannot console him and wonder if he wouldn't be happier to forget about trying to live. I only hope Daniel is right about the soothing effects of water today.

By nine thirty we are rolling into a car park among the trees on the south bank of Lake Bohinj. This is a bigger stretch of water than Lake Bled and more isolated, unadorned and melancholy. Bedrich and Anita opt for the two-hour tourist boat trip along the lake and back. Leon decides to walk the path around the lake. The others hire boats, but Adam wants to swim. I'm about to join him when I look at his face. There's something remote and peaceful in his eyes as he looks across the waters. I too stare at the inky depths, but the only message I receive is one of cold. I make a finely calculated decision, taking into account the probable iciness of the water, and my feeling that Adam needs some space without me. I opt to go rowing with Ben and Vicky. My hope is that Adam, free of me for a couple of hours, will swim away his melancholy.

Ben, looking pleased, hands me into the small, solid craft. He offers me an oar, but I climb into the bow, where I will be behind him as he rows. Vicky sits facing him giving steering instructions. As he dips and lifts the oars, I watch the water breaking over the blades and day-dream. I can feel my hair lifting and settling with each tug of the oars. Ben turns occasionally, to check, so he says, that I have not fallen overboard. If he interprets my fatuous smile as a tribute to his skills, I don't mind.

The September sun, weak when we first set out has now warmed up the day and the lake seems so spacious and empty that we have the sky to ourselves. Ben may be right to worry. I doze a little as I feel the sun soothing my muscles and my spirits. A couple of times I jerk awake as I feel myself slipping or as drops from the oars splash on my arms, but I'm never really in danger of falling in. This is the right choice; I need this bit of slack in my life. I only hope some of the sun's goodness is reaching Adam too.

As we come paddling back in the late morning we can see the others in a clump on the Eastern shore, then someone, Lindsay, comes running up with a stranger. A small emergency; it looks as though someone has cut their foot or something. Then, as we get closer, I realise that Daniel is kneeling beside a body. I assess the remaining figures and even from a distance know who lies on the ground. Daniel is giving Adam the kiss of life.

We pull the boat onto the shingle and Ben and Vicky hurry forward. I stand rooted on the shore. I want to run in the other direction, but there is nowhere to go. I walk up a path past an array of traffic signs for walkers forbidding everything from butterflies to bicycles. Red lines, slash, slash, slash across each pictogram. That's my mind; every path has a red line across the entrance. I reach a hut in a nearby field and sit down leaning against the far wall. I can no longer see the lake shore. From the top of the mountain on my left there are paragliders tossing themselves into the void.

I start picking a bunch of the pale, starry flowers that grow all over. They are weeds, but I pluck them with care. I cut off the ends of the stems, tidy the leaves, remove the dead heads and concentrate on making the perfect bouquet. My mind is as blank as the endless blue sky above me. It's as if, after all the weeping and mental scurrying, something has stretched too far and snapped. Somewhere in Adam's action is a message I do not want to receive. If I keep my mind closed, I will be safe.

Time, possibly an hour, passes. Then Daniel walks around the corner of the hut. 'Grace? They've taken Adam to a clinic in Bohinjska Bistrica. He's alive. Ben has gone with him.' This seems odd, but everything is odd and I can only stare. 'Ben speaks the language. It's too early to tell if Adam will be OK.'

He sits down beside me and I pass him the bunch of flowers. He takes them and continues, 'Adam may have passed out while swimming. You're both living on air and no sleep, I should have thought of that when Adam chose to swim.' He picks another flower and adds it carefully to my posy. 'The other possibility is that he planned this, or took a chance that walked up to him. He may be so happy that he wants to stop here and now, or so anxious that he cannot face the future.'

I look hard at the flowers. Dear Daniel reaching, as always, for the nub of the matter, no messing around the edges. He passes the flowers back to me. 'You may never know the answer to these questions for sure.'

Wham! There you have it. Since that moment of realising that the body on the beach was Adam, I haven't dared ask myself a single question. Now they flood in. If Adam dies or is already dead, I have seven days that I cannot bear to contemplate ahead of me, then I cross the border with the others – decision made. If he lives, though – that's the snake-pit. Could I ever trust him again? Why did he do it? Scared of living with me? Scared of his Uncle? Scared of going to Brazil? Scared *for* me? What if he survives and we go to Australia or Canada and he decides he can't hack it after all? Anyway here is Daniel ahead of me with the killer answer – you may never know. I can feel his arm around me stroking my shoulder, but it feels like something happening to another person.

I open my mouth, but my tongue is dry and sticky. I swallow. 'Adam nearly jumped off the cliff edge that first afternoon in Rogatec. *We* nearly jumped. That's how we... got together.'

'Uhuh. Grace, I don't *think* Adam intended to die today, but I could be wrong. Will you come to the clinic? You could at least be with him whatever the outcome. And if he should come to himself, you would be able to hear what he has to say?'

'Do I have any choice?'

Daniel is smiling very sweetly. 'You can do anything you want.'

'What if I haven't the faintest idea what I want? I can't seem to engage my brain at all.' Daniel squeezes me.

'Funny, I thought you would be double thinking. Shock takes people different ways. Don't worry. I'm always astonished by how little I know about what goes on in people's heads.'

'But you're really good at that, Daniel. Didn't you know that my brain shut down hours – is it hours? – ago?'

'No, I didn't know.' He takes his arm from around me and rubs his face with both hands. The hopelessness of the gesture destabilises me yet further. I put both arms round him and cling on.

'Poor Daniel, I'm sorry. We put everything on your shoulders. We treat you like our mother, father or teacher. How old are you?'

His head is heavy against mine. 'Thirty-six.'

'Only a year older than me.'

'Sometimes I feel as though I'm sixty.' He takes my flowers and lays them one by one across our knees. 'When I was living in Switzerland, in the summer we would go up to our cabin. Dad would go up there first with my uncle to help take the sheep up to summer pasture. Mum and the cousins and I would join them for the summer festival. We picked flowers so like these ones.' He lifts one to his nose, I do the same, it smells only of greenness. 'I remember the year I decorated my own hat for the first time. And the mule; when I was very small I got to ride on it, the hair so warm and smelly against my bare legs. This feels like another century, another life.'

We sit silent then Daniel lifts his head with a sigh. 'Dear Grace I shouldn't lay this on you, and I fear I may be being selfish, but please, if Adam survives, give him another chance, whatever the reason for today's event.' I nod, too numb to make a decision but willing, if he asks me, to swim the lake or anything else for him.

### Ben in the clinic

Back at our *pensione*, Daniel orders a taxi to take me to the clinic in Bohinj Bistrica. Ben will be there and has volunteered to stay with me, as he's the only one with more than the odd word of Slovenian not to mention several other languages if necessary.

At the clinic I sit in reception feeling like an ant in a mausoleum. I've been in this place before: sitting on my bedroom floor after Oscar died wondering where all the heat in my life had gone. I remember thinking I've done it now; I've brought on my personal ice-age. Twenty-five years later, I have turned the happiest days of my life into another ice-age. Now the questions crowd in. What have I said, done or not done to make Adam need to die now?

Ben puts a cup of coffee in my hands. The woman in reception speaks good English and she's kind, but there is an emergency on and it's only a small place. We've been here nearly two hours and have still not seen Adam. He may be dead already for all I know.

Then this official appears and says, according to Ben, that Adam is still alive, but asleep – or perhaps in a coma – and should be left undisturbed for many hours. He is breathing on his own. They think he will be fine when he wakes up, but no promises are made. Brain damage... lack of oxygen... minutes without breathing... lung damage. The words are all tendered, filtered along the angles of Slovenian to Austrian-German to English. With meanings distorted at each linguistic turn, the reassurances and warnings might as well swap positions. They could be giving us bad news. Although Ben assures me that these alarming terms are used only to be dismissed. I walk out less well informed than when I walked in.

We plan to go and look for a taxi back to the *pensione*, but then discover a café next to the clinic. I'm feeling faint by this time, both of us having missed lunch, Ben ushers me in and orders coffee and rolls. Knowing my penchant for ice cream, he orders a vanilla confection. I cannot swallow the bread, so Ben obligingly eats the rolls. I try to spoon down the ice cream, but gag as the sickly fluid swells in my mouth. I drink the coffee

Ben is good. He doesn't try to force me to eat. He reassures me, putting the best gloss on what the clinic has said – or might have said. Then he shifts the subject, but not too far.

'Are you still going across the border?'

'No. Yes. I don't know.'

He laughs, 'Well that's settled then.' Ben tweaks one of my curls. 'You're manifestly healthy – and attractive. I think you should go back home and if you did, I might be able to help.'

'For heaven's sake Ben...'

'I know – Adam. Assuming he does survive, do you want to bet against him crossing the border?'

As he talks, I experience a revelation. Nothing, not Ben's green eyes, not a win on the lottery, not even, perhaps, the knowledge that maybe I was not responsible for Oscar's death, will make me go back home. Nothing, that is, except for my perverse passion for Adam. Ben rambles on, unaware of the great light I have seen. I, lacking the energy to stop him and thinking maybe he needs to talk, sit passively, my mind assessing my new discovery.

I'm still feeling weirdly detached. I compare the excitement generated by Ben's charm with my heart-shaking craving for Adam. It makes no intellectual sense but it's Adam's wounded surliness, his blasted open vulnerability, his neat practical competence and his trembling, fragile dependence that occupy me. Ben needs me like he needs a fancy car. Adam needs me because he is missing an essential organ. If he should cross the border and I went home, I would die of an old-fashioned broken heart. I think I can feel the cracks already.

Ben takes my hand, playing gently with the fingers. He has that perfect touch of the fatherly that makes the gesture acceptable under the circumstances. He isn't to know how precisely I can compare this to Adam folding and unfolding my hand in an agony of indecision as he tries to suggest that we might perhaps find a deserted place, somewhere without the internet...

No, Ben is on a losing streak and I cannot tell him. He pats my hand and lays it carefully down on my knee again. Turning me by the shoulder to smile his green smile into my eyes, he suggests, 'Grace, we're young, perhaps we could find a city, somewhere new and different, to start again. I speak French, Spanish, German...'

'And Greek?'

'No, we couldn't live in Greece.'

'Ben, I'm sorry. It's incredibly simple for me, if Adam lives and then crosses that border, so do I; if Adam dies here in this clinic, so do I.' I stand up and set off towards the exit. Instinctively I turn in to the clinic again, but there's no news.

Ben follows, his phone buzzing. He checks it, makes a grimace, mutters, 'Well, well!' and switches it off completely.

He turns and stares at me with the faraway gaze of someone dealing with a crossword puzzle clue. I move to leave the building and he catches my hand. 'Hang on a mo. I think... yes, I think I'd like to tell you some other stuff I haven't yet talked about. Don't tell the others. Once I've crossed the border you can tell anyone you like.'

'But...'

'Of course, you think you are not going home either, though I have my doubts.'

There are some sofas in the clinic lobby. Ben flings himself down on one and grins up at me. He can do that; turn from persuasive know-all to little boy. I have no trouble now imagining him seducing a Greek schoolgirl. 'Anyway,' he goes on, 'I'm in confessional mode. You want to hear how to mess up big time? Not only do I have Eleni's brother after my blood, but there are one or two other less civilized people queuing up to take pot shots at me. If I could trust them to make a good job of it, I might hang around and let them get on with the deed. The trouble is, I have this thing about physical pain. I think some of these guys – and they include the police – might just want to make me very sorry before they give me the last rites.' He holds out an arm to invite me onto the sofa.

I stand gaping down at him. 'You mean Adam was right?'

He grinned. 'Depends. What did he think?'

'Well, he reckoned you had screwed someone over and they were after your blood.'

'Spot on!' He beckons, 'C'mon Grace, keep me warm. How can I bare my soul, with you staring into it like that?'

In my pathetic state, I drop into his casual arm. He chuckles. 'That's better. As far as I can see, I'm the only real criminal in this ship of fools... though I reckon Leon's probably dabbled in things he should not have. The rest of you are innocents. I've not exactly killed anyone, but only because I'm a coward. If I could've done so without jeopardising my skin, I would. None of the rest of you went to boarding school; it's as good as prison for picking up criminal tips. I went to one of the best. Machiavelli would've been proud of my development. I learnt survival any way I could. I was blonde and sufficiently cute to attract... favours. At fourteen I could write in miniature code and get ninety-five per cent in exams (note ninety-five not one hundred, always leave that little human margin). I soon discovered I didn't need to cheat, I have a nearly photographic memory, but I found I could sell my talent to others for money or favours.'

In the cushion of his arm, I feel completely at ease, no sense that this is a bad man. 'Ben, aren't these things that some kids do? They don't make you a criminal.'

'Look who's talking – and you tried to make us believe you were a child killer!'

'That was different I did actually kill someone.'

'No you didn't; you fantasised about killing someone, who eventually died in an accident.'

'It doesn't matter what I did. Surviving at school doesn't make you a criminal.'

'Ah, but you see, I enjoyed it. Not the danger, but the hidden cleverness of it. I never felt bad. My mother said that I was genetically amoral. If someone else got beaten because of something I'd done, that was fine by me. I only really care about things that are actually happening here and now. Besides that was just the beginning. I started betting on horses before I left school and one thing led to another. There's a lot of money and fun to be had out of dog racing and then there's dog fighting, hare coursing, cock-fighting and... Anyway, you meet some extreme types in this world and they don't appreciate late payment, for instance.'

'Why are you telling me all this now and exposing your... your misdeeds?'

'My crimes? Well it doesn't much matter what I do now, does it?' He strokes my arm; again he treads that thin path between friendly comfort and suggestive touch. He decides to cross it. 'I'm comfortable here, like this. If I could persuade you to further comforts...' I shake my head in disbelief, 'fine, if not, I'm reasonably content.'

'Ben, I still don't understand. If you like to be so comfortable and don't like danger and don't care what other people think or feel, why are you doing this? Why are you going to die?'

'My darling, lovely Grace, there are no less than five sets of hoodlums out there. Some are clever; some exceedingly stupid. More importantly, all of them are cruel and, maybe with some justification, they're after my blood. I don't think any of them have in mind a quick or clean end; I've cost them too much money. They've had a couple of pops already and I didn't enjoy that much.'

'The scars on your back?'

'That, and others less visible. The balance has tipped. I'm now the fox in this hunt. I've run out of cover, I can't be bothered to find more camouflage and I'm tired, I don't enjoy it any longer. I work solo. This has been in my favour most of the time, now I lack decoys or henchmen to take out the opposition. They will catch me in the end. I have this weird personal preference to die at the moment of my own choosing, and by as pleasant a method as possible. I don't think the clowns I have been tangling with will like that very much. I've had a couple of goes myself, but I didn't quite make the jump, so this is third time lucky. I'm easy about many things, but there are a few others I like to keep control of, my skin and my life being among them. Even if the police get to me first, it would mean incarceration for life. I can't face that one. Another boarding school hangover, I guess.'

I'm struggling to take this in. This solid, warm, steady body supporting me belongs to the kind of person I fear and despise – a manifestly nasty piece of work. I have more trouble believing this version than the story of his lost Greek love.

'Ben how much of the story about your girlfriend and the miscarriage were true?'

'Oh that was true, up to a point. Eleni was underage though, and so naive. They're well protected these Greek girls. But that leaves them vulnerable when they come up against someone like me. I bribed Eleni's little brother to disappear instead of chaperoning us. He knows damn well who's responsible for what they see as the family disgrace. He sends me regular warning texts.'

'Was that him just now?'

'No. He thinks I am in Scotland. No... that was... Never mind.'

'What about being adopted?'

'Oh that's actually true. And I do have a little brother but… well never mind the rest, it's complicated.'

I turn to stare. He returns my gaze, openly, frankly, a half smile on his lips, the creases around his eyes deepening at my expression.

'My face is my fortune, you know. I discovered that by stealing Smarties from the local newsagent's counter when I was less than five. It is really true, you can smile and smile and still be a villain.'

I finally persuade Ben, after further lazy offers of comfort and distraction, to set off for the *pensione*. As we leave the clinic Ben drops something that makes a hefty clonk into the rubbish bin. It could have been his phone, though this seems unlikely. I almost ask, but he is striding off looking for a taxi.

I feel utterly destabilized. Even my feet walk with a sense of disbelief. In the taxi Ben repeats his command to tell no one, or I might put the others in danger. I sit clutching the taxi handhold, my mind a river of confusion snagging over fears for Adam; anger at Adam; disgust with myself. On the surface of these, Ben's revelations seethe like a layer of dirty foam.

# Night trek

Back at the *pensione*, I try to avoid the others and talk only to Daniel. He's already rung the clinic, because we have been away so long. There's no change. Adam is resting and all the signs are good so far. The others appear and surround me with warmth. They're about to set off for a meal out, but I want nothing except my bed and remain steadfast in the face of their kindly persuasions.

I sit in the bar with the cheese and ham roll Anita has insisted on ordering for me. It looks like solid rock as far as my throat is concerned. How can I swallow when I can barely remember how to breathe? I start to tear up the roll with the foolish intention of creating pieces small enough to bypass the lump in my throat but I forget what I'm doing and sit imagining Adam ploughing into the middle of the lake and then... stopping? My head will not compass this; a swimmer cannot stop himself from trying to breathe air. Perhaps he did faint. I should have persuaded him to eat breakfast this morning.

My eyes prickle and I abandon the porridge I've made of the bread and flee to my room. I turn the lock on my door and then undo it. For the last week I've left the door unlocked so that Adam can rejoin me after a quick visit to his toothbrush. Tonight I fall down on the bed and push my face into his nightshirt.

This is a foolish idea; the smell is like being punched. I curl round it and lose all possible coherence, indulging in endless tears. I'm not sure I ever knew pain like this. It was different after Oscar died; the pain of being hollow, gutted. This pain is volcanic.

I should be glad Adam is still alive; instead I am thinking, like a teenager, he didn't love me enough. Then I imagine him lying in a pristine hospital bed, and shiver as I pull the covers over my clothes. He might at this moment be cold, bare, even dead. I should have stayed with him. Tears continue to leak out in a feeble, pointless, stream until everything: my hair, the pillow, my shirt collar, Adam's shirt and the duvet are all damp. I switch off the light. An hour later, still weeping, still dressed I begin at last to drift towards sleep, repeating like a sort of mantra, 'Stupid woman, stupid woman...'

'Grace?'
There's a crack of light at the door.
'Grace?'

I jerk awake. 'Adam?'

'May I come in?'

'But you're… in the clinic.'

'I discharged myself.'

'How did you get here?'

'I walked. Can I borrow a jumper, I'm a bit cold.'

I reach for the bedside light and stare him. He stands there in t-shirt and shorts, shivering. 'Oh Jesus!' I croak. "I'm going to run a hot bath. Put this round you and sit still.' He sits on the edge of the bed and submits to being wrapped in the duvet. 'You didn't really walk did you? It's six or more kilometres.'

His body shudders. 'I think I walked seven of them.'

I head to the bathroom, but he grabs my shirt and reaches out to turn my chin towards him with the other hand. His touch is icy and I can't help but jerk away. He lets go but stares at my face. 'What've I done? What *have* I done? You're still dressed; it's 2 am?'

I've forgotten my four-hour weep. I look away wearily. 'Let me fill that bath. You've got to get warm.'

'Please don't go. Lie down beside me. I won't touch you.' I dither between good sense and the desire to respond to his pleading. 'Please, Grace, I'm warmer already. Just lie here.' His mouth distorts. 'Your poor face.'

'Ugly as sin isn't it?'

'No. It hurts. I'd forgotten how much.'

I half smile at the echo of my own rediscovery. 'I'd forgotten too; loving hurts out of proportion. Pinching a finger feels like a car door slammed on your hand. We're a couple of idiots. Daniel made it so easy for us and we've really fucked up.'

'You could've had a fling with Ben and no pain. I'm sorry.'

'I've always been a sucker for punishment. I turned Ben down again today.'

'Today!'

'He offered to console me. You really got him sussed, I'll tell you another time. Come on lie down. I'm going to pile on some coats and this cover.'

Adam leans over and fumbles at his shoelaces, but his hands refuse to work.

I kneel down to untie them and when I look up his mouth is open and stretched in a rictus. Tears fall onto my face. 'Oh Adam, you *are* sick. I should wake Daniel, get you back to the clinic.'

'Why bother? There are so few days to go. That's why I discharged myself. I want to be with you while I can.'

So he's decided to cross the border. I can't deal with that now.
Anyway it's no surprise. I push him back onto the bed, trying to
wrap him and rub him and pacify his shaking body all at once.
Later he says, 'And I know that's not fair to you. I'm sorry. It takes
courage to live. More courage than I have.'

After a while I lie down beside him, still dressed, and pull a bit
of the duvet over myself. Adam reaches out to push the wet strands
of hair off my face and I flinch. He pulls back, so I have to reach
out and grab his hand.

'It's all right, you're still freezing, I should've run that bath.'

Adam falls asleep; I keep vigil. Now I know that we will cross
the border with the others I don't want to waste time sleeping.
Every now and again I touch the back of his hand to check his temperature. I can smell the arrival of the morning through the tiny slit
of window I left open. Eventually the *pensione* begins to stir and
I'm unsure if I've slept or not. I have the sensation of having spent
what was left of the night clinging to a ledge on a mountainside. I
know it's illogical to grieve. Grieving is what the living do for the
dead and I will die at the same time as Adam. Yet what I'm feeling
as my eyes travel continuously over his half-lit cheek, his lashes
at rest below the shadowed lids, is anticipation of grief. I'm also
frustrated to recognise the rightness of Imogen's statement, that
you cannot stop someone choosing death.

I creep out of bed and shower. Adam sleeps on. I'm almost surprised to find that day has started. Yesterday was so catastrophic I
expected the world to stop with us. The perversity of my reactions,
having come to die, is beyond excuse. I know this as clearly as I
know my mental pain, perhaps the suggestion that the two halves
of our brains behave differently is not as bizarre as I once thought.

I check, yet again, that Adam is breathing and then go down
early to breakfast. Daniel is preparing to visit the clinic. I tell him
about Adam's return and then we both go through prolonged ex-
planations with the staff of the *pensione* trying to ring the clinic
and reassure them that we have Adam safe and that we will pay for
yesterday's treatment.

Imogen appears, her face is paler than usual and she asks if we
have news of Adam. I tell her he's asleep upstairs and my heart lifts
as her dimples reappear.

'I'm so glad.' She looks it. 'Things have happened so swiftly, neither of you has had a chance to catch up with yourselves... to integrate your new feelings. Give it another chance, Grace.'

'If only... I don't... I tried... ' I say, then realise I'm not capable of coherent speech and turn back upstairs.

We have to be out of our rooms by 10 am. I pack Adam's gear, dribbling tears over his socks as I fold and stow them in his ruck-sack. The others set off for the Mount Vogel Cable Car to see the Savica Falls, except Anita and Bedrich who walk around the lake.

## The kindness of strangers – Day sixteen

Two women, both with iron-tight buns and efficient eyes, run this *pensione*. They look too similar in age to be mother and daughter, yet too different to be sisters. Only the younger one speaks English. Daniel has bribed her to let Adam sleep until lunchtime.

It's nearly midday by the time we come down; Adam has not eaten for twenty-four hours and he doesn't exactly have surplus fat to live off. We go to the restaurant, but struggle to read the menu. The older manager approaches us. She shakes her head at Adam and wags a finger. Having no language in common, we don't know which part of our story she's referring to. Talking as though we understand every word, she starts to suggest things from the menu. Adam puts a hand on her arm and looks at her in despair, gently shaking his head. She looks from one to the other of us, pats his hand and then, inclusively, pats mine. She stalks off, taking both menus. I shrug at Adam in a silent gesture of what-the-heck and even get a glimmer of a smile out of him.

Bare minutes later two small plates of sliced tomato with a light dressing and a crust of bread appear in front of us, flanked by glass-es of wine the colour of blackcurrant juice. The woman gestures to us to eat and disappears. Ten minutes later she reappears with two small steaming herb omelettes. She nods with pleasure as she removes the empty tomato dishes. A little later yet, she reappears with tiny egg-cup-sized helpings of a green ice cream with delicate home-made almond biscuits. Adam's face trembles into its beautiful smile. She pats his arm, rewarded. I grip her hands, smiling, but with tears threatening to spill I cannot find a single word of Slovenian with which to thank her. She must think we're barmy, but she pats us both again.

I ask Adam if he wants coffee, but our wonderful hostess is having none of it. She shakes her head at the suggestion of coffee and by now we know our status as obedient children. When the others arrive back we're sipping some fruit cordial of unknown origin – rosehips perhaps? I see Ben in the distance and only realise later that I could have felt self-conscious after the revelations of the previous day. Actually, I'm struggling to join yesterday to today at any point, never mind placing these two days in any bigger context. We pack our bags into the coach then find there's a game in the offing before we return to Ljubljana.

On the grass behind the *pensione* we gather in a circle. It's a trust game and we have to allow ourselves almost to fall before being caught. We all take turns. Leon and Bedrich, as the most solid men, are a little anxious and never fall wholeheartedly. Adam is too trusting and too fragile. My heart jerks each time I see his body falling. Ben, in contrast, trusts no one. His feet step out each time he is pushed. After the exercise I stop feeling like running away and more like clinging to the others.

Imogen asks, 'Adam how are you feeling now, any ill effects?'

Adam shakes his head gently. 'I'm fine.' He looks at all of us and I see the suspicion of a blush on his throat. 'I'm so sorry for causing such a stupid commotion.'

There's an ambiguity here about whether the trouble he caused was intentional or not. No one, including me, asks him directly whether he planned to take his own life in the lake. I'm not sure if this is English reticence, fear of the answer, or simply that we know the answer and don't want to force him into admitting it.

Trust is indeed a great thing. I love these people, who have chosen not to hassle Adam. I walk over to the edge of the hill where the *pensione* sits and looks westwards in the direction of the lake – now out of sight. In the twenty-four hours since we arrived here my life has flipped over. This thought makes me remember my mother. Should I call her before I cross the border and make sure she doesn't suffer further through me. What if she tries to stop me? Of course I needn't tell her what I'm about to do. I could simply say that I'm sorry and that I... that I love her. Could I say that?

'Grace...? Cooee! Are you coming with us?'

'Sorry! Anita, I was... I was wondering...'

We climb into the coach to return to Ljubljana for our last week. Daniel sits across the aisle from Adam. Almost as the coach starts up, Adam leans over. 'Daniel, I want to let you know straight away. I *will* be crossing the border.'

Daniel looks at Adam then at me. He's very still for a moment and then he nods. I feel as though I'm driving cold iron into his heart. The frozen look passes and he says, 'And you, Grace?'

Adam replies. 'Grace will obviously make her own decision.'

'I shall go too.'

Adam shakes his head in frustration. 'I can't persuade her otherwise.'

'It's very simple. I was always going to cross the border anyway. If Adam could find a way to live, then yes, I might change my mind. Adam's staying might have persuaded me to stay, but Adam's going hasn't made me go.'

I expected to sleep on the bus – especially with all that wine inside me, but instead I lean sideways and watch Adam watching the landscape. He's not looking forward to our last week inside the city again. Why did I ever think we had anything in common? Where do I start? I was brought up in suburbia, he in a forest – as far as I understand it. Home, job, schooling, interests are all different, yet they seem irrelevant now.

When we reach our hotel I have no energy to unpack. I don't understand how I'm crossing a room with the same shirt in my hand as a week ago but as a different person. I walk into the corridor to see if Adam is real, but I don't even know which is his room.

I stand stupidly looking up and down an empty passage until, like the unexpected answer to a prayer, Adam appears at one end, carrying his bags. I beam and run to him. Leon and Adam are swapping rooms. This will bring Adam next to me and Leon will be next to Vicky.

Vicky and Leon have become fast friends, listening to music and walking together. From the day I helped her choose new clothes, I have fantasised that they are lovers but if so they're both very discreet. I did dream that they would go home together, but with Vicky being married and with her disease, I don't know. Anyway, my dreams are the least reliable source of reality, especially now.

I make a discovery; when you're seriously short of sleep you hallucinate. At least I think this is what's happening to me as we walk the now familiar route through the damp city to Preseren Square. Lamps sprout comet tails, shop windows bulge and spill red peppers and grapes or green strappy sandals and black zip-up boots onto the pavements. I have to let go of Adam to hold my head in my hands and then catch hold of him again to stay upright. When Bedrich speaks to me I lean in close then move away again as he refuses to come into focus. No one, not even Adam, seems to realise that I'm non-functional.

In spite of recent rain it is still warm enough for us to stay outside for our evening drinks. I sit watching their faces in the dimness of candles and soft streetlights. I suddenly see that Anita has a perfect complexion and Bedrich's sleepy eyes are smiling. Kip is standing by the river wall looking out into the night like an ebony god; Ben, staring out across the square, might have been wheeled out of a workshop in Ancient Greece. He's almost as silent as a sculpture tonight. This is uncharacteristic, I wonder if any of the cheerful students and tourists at the neighbouring tables are after his blood. They could be the angry hoodlums he has swindled or the low-life he has double-crossed. I try to spot any suspiciously bulging pockets, though in this country a cross-bow might seem more appropriate than guns.

Out of the sky an enormous concoction of pink and white ice cream and strawberries is lowered into my vision.

'Jesus! Did I order this?'

Imogen says, 'Yes'

Anita says, 'No, Adam did.'

Adam holds up a hand saying, 'Not me.'

I look round, but no one is owning up so I push the pink mountain towards the centre and under the assault of at least ten coffee spoons it disintegrates.

## Norodna Gallery – Day seventeen

It is day seventeen and Adam and I both make it to breakfast today, a rare event. Ben does not. He has sometimes missed it and even occasionally he has breakfasted early or gone out for a run or something. We're going on a longish journey south-west this morning to see Otočec Castle. I can snooze beside Adam on the coach.

We're supposed to assemble at nine fifteen, but people are less prompt than they used to be. By nine thirty everyone except Ben has appeared. This has happened before so we hang around expecting him to show up. Vicky talks to Daniel; Adam grabs a paper; Imogen starts a conversation with the receptionist.

I daydream, but it's one of those mind-wanderings where fantasy segues into anxiety as I imagine Ben running and being chased by someone out of The Godfather. I find myself watching the window with an uneasy prickle in my chest. Ben now seems like two people: the charming extrovert who travelled with us for the first fortnight and the edgy, criminal, guy who talked to me in the clinic near Bohinj. When he's not there I feel almost scared of him. When I bump into him again he feels like an old friend.

Eventually Leon volunteers to go up and see if he's overslept. He finds the Do Not Disturb notice up and knocks hard, but there's no answer. In the next half an hour we phone Ben's mobile fruitlessly and everyone checks for messages. Perhaps he really did throw away his mobile phone in the clinic, but that was the day before yesterday. Surely I saw him with a phone in his hand last night? Then Daniel speaks with reception; they've not seen him and have no information. Remembering certain details of our conversation in Bohinj, I begin to feel nauseous.

Daniel and Leon go up to Ben's room with the cleaner. Leon returns to tell us that the bed is empty but looks slept in.

Kip says suddenly, 'D'you think something was up with his phone? He went into that mobile shop yesterday, maybe he bought a new one. He didn't give you a new number, Dan?'

'No.'

I stand for a moment unravelling my scarf as I try to decide how much to say.

Adam says, 'He talked to Grace the other day.' He turns to me, 'I wonder if...'

'His phone definitely worked then,' I interrupt. 'He had a call he didn't take while I was with him. He told me things,' I shiver, 'but I have a feeling that it's better if I don't tell you. I don't mean to be difficult, but he did ask me not to and then... you might feel obliged to do things that I'm sure Ben wouldn't want... things that would certainly be a problem for the rest of the group.'

Daniel gives me a considering look and passes a hand over his face. 'OK you must follow your own code. Do you think perhaps you could talk it over with Adam? That way you share any responsibility you might feel.' He turns to the others. 'Does anyone have any more suggestions?'

Vicky looks round then says, 'I suppose we should go to the police?'

I shake my head and Daniel says, 'Not yet, I think. He might roll up any minute.' He nods to Kip. 'Park the coach again. We'll stick around. We may have got this wrong; he may have gone for an early run and sprained his ankle, or simply got lost, for all we know.'

Vicky looks at Leon. 'You don't think he's gone to ride that cycle track round the city?'

'What track?' I ask.

Leon answers, 'I wonder. Yesterday I was telling Ben about the POT. It's the cycling path that runs where the barbed wire used to surround the city in World War II. We talked about hiring cycles and doing the circuit, but I didn't think he was that keen. Anyway, why would he go and not tell any of us?'

Daniel leans on a table and sighs. 'I can't imagine. I think we'll postpone the trip to Otočec. I'll go on searching, but I'd like the rest of you to chose one of the several places in Ljubljana that we haven't yet visited. Could everyone with a mobile take it and keep it on.'

Imogen says, 'I've been wanting to visit the Norodna Art Gallery – The National Gallery. Does anyone else fancy coming?'

Leon shrugs. 'I don't mind. Vicky?'

The rest of us tag along, not having anywhere else particular in mind and feeling like sticking together. We're a little lost without Daniel and the atmosphere has changed. Adam's near brush with death has sobered us all. Now Ben's disappearance has put our half-hearted tourism yet further down the list of priorities. All we can talk about is where he might have gone, what he might have done. I feel the weight of my knowledge and long to get Adam to myself. I haven't yet told him everything Ben said to me.

As we're leaving the hotel, Daniel appears, looks swiftly round and puts a hand on Adam's arm. 'Adam could you give me a hand checking some possible leads. We'll catch up with the others later.'

Desolated by Adam's absence and never a fan of old paintings, I drift round the exhibits, revolted by the endless scenes of religious tortures. I am half asleep on a bench while Vicky is studying nearby paintings, when an ungallery-like squeak rouses me. I look up to see Lindsay in front of a picture, clutching Kip's sleeve. She turns to us. 'Hey, Grace, Vicky, come and look at this.'

Vicky raises her eyebrows. 'Superb! Apart from those exotic paintings in the Ptuj gallery, the only older paintings I remember depicting black people are of the three Magi or sometimes a cute little page in the train of some aristocrat. They usually look sort of... exaggerated too. This is different.'

Lindsay's find is a portrait titled Black Lady. The lady looks stunning: wistful, yet with a strong beautiful face. She has a soft green dress cut low, with a foam of white lace across the bosom. The dress is vague and impressionistic, but her face is finely painted and has a gentle haughtiness about it. It's dated 1895.

Kip is hopping from one foot to the other making casual 'not bad' noises, but Lindsay is thrilled. 'I guess there's a whole lot of history about black people in Europe, that we never get to hear. All we hear about is the slavery, like newspapers only giving you bad news. This must have been an important woman. She doesn't exactly look happy, but so dignified, so clever. Kip, do you think perhaps the painter was in love with her?'

Vicky says, 'Where do you think the painter was from, Europe, Africa, America?'

Lindsay peers at the label. 'Anton Azbe? Doesn't sound...' Hearing a whimper, Lindsay turns to Kip again. 'What's the matter?'

'I think someone – Nemesis, that's the guy – is following me around. She's a ringer for my mum. A straight image. She looks... like Mum watching Mark when he's just fallen asleep. I don't think...' Kip sets off at speed, with Lindsay trailing behind.

I ask Vicky if she knows what happened to Kip's mother.

She purses her lips in frustration. 'Yes, I asked Kip, it's the saddest thing of all. She died of heart failure due to undiagnosed Pernicious Anaemia. It's totally treatable in the early stages, but she was concentrating on Kip's brother.'

Vicky follows Lindsay, but I stand in front of the portrait. Tears are dripping down my nose. Crying is now my prevailing mode. I have no tissues and use my sleeve. Imogen finds me there, stuffs a tissue in my hand and inspects the picture that has upset me.

'Beautiful.'

I sniff. 'Kip says it could be his mother. Why do you never see paintings like this?'

Imogen shakes her head. 'They get lost. You saw the collection in Ptuj. There are lots of very wonderful paintings and sculptures of people of all colours tucked away in galleries all over Europe. You should see the stunning African busts by the French sculptor, Cordier, in the Musée d'Orsay in Paris. The trouble is that the large expanses of white flesh on so many canvases simply take the eye. Half the time you spend in galleries your eyes are riveted to variations on the bosom of the Virgin Mary.'

'You're right; I've never seen so many nipples in one room in my life before.'

In the end I leave the gallery reluctantly, buying three postcards of the Black Lady on my way out. I could send them anonymously to certain people before I cross the border. I'm still pretending to myself that I might phone my mother. I expected these last days to bring peace, all the unknowns sorted, all decisions made, each of us clear about our destiny. Yet our different stories seem to be converging then diverging in the most unsettling way. Kip, who seemed so alien in this land, suddenly has stronger connections than the rest of us.

## Ben, Leon and Imogen

We are all subdued at lunch. Ben's absence brings a cold draft of reality into our lives. Vicky suggests that he might have gone and got it over with. I wonder if she's right. If he'd felt the net closing in he could simply have found a quiet spot and taken his collection of drugs immediately and alone. The thought lies heavy in my stomach and I have trouble swallowing. The whole point of coming, as I'd originally envisaged it, was to be able to go through with dying without being alone, and with enough advice to make sure it worked.

'Daniel,' I ask, 'do we know if he has all his drugs with him?'

'Well, he has his over-the-counter ones, but not the anti-emetics. Though he may have a supply of his own.'

I don't say anything, but if he is the kind of guy he led me to believe he was, he could have dozens of drugs on him.

Imogen nods. 'It's possible. Yet he's so gregarious... I can't see him...' She leaves her sentence uncharacteristically open.

This direct mention of practicalities is the first time the act of killing has come up since we individually discussed methods with Daniel before we set off. Reality is a cold, even an ugly, place to arrive. I feel a gulf as wide as the Red Sea opening between the two going home and the rest of us. In spite of reassurances, I worry about when Daniel will abandon us. Will he go home with them or will he escort us across two borders and hold our hands to the last?

We all swap glances, but no one wants to pursue this line of thought. After his revelations the other day, I ought not to care two hoots about what is happening to Ben. I know that he must have hurt a lot of people in his life. I don't think it was only money he played around with. I push my plate away.

Daniel says with decision, 'There's nothing more we can do lingering here. If you get the coach out, Kip, we'll drive along the Krka river to Zuzamberk Castle and breathe a bit of ancient stone.'

The coach seems half empty with Ben missing. It can't simply be that he was the tallest of us. His voice had – or do I mean has – a cheerful and characteristic ring to it. We miss the sound; his going has torn holes in our security.

We stop the coach to get out and stare at the flow of the river, which is, as promised, picturesque. The Calc-tufa falls, with their horseshoe-shaped steps, trees growing mid-stream and mini cascades stretching from bank to bank, are novel enough to distract. Adam and I stand, hand-fast and silent, gazing at the quiet circle of water below the frenetic walls of foam. It's another of those moments when you pause between past and future and have an aching desire never to step forward. Daniel gently taps Adam on the shoulder and we turn to see the others are back on the coach, waiting. And so is the Ben worry.

The castle itself is both eerie and splendid. It's been built over several centuries and successively battered and rebuilt. It's now undergoing prolonged restoration. Parts of it are finished. These appear thuggish and enclosed and then you round a corner to find an untouched elevation: a row of windows with the sky washing in and out. I try to take some comfort from its ability to survive calamities and continue to exist long after our decisions are history.

We return to the hotel full of hope, but there's still no sign of Ben, no clues and no message. That night Daniel calls us together after supper. 'We have to make a big decision. I think I should go to the police, but this will delay us all and I don't know by how much. The police may allow most of you to leave, as scheduled, in three days, but they may not. I shall have to stay. Can anyone throw any further light on the situation or suggest alternative actions. Grace, you say Ben talked to you about himself. Do you feel there is something we could or should be doing?'

I drag my hair back and hold it off my face. Here's a responsibility I'm struggling to know how to handle. 'It's true Ben talked to me, but he told me not to repeat what he said. There were some people he was... avoiding. I'm worried they might have found him.'

Leon speaks sharply, 'What d'you mean?'

'Well, he mentioned some problems... he asked me not to talk about them.'

'For heaven's sake,' Vicky leans over the table, 'there are times to respect confidences and times to be sensible.'

'Is he on the run?' Leon says bluntly.

'I don't know,' I wail, 'I really don't know. I only had the one conversation, while we were waiting in the clinic. I was thinking about Adam. I didn't take it all in and I didn't really believe it. All I know is that he definitely told me not to repeat it.'

Adam says, 'From what Grace said, the question is did he choose to go? If so we should let be. The only worry is if he was taken by force.'

Lindsay gasps, 'Force? Do you mean he had enemies? Is that Greek family after him?'

Leon shakes his head. 'There was no sign of force when we checked his room this morning. He left some of his gear, but nothing essential and his room had not been ransacked or anything. I think we'd have seen some sign if he went unwillingly.'

Daniel nods, 'Yes, true. His door was locked from the outside, he had most of his kit with him; money, passport and everything have gone. None of us have seen him with any strangers. Has anyone anything to add?'

Adam looks at Daniel. 'I think we should let well alone. He wouldn't want his name given to the police – I'm sorry if I've said more than I should Grace.'

Daniel looks at me but I have nothing to add. 'OK does everyone here accept Grace and Adam's advice? Taking no action is uncomfortable, but I've never seen any sign of Ben doing anything he didn't want. So we must assume that if he has left us, he chose to do so.'

Later we swim, and yet again the pool seems to have Ben-shaped spaces in it. I am also anxious for Adam as we face water for the first time since Lake Bohinj, but he swims as though he's never had any problems. I suppose that his near drowning in Bohinj is only the tiniest per cent of his experience with water. I don't think I could be so cool. I love water, but even this safe, small pool is sending ripples of anxiety through me.

When we return to the hotel lounge there's an atmosphere. Kip, Lindsay and Anita are absent, but everyone else is around. Leon, Daniel and Bedrich are in deep discussion with Imogen.

'What's happening?' I ask, 'Is it Ben?'

'No.' Daniel turns, smiling. 'Imogen has done great kindness.'

I'm puzzled as Leon is sniffing and blowing his nose. He struggles to speak, 'Imogen has paid my fare and everything so that I still own my cello – so I could go home.'

'This is not a bribe, Leon.' Imogen insists, 'I merely wanted you to be free to choose.'

Leon mops his eyes. 'I had no idea I would miss my cello this much. I think I have to return. Thank you, thank you.' Imogen's silver head almost disappears in his great hug. 'I wish I could take *all* of you back with me.'

Adam and I hug Leon too. I feel like exploding with delight. Leon is actually blushing. I didn't know he could. Underneath my joy is a tiny stab of melancholy, he will be on the other side of the gulf that I already feel between Lindsay and Kip and the rest of us.

The conference we came upon is not only because he's returning; it seems he also has big schemes. Imogen is talking about financing a charity and Leon wants to run it. They're pressing Bedrich for advice on how the daily stresses of caring for a sick relative might be relieved. Everyone is buzzing with ideas and details and the plans are clearly advanced. I feel like someone who has been off sick for a week and missed a major event. There is something odd about it all though, I think it's seeing Bedrich talking without Anita at his elbow. She usually speaks for him. I never know if he prefers it that way or doesn't have any choice. When I check my watch I realise it is nearly midnight. Anita and Bedrich usually turn in around eleven o'clock.

The discussion must have stimulated Bedrich because before we go to bed our big, sleepy Gumby cat suddenly lifts his voice. 'Please, I have one special request. I would like to go and see the trains before I die. The museum of trains.'

'How can you have a museum of trains?' Lindsay queries. 'I mean, are they in a building, or what?'

'Yes, they're in a big shed.'

She shakes her head in disbelief. 'OK I'm game.'

Daniel grins. 'That's tomorrow sorted then.'

# Round the mulberry bush – Day eighteen

We're standing at the window of our hotel room; Adam's chin rests on my shoulder, his arms are wrapped close around me. Neither of us can stand alone these days. We pretend in public. I don't know how much we succeed. Although he has officially recovered from his drowning experience, Adam seems to me hourly more fragile. In private he barely lets me go for a second. I am not sure if this is a need to pack our entire relationship into the vanishing time-gap left to us; a fear of the approaching border; or an apology for his decision.

We're due at breakfast. I know we must not miss it if we're to get through the day, yet eating does seem completely pointless. I feel safer here, attached. I, too, have become dependent, insecure unless Adam's hands are in contact with me.

'I've been thinking about my mum,' I tell him. 'I think Anita may be right. Perhaps I'll send a card. Let her know it's not her fault. Let her know I'm happy.'

'But are you happy?' His voice vibrates softly by my ear. 'How many times did you cry yesterday?'

I rub my cheek against his. 'That's a sort of self-indulgence. Something inside me has broken – not in a bad way. I think a dam that should never have been built has burst. I think the weeping may be due to years of not weeping. Compared with how I was before this trip, I'm deliriously happy. Could you doubt it?'

'Easily. I'm in love and I'm going to kill the person I love. My insides drain away even as I say it.' I make a noise of protest, but he goes on, 'the only time I forget is when we're making love. Then afterwards, I have to remember all over again and it's even worse.'

'Adam, you're no more killing me than I'm killing you.'

He murmurs into my ear, 'No, I'm failing to save you – different but no better.' I'm silent. 'I know what I've done. I can't undo it, I can't unmake our time together...' He turns me and his arms tighten. He presses his mouth into my neck, but when I wriggle he loosens his arms. 'Am I giving you claustrophobia?' He turns me a little further and lifts my hair so that he can see my face. 'Shall I go away for a bit?'

'No, it's not that. I just... I don't know how to get through to you. You can't cram a lifetime into three days.'

'You've had enough, Grace. I'll go for a walk.'

178

I clutch his hand. 'No, stay.' I look out of the window again; it's another photogenic morning. 'This is the oddest holiday; no one has a camera, no one is taking any photos. Well, except Lindsay on her mobile and they're all of Kip.'

Adam abruptly lets go. Instantly forlorn, I almost fall over.

'Wait a sec.' He disappears to his own room and returns two minutes later. He stands in the doorway arms flung out like a magician, a digital camera in one hand. 'Voilà!'

He poses in laughing triumph, with no idea of his magnetism, his flame-like attraction. I walk towards him, utterly destroyed. By the time we think of the camera again, we've missed breakfast.

We take the camera with us that day. Adam allows no photos of himself. The only clue to his whereabouts must not come until after his death. He has the notice ready to send off to the local papers and to the police.

When we finally join the others on this, the eighteenth day, it looks to me as though Daniel's not slept that night. The light in his eyes at Leon's change of heart last night has faded; he owns up to feeling very unhappy. He's never yet lost anyone on a trip. As we stand dithering in the lobby of the hotel, the hotel owner reappears with an unstamped postcard for Daniel. It has been left on the reception desk. It simply says "All well!" and then something indecipherable.

Daniel stares at it. 'I think, but I'm not good at these things, that this is Ben's writing.'

Lindsay reaches out a hand. 'Let me see. I know something about this. Have you got a sample of his writing somewhere, Dan?'

'Yes, yes, I'll get it straight away.'

Leon frowns. 'What do you know, Lindsay?'

'The training course I am doing with the police includes forensic graphology…' she looks up as we make various querying noises, 'you know, collecting clues about a person from their handwriting.'

I gape at her. 'Lindsay, you didn't say.'

She smiles softly. 'You didn't ask.'

'I'm sorry.'

'There's no need to be sorry. Kip's the only one who asked. I guess I look as though I'd be hopeless at anything.'

We protest as Lindsay picks up the card and runs her fingers across the back. 'What I'm really training to detect is the state of mind of the person writing. There's very little to go on here, but the biro hasn't indented the card deeply and the writing looks firm, not shaky. If it is Ben, he may be OK.'

Daniel reappears with a form with Ben's name and address and a note about some drinks from a mini bar. 'This is all I could find quickly. Will it do?"

'Let's see.' She puts the card down on a table.

We all bend over, then, as Lindsay waves us out of her light, stand back. After a minute she says carefully, 'I think so. I wish I could say with certainty, but there's no capital 'A' for comparison. The 'l's do have the same slope and start from the top. I'm almost sure. These last letters are in a different script - not English.'

Imogen, arriving at this point, stares over Lindsay's shoulder and smiles. 'That's Greek, it says, roughly, *"au revoir"*. Where did that come from? I assume it's from Ben. Looks like he may turn up again.'

'Thank God!' Daniel sits down on the nearest chair. 'I do hope you're right.' He runs his fingers through his hair. Imogen waves the card at him. 'I'm sure it's him, without even knowing his writing. Using the Greek is his style. Whoever he's hiding from probably won't be aware of his Greek connections, whereas everyone here knows about them. Clever.'

I watch the colour returning to Daniel's cheeks. He's all that holds our strange band together. I feel retrospective fear at how close we've come to crashing this project. So that must mean I still want to go ahead.

## Trains and zoos

Daniel leaves a message for Ben with reception, as he does every time we leave the hotel, and we prepare to set off for the train museum. Enthusiasm does not predominate. Lindsay and Vicky suggest that trains are boys' toys and that they should be excused the outing. Even Leon says that, trains not being his thing, surely he could go and hang out quietly in Preseren Square and make plans until we've finished. I feel desperately tired and would love to stay in, but Bedrich's dog-like gaze pricks my conscience and I try to look keen.

Daniel is firm with us all, but it's a less than eager crowd that stumbles through a dull suburb of Ljubljana and finally approaches the barrier of what appears to be a disused factory. I see Vicky looking hopeful – perhaps it's closed. There's an uninviting silence as we push through the entrance door, but inside a cheerful girl greets us in impeccable English. She escorts us to a door in a shed, unlocks it and tells us to come and see her when we are finished and she will open up the other building for us.

We file in and there we are, ten of us, in sole possession of a gigantic semi-circular shed, our noses up against fifteen or so shining, functional locomotives. For at least thirty seconds, like town children at the seaside, we stand motionless breathing loudly. The potent mix of oil, metal, paint and sawdust causes those who remember it to make plaintive aahhs; the others to flicker their nostrils like excited horses. Bedrich looks more and more beatific.

We spend ages in that shed. The Fat Controller could have come and patted us on the head and we would not have been surprised. The engines are there under our hands, and looming above our heads; ranks of outsize cast-iron wheels; curved steel bodies, riveted and bolted, strung across with rods and shafts and wires and cogs. Every part, from chimneys like ships' funnels to nuts the width of a thumb, essential to the working of these Leviathans. Close up, the engines all look hand-made. You can see that the metal sheets are beaten, the rivets individually hammered home.

There's also plenty to read. Each Colossus has a life history; each has travelled through many countries or altered nationality as borders shifted around it. They should look world-weary, but they stand there, solid, proud and ready, oil gleaming on all their working parts.

Bedrich climbs into the cab of a green giant and lovingly fingers the controls. Anita sighs, 'I wish we had a camera.'

Adam dives into my handbag and is on the footplate in seconds. In a sweet moment he captures Bedrich smiling in shy pleasure as he poses as a train driver.

After nearly an hour wandering, reminiscing, sniffing and touching, we reluctantly leave the great shed. We go on for another hour through buildings housing the rest of the museum. Here uniforms, signal levers, point controls, track repair trolleys and all the paraphernalia of the railways are displayed in touching distance. We walk slowly through, still awed by the presence of the monsters in the shed behind us.

As we finally return to the dusty sunlight of the real world, Bedrich takes Anita's hand and kisses it. Such an old-fashioned gesture but carried out and received so tenderly that I wonder if they, too, are coming back to life.

We leave the train museum, dawdling among the rusting engine hulks left out to pasture in the grounds. I sense a general reluctance to return from these solid creations to our usual abstract subjects. We're weary now of long hours in the burrows of self-investigation.

We walk to the Tivoli Gardens for lunch. The sunny atmosphere prevails and we smile a lot and talk little as we eat. Then Adam suddenly says, 'There's a zoo nearby!'

I turn to Daniel; he smiles happily. 'Shall we go? We can walk across the Gardens from here.'

Everyone is half grinning pretending this is a childish idea, but really contented that someone else suggested it. There's rain in the air now but it's so light and the atmosphere so balmy, we all walk without extra covering. My hand is warm in Adam's, my face pleasantly cooled by the surrounding moisture. There are only two days to the end but we're wandering along like holidaymakers again. Perhaps Anita is clinging a bit tightly to Bedrich, but Imogen is skipping from plant to plant in a positively carefree manner. We pause for an elderly couple with a wheelchair filling the path.

Leon, who is leading, turns and says to Daniel, 'It is odd that we talk about our death in relation to the people left behind. None of us talk about *our* feelings about death.'

Imogen answers, 'Well we thought that through before we set out.'

Vicky says, 'For me it is simply blessed oblivion, not walking around carrying the burden of my future.'

I add, 'For me it is the opposite, no longer walking around dragging the weight of my past.'

Adam says slowly, 'Not having to face the future – not *my* future. Feeling I have balanced the equation.'

Bedrich says hesitantly, 'For me too the question is of balance.'

There is silence. I notice everyone walking with heads down, thinking again, instead of sniffing the air. I feel resentful towards Leon. It's all very well for him to bring this up; he's going home now and no longer has to deal with these feelings.

Lindsay takes Kip's hand before asking, 'I worry about those crossing the border. Is anyone here, who's going to die, feeling frightened or sad?' She looks at Daniel. 'Is it all right to ask, Daniel?'

'Of course.'

We wander on and I hope someone will answer. I'm not frightened, I don't think. But I am sad. I can't say so, because of Adam.

Adam suddenly squeezes my hand. 'Grace is sad.' We all stop and everyone turns to look at me. 'That's true, isn't it, Grace?'

I open and shut my mouth, then wriggle. 'I can't explain easily. I came here to die. I wanted to die. I still want to die. I don't mind dying, *but* I have this unreasonable objection to Adam dying. I can see another possibility, of living together, and sometimes I feel a little sad not to try it. No, don't turn away, Adam. There's another side to this. There's something perfect about stopping completely in a couple of days. If we live on we might never be this happy again.'

We're facing one another and he simply leans his head down on mine. I can feel the softness of his hair and the heaviness of his head on my forehead. It is a strange moment of rest and honesty for both of us.

Anita bends down and picks up a leaf, turning it over. 'Well I think it's wrong to take your life without sufficient reason. But for me yes, I'm scared. I think we'll face hellfire and my soul shrinks from this, but I will hold to my faith and resolution. I'm not sad, though. My God will be waiting for me – and my unborn baby – and I have faith.'

Vicky huffs, but Daniel says unexpectedly, 'Hold onto that faith.'

Kip asks, 'Anita, couldn't you please your God somehow, I mean instead of making him angry – like, maybe, start up a charity or something?'

Bedrich, who is watching some children in a playground, jerks round. 'What's that!'

Kip steps back. 'Sorry?'

Anita clutches her bag, eyes wide. 'What is this, Bedrich?'

'It's nothing.' He makes a throwaway gesture with one hand. 'I talked with Leon and Imogen. They want to begin a charity and last night I am giving them some advice.'

'So?'

'Nothing. I thought Kip is misunderstanding, but he wasn't there.'

Anita is confused. 'But Imogen, are you going home then?'

'No fear. I have some money though, and I believe Leon has the energy to make it do something useful. This makes me very happy.'

Bedrich adds, 'You could also give Leon some advice, dearest. He is thinking about young people, particularly those in care and with extra problems. How to help them.'

Anita reaches for Leon's arm, saying fiercely, 'To help you must help those who are caring: with education, with rest, with equipment... with so many things. The carers – these you must help. There are children, too, little ones who are caring for sick parents.'

There's longing in Vicky's voice as she says, 'I only wish I could come and help.'

Leon turns and grasps both her hands. 'Come home with me, Vicky, help me with this charity. I'll look after you.'

Vicky shakes her head. I'm sorry Leon, David is at home and besides you have no idea what is ahead for me.'

Still grasping both her hands, Leon opens his mouth, but she shakes her head and he lets go.

When we reach the zoo it's small and friendly. We wander from the elephant's house to the tiger enclosure. We have a staring match with a tiger, who stares impassively back at us. He wins. We watch seals being fed and for a few minutes I am somewhere else, not in my body, not searching my mind, simply delighted by the seals' delight and by Lindsay feeding Kip jelly beans as if he's a seal.

The rain has cleared and in the damp sunlight the neatly kept greenery, the animals and even the people glisten. The air is full of tiny insects dancing. As we set off on the longer trail to the uplands of the zoo, I realise that the conversation has changed too. Leon, now an outright convert, and still pressing Vicky, is bursting with forward-looking plans.

Instinctively we make two clusters: returners and those going on. We feel safer with our own kind. Kip and Lindsay are so gentle towards us that I feel a kind of pressure from their pity.

We're admiring a miniature zebra when Lindsay suddenly shouts, 'Ben!'

We all turn like wheeling birds and start to move towards the figure Lindsay is pointing at. He's at least 100 metres away and appears to be jogging away from us. It's Ben. He doesn't turn or break step, even though we all yell together. Kip starts to run after him, but Daniel calls him back.

'Don't Kip. It may not be... I'm not certain it's Ben. If it is him he must have heard us shouting and chose not to respond. We can't force him back.'

Adam frowns. 'That was Ben but…'

Leon interrupts, 'It can't be. He wouldn't go jogging in a public park if he's on the run. It doesn't make sense.'

'I don't think we should assume anything,' says Imogen, 'I agree, I think it was Ben, but about everything else we're guessing. He may have chosen to leave us early because he didn't want to go ahead. I don't know what he said to you Grace, but we must keep in mind the possibility that it was a false trail.'

'I never…' I stumble, 'it never occurred to me. You mean it might not be true? He was so convincing at the time, but whenever I think about it now, I can't match up the person we all knew with the person he told me he was.'

Imogen laughs, 'My theory is as likely to be wrong as our previous assumption. I think we keep an open mind. The card said *au revoir.*'

## Bridges and storms – Day nineteen

Adam and I arrive at breakfast bug-eyed on this, the nineteenth day. We're due to go on a boat trip in half an hour. This is an overwhelming relief. I can sit and doze.

I half expect Ben to reappear after yesterday's sighting, but there's still no sign of him and no further communications. If Ben's enemies have really unearthed him here, then maybe Adam's fears about his uncle are justified. He might track him down anywhere in the world. If so there's no escape. On the other hand I would be happier if Imogen were right and Ben had made up his story so as to escape from us.

We cross the Dragon Bridge and descend to the quay to catch a boat. The dragons watch our progress and I cannot help remembering the last time when Leon and Ben started a silly conversation about the tradition that the bronze dragons lash their tails when a virgin walks over the bridge. They made Lindsay blush and it was only later that I wondered if perhaps she really was a virgin. There's something innocent and buttoned up about her – or there was. I watch her striding ahead now, in her loose skirt and comfortable sandals, chatting to Leon. She's laughing; I think she is remembering too.

I climb down into the boat and sink onto the hard plastic seat with relief. My legs are trembling, even putting one foot in front of another has become an effort today. This beautiful, gracious city can glide past me and I don't have to move a muscle. I feel cosy here with just us and a few other random tourists tucked into this boat, water all round and the high embankments of the Ljubljanica guiding us up stream.

The water smells of wet vegetation as we chug alongside the great colonnade that fronts the river edge by the market. Yet I'm enchanted by the whiteness of the architecture. This trip is a bridge celebration. Although the Dragon Bridge is made of reinforced concrete, the great green beasts guarding it make it into a fairy tale structure. This feeling grows as we pass under Plecnik's Triple Bridge.

Imogen reads from her guidebook, 'Here it is, "... a grand celebration of the balustrade in multiple layers of pale stone with steps like layered petticoats descending to the riversides", not bad!'

We drift on, passing under the Cobbler's Bridge. Then the high walls drop away, paths and green edges appear. This is a river again no longer a city highway. I can see allotments and cottages. There's peace and industry here. We turn and head back. Adam, beside me, eyes calmly fixed on the tour guide, seems at peace too. The sun is out and feels warmer than usual. The white stones of the monumental parts of the city reappear. My eyes close.

After an early lunch on our return, we're back in the hotel and Daniel leads us down to the same small, carpeted room that we once used for the blindfold game. As before we take off our shoes. Daniel smiles at us. 'OK today you're going to get a chance to chuck out some of the emotions that you've been going through. I'm going to give you an emotion cue such as "restless" or "cheerful" and I want you to show this emotion on a scale of one to ten. So happiness at level one, might be the barest smile or perhaps a light-hearted stance. To show level ten of happiness I want everything from you; loud, crazy, over-the top wild and grotesque will be fine.'

Anita makes a face. 'Oh dear, I'm no good at these acting games.'

'Anita, bear in mind that we'll all be doing this simultaneously, so there's no audience. The only the person you can embarrass is yourself.'

'Yes, but I'm the person I care about embarrassing.'

To general laughter Bedrich grabs her in a big hug. He says, 'I make a deal. I'm embarrassed for you and you enjoy yourself.'

Daniel grips Bedrich. 'OK, let's start with Embarrassment.'

We work through Surprise, Curiosity and Irritation while becoming increasingly uninhibited and come at last to Joy. At level eight of Joy the noise in the small room is soon overwhelming. Leon is doggedly singing the Hallelujah chorus. Kip joins in and then Imogen, taking up his line, goes into Beethoven's *Ode to Joy* - *Freude! Freude!* Leon and then Lindsay and Kip follow her lead and the four of them stomp round flailing their arms and yelling. Daniel joins in. One by one the others succumb to the wild chorus.

I try to join in, I yell *Freude* but something inside me flips. I don't feel joy; I feel anger, overpowering, screaming, eye-scratching-out anger.

I grab Adam and pin him to the wall yelling, my mouth inches from his ear as he turns his head away from me. Tears stream out. 'I hate you. I hate you because I love you. I hate you because I don't want you to die. I love you more than you can imagine, more than you could ever love me. I want you to love me the way I love you, so that you want to live again.' I grasp his head and turn it so that I can yell directly into his eyes. 'I hate you for not wanting to live, I fucking hate you and I fucking love you and I want to die now so that it's all over.' I start to kick him and pound with my fists. He does nothing to protect himself and this infuriates me further.

I don't really remember much more. I'm on the floor, still screaming, with my own arms somehow tying me up and Kip talking into my ear. 'It's OK Grace, it's OK now. Big breaths now; in, out, in, out.'

I think Adam's on the ground too, because he's suddenly kneeling above me crying, 'I'm sorry, I'm sorry. I do love you. You know I love you.' But merely hearing his voice makes me boil up again and scream. I really hate this man.

In another life I hear Daniel speaking calmly, he says, 'Imogen could you stay with Adam and everyone else go up to the Café, we'll join you in a bit.'

Adam disappears. Kip and Leon, half carry me up to bed, then Anita comes and Leon leaves. I'm now a limp heap on the bed. Kip gives me a glass of water and holds it for me to drink. It's difficult to open my mouth. The glass clinks on my teeth. I'm my eight-years-old self with flu.

They sit me on the side of the bed as they undress me like a doll, put on a nightshirt and tuck me into bed. Kip pats my hand;

Anita leans over and kisses my forehead. Then they potter around the room talking quietly until I must have fallen asleep.

I know nothing about how the others react until later when Adam tells me. Apparently when Leon came downstairs he said to the group, 'I've seen a man act like that after he heard that his son had died of asthma, we couldn't understand it, it was like he was fighting drunk, but he wasn't – drunk, I mean.'

Daniel then explained to the others. 'What happened today is a hazard of stripping away inhibitions. It can and does happen to anyone. An older bit of the brain takes over and you end up with a toddler in an adult body. Like, as Leon so acutely remembers, a fighting drunk.' He has a hand on Adam's shoulder all this time, he goes on, 'A person who's short of sleep and/or food, like Grace, is more vulnerable. In three hours time, if you take her a cup of sugary tea, she'll be herself again.'

## After the storm

Next thing I know, there is Adam with a cup of tea. For an innocent moment I am stunned with joy simply to see him, then I remember. Horror flames in me and I pull the covers over my head wanting to die on the instant.

He peels back the clothes. 'It's all right, Grace, really.'

'Oh God, I'm sorry. I've never done that – or anything like it in my life before. I swear it. Adam I'm so sorry, I don't know what happened.'

Then I'm tight in his arms, not lover-like arms, but secure and consoling, petting and murmuring as yet another cataract of tears drenches his shirt and me. I do eventually hiccup to a standstill and drink my cooling tea. After this Adam becomes practical.

'Do you want these clothes or something different? Leon wants to show you something. '

I dress slowly and there's a moment when I sit half dressed on the edge of the bed and Adam's face starts to crumple in a way that I now recognise and his hand is warm on my neck as he leans down to kiss me. A tiny bit of hope stirs inside, but there are footsteps in the corridor and he stands up again. 'Leon's waiting.'

I want to forget Leon, but push my resentment aside. During my earlier distress I had been distantly aware of Leon's kindness as he turned me into a parcel in order to remove me from the games room. When we finally go downstairs Leon is on the hotel computer, he has some kind of DVD on. He calls us over. 'Grace, come here. I want you to watch this. It's from an opera.'

'Oh Leon, I don't really go for opera at all.'

'Don't worry, it's very short. It's a moment when a young woman is going to leave the man she loves beyond anything imaginable. She's led a tough life and then this man appears. Out of all the men she has known, he's her first genuine love. They've been wildly happy for a month or so. She's dying of tuberculosis, but her lover's father bullies her into giving him up. Grace, I know how weird you must feel about this afternoon, but your passion reminded me of this. We can understand how you felt.'

He switches on the player and a girl in a pink dress sings and sings – her whole body sings in an extraordinary convulsion of love – to a man who doesn't yet know that they have no future together. He cannot make sense of her despair.

'I only wish I appeared as passionate, as beautiful or as convincing as she does. Can you rewind?' I watch Violetta begging Alfredo to love her as much as she loves him. We watch it three times. Adam wants to go on to the end, but we're called to supper.

It does help. For a moment I think that I'll get the DVD for Adam. I even memorise the opera, La Traviata, and the singers' names, Anna Netrebko and Rolando Villazón.

Then I remember.

Why can't I go back to that place of only two weeks ago, when I had no Adam and no doubts at all? Back then I knew it would be easier to go forward than to go back to my old life. If I'm honest, I know that even if Adam consents to live, we could have as many hassles together as we had before in our separate lives, all the reasons for wanting out will remain... except that Adam would be there – a reason for living, where there was none before. I ought to admit that I *can* love and go back to the world and try again, but it would be easier to die with Adam than to live knowing him dead.

At the end of the day we return to the now horrendously familiar carpeted room in the hotel basement. I find myself shaking as I enter. It's only a few hours since I disgraced myself here. Adam squeezes my hand. Imogen gives me a hug, Vicky strokes my arm. How we've changed in two weeks. I love these people – all of them.

We lie down. There seems to be more room than I remember, then I recall Ben's absence. Once again the size of the space

189

he might have occupied is in itself a disturbance. As we lie there Daniel talks us through a relaxation exercise. His voice leads us tenderly to a warm spa and immerses us. He's still talking when I drop off and dream, perversely, of maps.

The next part is more difficult. We sit and attempt a simple ten-minute meditation. On a scale of one to ten, I remain at level one. My mind refuses to stay focused on the present, even for as long as an in and out breath. I try. Obediently I allow the thoughts to come into my mind and then pass on and out again, but I have no control over the next one arriving. Emptying, or rather focusing, my mind is beyond me. I try flooding my brain cells with a single colour. I have a blue six seconds, before the blue turns to the soft green-grey of the surface of Lake Bohinj.

Afterwards everyone except me votes for another session after breakfast tomorrow. Lindsay in particular is wildly enthusiastic. I feel stupid and irrationally betrayed by Adam. It's as if no one wants me on their team.

That night Adam and I make a stupendous effort to climb out of our personal vortex and give the rest of the world some attention. In particular we worry about Daniel and whether he becomes this drained every year or are we a spectacularly difficult bunch. It does not take us long to return to our usual subject matter – ourselves.

When we finally sleep, I dream non-stop. For the second time on this trip I have my old dream about Oscar and wake up with my teeth clenched, blood drumming in my veins. On this note I start my last day in Ljubljana. Still no sign of Ben. I decide that the sighting at the zoo was a mistake and comfort myself with the memory of the postcard. In some ways, it's easier for me with him absent, after his confession to me. The group, however, miss him.

## Meditation and music – Day twenty

We troop down to that dreaded room for a repeat of the meditation exercise. I have to remind myself that Adam seems to gain an atom or two of serenity from it. I especially like the relaxation at the start and once more Daniel barely suggests a mental journey before I drop into a smothering sleep.

When I'm woken I do wonder if I've been hypnotised, but it turns out all I have missed is an imaginary repeat of our boat journey. Of course, I slept through much of that as well. Now comes the difficult bit. I am sitting cross-legged on the floor and having another go at this mind-focussing business.

Is there a secret no one has told me? In the stillness my mind is a maelstrom of thoughts piling in like trucks at a rubbish tip. The pink girl from the opera is in competition with the maps of Slovenia that I was looking through this morning. Images flit across my mind, Bedrich talking to Leon; Kip jumping to try and reach a flower growing in a castle wall; Anita undressing me yesterday. My mother undressing me...

I try pretending that I'm in a car and the windscreen wipers, with each sweep, clear my mind. I look out of the clean windows and instantly find a landscape. Steep Slovenian hills, a rocky chasm and Adam...

No. I must think of an empty space before I ever knew Adam. I go back to my Devon cottage and concentrate on the empty field outside the kitchen window. Nothing but brown furrows, up and down. There's the barn in the distance. It's quite different from the barn in which Oscar and I played on that last holiday. If only Oscar had been less loving, less willing to obey, if only...

Time is up. The others have had a ball, or so they claim. I find it difficult to believe. How can they do such a difficult thing, or if it's easy, why on earth can I not do it?

Adam, seeing my disappointment, hugs me. 'Grace you have so many other talents, don't begrudge us this one.'

The relief of being outside in the soft September sunshine cheers me up again. The plan this morning is to wander round the Natural History museum. We collect on the grass in front of the imposing building waiting for Daniel.

Leon, never far from his music, fishes in his jacket pockets. 'Listen everyone. This, to my mind, is the sexiest music ever composed.' He looks round then grins. 'I'd love to know what you others think.' My mood goes up a notch.

He pulls out his mini speakers and sets the iPod up to broadcast. The opening bars of Milhaud's *Creation du Monde* have a low, slow beat and a saxophone tune that dissolves my insides. As the sounds spread out they seem to enter through my skin.

Imogen says, 'The trouble is you've put the idea of sex into our heads. Of course we're thinking of it – flawed research,'

Leon smiles, shaking his head. 'Please Miss, this isn't research. I'm simply sharing my passion.'

'Well it does it for me,' I volunteer and tip my head back for Adam's kiss. I emerge from this startled, because instead of the light public brushing of the lips I had expected, it is long and deep. There's general laughter.

Adam gives us his lovely beam and shrugs. 'Blame Leon or the guy on the sax.'

I turn to look at Adam. His face is so fine drawn that it's almost transparent now. I suspect he's decided that for the last hours of our lives we might as well behave in public as we do in private. Well, so be it. I cannot refuse him anything now.

The music continues with its stirring beat and unsettling tunes. I look round. This is our last full day. The anxiety and the fluctuations from childishness to paranoia of the preceding day seem to have dissipated.

As we're cuddling and laughing on the grass, I become aware of a shadow. Daniel stands there watching us. He's blowing his nose, but smiling. It's the kind of smile that makes me want to cry. Vicky and Imogen pull him down and insist he listens to Leon's music. He does this with eyes shut, a real smile curving his lips. There's nothing but the sunlight on Daniel's face and on the tiny upwards lift at the corners of his mouth. My mind is blissfully empty. This may be the nearest I will ever get to meditation. I'll settle for that.

## Dead and living history

In the museum we become children again. We can't help it. There's a skeleton of a mammoth and Adam's camera catches us fooling around in front of the monstrous bones. We wander, giggling, past cases of stuffed animals. A bear with its kill; badgers – I didn't expect them in Slovenia. A whole case full of skeletons illustrate the evolutionary links between human and hedgehog. We're clearly the same beast, with a ribcage, breastbone, tail, all basically identical to the hedgehog, merely bigger. I shall never look at dinosaurs or hedgehogs again in quite the same way. Of course I shall probably – no I shall certainly – never see one again.

I'm still standing mulling over this thought, when Vicky asks, 'Do you mind? I mean mind not seeing one of these again?'

'Yes, a bit, but there are a lot of other things I'll be glad never to see, so all in all it'll work out. I'm grateful I'm getting a chance to see so much on our last day.'

Adam is wandering, nose glued to the glass cases, but always with one trailing hand on my waist, my shoulder or linked to my fingers. Vicky is really getting a lot out of this too. She likes the geological specimens. Every possible colour and shape of rock is displayed, from a lump of Cinnabar, through hematite and amethyst, to Dolomites as smooth as though they've come out of a mould.

The Slovenes even have their own living fossil, a primitive newt-style beast, related, I see, to a salamander. It looks very pink and vulnerable, like some infant dinosaur newly out of the egg. There are thousands of miniscule soft grey birds, stuffed but almost fluttering on their branches. A thorn tree is covered in bright finches – I do wonder for a second if these are alive. There are ducks of every variety marching in pairs like a crazy Noah's Ark. I wish I'd attended to this kind of thing more as a child.

Even as this thought passes through me, we are swamped by schoolchildren and become part of their chattering stream. Anita, struggling amongst them, abruptly starts to cry. We make a quick exit with her protected in our midst.

Most of us are looking forward to simple oblivion; she is staring into an abyss of excruciating pain. I feel powerless to help, but we all try and comfort her.

As we settle at tables for lunch, Imogen presses a card into my hand. 'You said you would get in touch with your mother. I've bought a lovely card with those finches on it, but I've no one to send it to. Take it.'

Anita, too, presses me to write to my mother, and I don't want to refuse her anything. Bedrich passes me his pen, I think I see the suggestion of a wink. Before I think too much about it, I scribble on the card. I tell her Slovenia is well worth visiting, that I am happy – I freeze over this astonishing, and true, statement, then realise they're all waiting – that I have some great new friends and, at Adam's suggestion, I sign out with "love you, Grace".

I'm happy with this compromise. It sends the message, but not too heavily. I don't know if it's true, but I want it to be. I want her to love me first, but maybe Anita's right and she does. I don't know. I am about to put the card in my bag to think about later, but Lindsay points out that I haven't put on an address. I do so dutifully and as my pen finishes the word UK, Leon snatches the card out of my hand and Imogen puts a stamp on it. I reach out for it but she passes it to Bedrich who hands it to Kip. Kip leaves the restaurant and nips down the road to a post office. It's a conspiracy. Everyone's laughing. I am laughing too, but scared inside. It's done.

Daniel says, 'That was a real kindness to your mother, whether you meant it or not.'

I am still sort of laughing. 'I think everyone here is being kinder to my mother, than I've ever been.' Tears fill my eyes yet again. 'No. You're all being kind to me. It's you lot I love.'

After lunch we set off for yet another visit. Daniel's keeping us on the hop today. Maybe he doesn't want us to focus too closely on tomorrow. Odd though, as he usually encourages contemplation.

We spend a couple of hours in the weirdest museum I have ever faced – The House of Experiments. It really is a house, but inside its small spaces it's pure hands-on fun – the antithesis of the Museum of Natural History.

We are playing with giant bubbles when Anita has another wobble, she is missing Ben, she says. He would have loved the fun. It is true that he always made her laugh; yet I thought she disapproved of him. We all work hard to fill the gap and succeed so well that when we leave, it is as a giggling group. We head towards our favourite café for a last ice cream fest.

As we polish off our ice creams and begin to look towards Daniel wondering how to end the day, he surprises us.

He says, 'I'd like us to take a bus out to the cemetery.'

'The cemetery?' Kip echoes, and we all stare in astonishment.

Daniel nods. 'Tomorrow, by choice, is for some of us the end of life, the last sunrise. Some of you have remained certain that you wish for this – to die before your natural end. We will now walk amongst a throng of people who would, every one, probably have lived longer given the chance. I want you to take every opportunity to be clear about your intentions. It's simplistic to say there's no return after death, but I want you to absorb this fact with all its implications. I have, as I've always made clear, no problem with anyone choosing to quit this life. I would have a problem if any of you do not understand fully the finality of your actions and what it is you are voluntarily giving up *for ever*.'

The experience of the cemetery is sobering. Plecnik, the architect of much of Ljubljana, has had total freedom here. The dead are remembered in a great open colonnaded villa. The white stone gives the building a strange lightness. It's a soothing place to walk with much calming symmetry in its layout.

The cycle path of Remembrance and Comradeship runs through here. I am glad to have seen it. At first I feel slightly resentful that Daniel should bring us here on our last day, but now I understand. Beneath our feet are many hundreds of people. I make myself imagine the worms then I think of those who are no more than dry relics such as we saw in the Natural History Museum. I have no trouble with this concept. My human skeleton is rather less important than that of the hedgehog we studied this morning.

The other aspect of this place, apart from the battalions underground is the aboveground aura of peace. I wander, my hand in Adam's, absorbing this. I look at the others wishing to spread this feeling amongst them.

Sadly Anita is very stressed now and none of us seems able to console her. Daniel is walking apart with her and Bedrich is following behind them. She seemed so happy yesterday in the train museum. I wonder what has come up at this late stage. If I had to choose which of our group I would be slowest to pull back from the crater's edge, it might have been Anita, yet her distress pains me intensely. Is she finally contemplating hell? Has her faith faltered?

This morning we saw the spoils of millions of years of evolved life; breathing, blood-pumping creatures, that had died and each had left a record in its own way. I suppose that's something to regret – not to have left a record. I messed up my life, but in the grand scheme of things it won't matter either way. Once I'm dead, I'll not even feel regret. I'm no more important than the ant I watched on that first day three weeks ago. Maybe I'm even a tad less competent, perhaps that's why I felt such a strong fellow feeling.

'Grace, what is it?'

'Uh? Sorry Imogen, I was remembering an ant.'

'Yes, this place gives you a sense of our status in the world; we're all ants. The strange thing is that we mourn the dead, but they're the ones free of pain, it's the living who hurt.'

## Revisions – Day twenty-one

I wake to find the bed beside me cold. Lying there rigid, mind tumbling, heart kicking and plunging, I have an image of Adam going somewhere quiet to take his pills. Like Ben he's decided go elsewhere, I might never see him again and I haven't said goodbye. What does any of this matter; I will be dead in a few hours?

Then I see his wallet, his file of papers and the camera on top of the chest and my brain starts to work again. He's probably gone to his own room to have a shower without waking me. I remember the warmth of the previous day, snuggle down and, amazingly, sleep for another hour.

I'm in the shower when he returns. I hear a noise and come out still wet with a towel clutched round me. Adam is standing uncertainly by the window. Something dreadful has happened; someone has jumped the gun, or worse, Daniel has disappeared. I stare, unable to imagine why he should look so diffident. Then I see his mouth lose control and a funny, shy smile comes into his eyes.

'Grace, do you really want to live with me?'

I'm so shaken, I drop the towel and, dramatically naked and wet, walk straight into his arms. 'Do you mean...? Are you sure, Adam? You won't change your mind?'

'I'm sure.' He holds me off for a moment to see how much damage I have done to his clothes. Then he starts laughing. 'Oh Grace, don't change.'

'But what...? Tell me why?' A shadow crosses his face. I clutch him. 'No don't worry. I...'

He's shaking his head. 'I *will* tell you but... Get dressed, love, and I'll try to explain.' Sitting beside me on the bed, he speaks in fragments. 'It isn't one thing. At least, I suppose, Daniel's the tipping point. Today I woke early and watched you sleeping. I knew I'd never see that again. I dressed. I don't know what I was planning. I went outside. It was barely dawn and the sky was transparent purple and green. I walked west until I reached the Tivoli Gardens. Then I went on and climbed the Sisenski Hill. Round me only grass and woodland, not so different from my childhood.'

Adam has one arm around my shoulders, his other hand is gripping his knee. 'Then I thought of you waking and finding me gone. I started walking back to the hotel. It was still so early with almost no one around. Then I saw Daniel. He was turning the corner by the Opera House. I ran to catch up. I couldn't see him at first. He was down on the pavement. He was crying, I mean *really* crying.'

I press my face into Adam's shoulder mumbling my shame, 'We've taken and taken from him and not given anything back.'

Adam pulls his arm from around me and grabs my shoulders; his eyes are alight. 'Exactly! That's why... but...' He takes one of my hands in his, runs his thumb over my newly bitten nails then turns it over ands spread out the palm, studying it like a clairvoyant. 'It was like finding the Eiffel Tower in a crumpled heap. Something that was never meant to happen. I went to hold him... Until this trip I'd not hugged a man since I was little. It wasn't like our games.'

The troubled look on Adam's face becomes acute; there's also puzzlement. 'I thought of my dad. I mean, I thought of him as if I was an adult and he was a child. I think I can feel how a parent – how my dad – felt. Oh God, I can't explain.' He closes my hand inside both of his. 'You need to understand. We'll both have to live with my decision.' He bangs his forehead on our hands.

I whisper, 'Ssh, it's all right, it's all right, Adam.'

He tries again. 'I only thought Daniel was blind tired – the same as you and me. Three weeks of us and years of others. After a bit he manages to talk. He says he can't face another year. Losing Ben and only three going home – but he respects our decisions. He's trying to smile. He says he's an optimist. We're laughing and crying on the pavement. This man with his dog sees us, looks scared and crosses the road.'

Adam stops. He runs his fingers over my hand again. Finally he takes a breath and says, 'I tell Daniel I'm still uncertain. He looks at me like I'm the Mona Lisa. He says I'd better not talk to him; he might try to influence me. I say maybe I want to be influenced. His face grows... younger?'

Adam is holding my hand to his mouth and talking into it, he says, 'You must, you *must* understand. Daniel's face was like he'd seen a vision. I felt this crazy sense of power – as if I could do some good,' Adam's voice is trembling, 'do something positive – for Daniel.' He stops, presses my hand to his mouth as if to stop anything else coming out and waits, head down, for a blow to fall.

I sit in silence. Adam's fear is confusing me, what is it he's afraid of, is he going to change his mind again or does he now fear that I'll change mine? 'Adam? Look at me. I'm feeling very stupid, what are you trying to tell me?'

Speaking very low, he says, 'Will you hate me, because I changed my mind for Daniel? I should have changed it for you.'

With a big sigh, I lie back on the bed. 'Adam, if Daniel asked me to go leap into the Victoria Falls in a barrel with him, I'd walk out of this door now. Don't ask me why. He is the father, mother, even the lover of my dreams. Here, look at me. Kiss me. Never worry about this again.'

Adam's face is still strained. He stands up and walks across to the window. He speaks with his back to me. 'There's something else, Grace. I was so sure I was going to die when I left England I wrote to the police. I told them everything. If Derek hurts some other child, it will be my responsibility. I had to tell them. They probably can't do anything to prosecute him now because Mum's dead, Amanda has emigrated and changed her name and would never agree to come back and I'll be either dead or on the run. The only hope I have is that they'll watch him. They will know he lied in agreeing that he murdered my father. I think they'll believe me.'

He stays with his back to me. He speaks very quietly. 'So, I'm wanted by the police for murder, and I have an angry sex offender after my blood, I've changed my name twice, but I have my original birth certificate with me. Do you want to change your mind now? I'll understand. In fact you'd be crazy to go ahead.'

I slide off the bed behind him and wrap my arms around his shoulders. 'No, I think you did the right thing. I'm proud of you. We'll be careful. When did you send this letter off?' I wonder what his real name is, then realise that I don't want to know. For me he is Adam.

'I posted it, without a postcode, from Scotland, before I left. I wrote in my old name. I imagine the police can track me down if they want to.'

I turn Adam round and we hold on to each other.

## Daniel

There's silence in the bus. The cluster of buildings signalling the border has appeared on the horizon. We pull off the road into a large parking area around a petrol station. Daniel stands looking down at us. 'We'll be meeting a hired car here in an hour's time to cross the border. Kip, Lindsay, Grace, Adam, and Leon you have all chosen to find your way home and have another try at life.'

Our change of heart is news to some of the others, Bedrich and Anita walk down the bus to hug and congratulate us. I can't help noticing that Imogen is beaming. I didn't know that anyone would care that much. The others are hugging us too.

Daniel continues as we gather outside. 'I make you a present of the bus. Kip has the keys. I've put all the papers in order so it is in Kip's name now.' Daniel reaches for Imogen and Vicky's hands.

'The rest of us; that's Imogen, Vicky, Bedrich, Anita and I will be travelling on as planned...'

Lindsay is clutching the coach door. 'Daniel... when will we see you again?'

'Well, this is my final goodbye too. I'm going...'

A universal gasp stops him. Vicky flings herself into his arms and we crowd round holding on to him as though we can tether him to the earth.

'You can't leave us.'

'Why, Daniel, why?'

'Everything you do is worthwhile, you have to go on doing it.'

Daniel pushes Vicky gently away. 'No, it's finished. I've paid my debt, or as much as I can manage. I'm going to rest at last. I'm so tired.'

'I don't understand, what debt? What can you possibly have done that you should need to pay with your life?'

'Because of me most of a family – three generations – died...' We freeze. Daniel opens his mouth as if he is going to tell us more then shuts it again. There's a stunned silence.

Vicky is still clinging to him, although he's not attending to her. She tugs at his jacket. 'It's not true. I don't believe you. You're making this up so we won't stop you. Daniel, it can't be true.'

'It's true. I made a bargain with myself to save four people, who would otherwise die, for every one of my victims before I could go myself. You five make up the last ones.'

My face is streaming. 'If that's how it is, I'll come too and you'll have to go back. I can't let you die, we all love you.'

Leon pushes in front of me. 'That's two of us then.'

Daniel puts both hands on Leon's shoulders. 'Please, please don't do this to me.' He is looking around. I see his eyes pass over the green field sloping upwards from the bus and then return to Leon, distraught but passive, between his hands. 'Wait.' He breathes deeply. 'I guess it's my turn. This will be the first time. Please, I beg you, let it be the last. Let's climb up here and I'll try and tell you my story. It won't take long.'

Sheep-like we stumble in his wake as he marches up the hill. As soon as he pauses and turns, Imogen pulls him gently to the ground and the rest of us settle in front of him. He strips off his jacket and makes Imogen sit on it. Vicky is leaning against him, tears bulge and spill from her eyes and she lets them fall.

Daniel gazes attentively at the sky as if speech will arrive from above if he waits long enough. His compact body is folded neatly; his arms rest on his bent knees. His dear eyes are still focused away from us. Nobody moves.

He smiles suddenly and makes his little characteristic outward puff of air. 'All these years I have ducked this moment. Now I know. All of you...' he pauses to look out across the hill, then down at our faces, 'not only you here, but all the previous groups, you have all had the courage to tell others what made you decide that life was no longer worth the effort. Only I've been too feeble to tell the truth.'

Vicky is shaking her head, Adam lifts a hand in protest. Daniel continues, 'In the last five years I've taken groups like you travelling. I've only taken people who were certain they wanted to die, and who convinced me that without my intervention, they would definitely go ahead. In each year some people have chosen to go home; the five of you returning this year make twenty-four. Saving twenty-four people doesn't begin to pay for the misery I caused originally, it is simply the bargain I struck with myself.'

He is shivering and we all huddle closer. 'Well imagine me at fifteen. I was as careless and uncouth as any other fifteen-year-old. My dad drove freight across the Swiss/Italian border and from the age of fourteen I often went with him during the holidays. They were good those journeys. Mounting the passes, weaving between the white peaks, slicing across chasms. I had a passion then for mega engineering, the sort that makes mankind seem all-powerful. The trains the other day reminded me of this pride. I idolised the creators of The Solis Cantonal Bridge viaduct and the Landwasser aerial rail. I loved the drama, the scale of the railway viaducts clinging to the mountain face, leaping across impossible gaps. I thought I was grown up. I smoked, I drank, I stayed up with my dad talking politics or sex with the other drivers.'

Daniel takes his eyes off the far distance and looks at us directly. 'There are no extenuating circumstances to what I did – or failed to do. It was back home in our village in... in Switzerland. One night I was boasting about my travels to the boys, the gang I'd grown up with, and we drank quite a bit. We had this stupid game we'd played since were small of kicking a big old can around the street, until someone got irritated enough to open a window and shout at us.

'This night, it worked like a dream; this old buffer opened a ground floor window really wide and bellowed at us. Vic… my friend lobbed the can straight at him. It was a brilliant shot and sailed straight through the gap, past the buffer. We scarpered and went to find another can to annoy someone else.

'Some time later, we were all going home separately and I passed that house again. The window where the can had gone through was bright orange. I couldn't understand at first and then I did. The can was only sort of empty, but I guess full of vapour. If the lid came off, or he lit a cigarette… I ran for home faster than I knew I could run. In minutes I was trembling under my duvet. I knew I should wake someone, but I told myself that the old guy was awake, so he would get everyone out. Even now, twenty odd years later, I re-live that night in these waking dreams, make myself get up and call for help, run back to the house, break down doors, smash windows, grab children and carry them into the fresh air.

'But I can't remake history. I did nothing. I said nothing. There were grandparents, a mother and three children in the house. The only survivor was a twelve-year-old boy, who had a room in the extension at the back. Five people died in that fire. When the police came round to find me and my friends, we showed them the can we had been kicking down the street *after* we saw the old guy. We said that he must have had the old petrol can in the house already. I don't understand why they believed us.'

There's a silence now, familiar to us all. Vicky is rubbing her head on Daniel's shoulder. At last Adam speaks, 'It's possible that something other than your can sparked that fire.'

'Of course, there's always the hope that you're not responsible. I doubt anyone here thinks the fire would have happened without our game, but that's not the point. I could have saved them, woken everyone, called for help. I went and shivered under a duvet while essential and innocent people; a mother, a baby, people in their eighties who had survived wars, all fried to death because of me. I have tried to figure out a way to live usefully with this knowledge weighing in my head, but I only have so much endurance.'

Daniel's hand covers his eyes. 'There's more. The next time I was with my dad on one of his trips, the men were talking about the fire and I found out that the father of that family had committed suicide, because he blamed himself. He'd been out playing cards when the family died.'

'What did you do then?' Imogen asks.

'Nothing, except to start falling apart. I became an expert on hidden guilt. A couple of years after that, I tried to take my own life. I saw what this did to my parents. More guilt. I had some help – therapy – and sort of got on with my life. Then I moved back to England, where I'd lived there for three years as a child, and tried the opposite; working hard.'

There's a long pause. 'What about the boy who survived?' I ask.

Daniel hangs his head. 'By the time I went back to Switzerland all I could find out was that he had gone to live with some Austrian relatives. I stopped searching a few years ago. It won't help him to know that, but for my cowardice, his family might have been rescued. He…'

Daniel stops abruptly and puts his head in his hands, but before we can speak he looks up again. 'Sorry, I don't want to bore you with my life story and I can't work out what I need to tell you to explain things.'

'What made you start doing this?'

'Well, after therapy I tried to be normal. I studied engineering, joined an evening drama class, volunteered with a mental health organisation. I deluded myself that I could balance the books and get away with an ordinary life, but I'm not strong enough. I can't.'

'What changed your mind, Daniel,' I ask.

'I met a girl.' He bends forward and plucks a couple of stems of grass, then laughs. 'Now I know how you lot feel. I didn't mean to talk about this bit ever. I found someone – maybe I was looking for her – as damaged as I was. She was an innocent whose father had committed suicide. Talk about a wake up call. I thought maybe I could help her and pay my debt by helping suicidal people. I retrained as a psychotherapist. I had some money that my mum left me when she died – we won't go there.'

He closes his eyes. 'I was fooling myself, my girlfriend left me soon after and is still battling it out with drugs, and I found it impossible to help people within the system. I moved back to Switzerland because my father was sick. He died five years ago. Although I've put immense effort into leading a normal life, everything I touch leads me back to my crime. I've had to go out to meet it instead. I'm sure you'll see how in each of your stories I have recognised myself. That's why you're all here. I'm so tired now, please let me go in peace.'

Imogen is looking at him consideringly. 'Daniel, if you're guilty, and if your crime is as great as you imagine, then frankly you've not yet paid the price. You could not pay in a lifetime of person-for-person exchanges. Can I suggest that you set aside what you see as your debt and look at the work you do without trying to match it to the scale of your guilt. At a personal level you've given me a happier ending than I could have imagined with new experiences at the close of my life. At a more general assessment, your work has incalculable value, you are beloved of all of us here and no doubt of every other person who has travelled with you...' Daniel shakes his head, '... and that includes the people you have taken all the way to the end. They, like me, will have felt happy with their decision. As for you lot here,' she waves at us returners, 'I don't remember seeing such radiance, such bliss, as I have seen fleetingly in all your faces. You cannot measure that in single units of debt. You could spread some more of that. Would that not balance the weight of continuing to live?'

'Dear, dear Imogen, how reliably you think things through. It is a clever argument, I have even toyed with it myself, but I've come to the end of some hidden resource that's essential for this work. It may even be that my reasoning is a cover. Perhaps I've all along wanted to quit, and thought out the most labour intensive way of reaching my goal or even perhaps of putting it off. It doesn't matter now. I know I will not, *could* not, do another year of this work.

'There are also some practical problems. Up to now I have been able to see people to the end and still make sure that the appropriate authorities are the first to arrive. This is not something you can repeat forever.'

'But Daniel,' Leon's hand is rubbing Daniel's shoulder and he looks up, 'couldn't you work without all this stress? I mean, there's veterans' groups in England, they're in desperate need of people like you.'

Vicky adds, 'You could help people without taking these journeys that sap your strength so brutally.'

Daniel shakes his head. 'I could, but it's simple. I don't want to. As Imogen once said,' his lips curve for a second as he looks round at her, 'no one can force you to live. I choose death. Please believe me, I really want to go now.'

We sit silently, unwilling to accept his decision yet unable to deny him anything he wants.

'Daniel?' Vicky puts a hand on his sleeve. 'Will you explain something?'

'I'll try.'

'I'm curious about how you chose us, there must have been lots more people who got in touch. I mean, apart from our particular stories, we're not a random selection of people are we?'

Daniel speaks slowly, pulling out thoughts he hadn't planned to share. 'No… I'm afraid I cheat. I'm self-indulgent when I decide who comes… You represent about two per cent of the people who get in touch. Apart from making sure that no one is included who might ask for and benefit from conventional medication or therapy, I have to choose people with whom I can work. I need – at the very least – to like all the people who come… I need to feel some of their pain. Of course, I don't always succeed in reading between the lines… I'm forever being surprised by human nature. I am confused by Ben, for instance.'

We wait in case he hasn't finished, then Imogen asks softly, 'Can you tell us about some of your successes?'

'Dear Imogen. OK. There was this boy, in his twenties. His father had committed suicide when he was about ten and his mother the day after his twenty-first birthday. He also had an uncle who committed suicide. His situation was a good and necessary reminder that what we as individuals think of as our peaceful oblivion can become someone else's burden. This boy felt appalling guilt for his mother's death in particular. The weight of it crushed all interest in life out of him. He didn't pair up with anyone on his travels with me, but when he listened to the guilt that each of the others in the group were carrying and how – in so many cases – these burdens were self-inflicted, he began to think his way out of them.' Daniel lifts up a stone and weighs it in his hand. 'It was exactly as if he had arrived with a pocket full of rocks and each day he left a handful behind. By the end he was unrecognisable. We all loved him; his enlightenment gave several others the courage they needed. He is still alive, well and happy.'

Vicky finally asks her question, 'Do you plan, when you select us, to put us into pairs?'

Daniel laughs. 'No. Though I've become accustomed now to this happening. The only time I planned it I was completely confounded; the female half of my imagined pair discovered her hidden nature and went home with another girl.'

This revelation causes a general chuckle and the atmosphere lifts. For a few seconds we feel that euphoria that comes at the end of a story, when the telling is over.

'Daniel?' Leon speaks hesitantly, 'is there someone... someone back in England that we can contact for you... for us? I need to know that this is not the end.'

Daniel nods. 'Kip has some contact emails for when you get home.' He stands and says quietly, 'We must go now.'

## Over the border

That's it.

Our mood is so fragile, we stand, each of us touching another, no one is left out. Daniel has an arm round Vicky, Adam round Imogen. We start walking down the hill. A taxi is approaching, I wonder if it is for us. As we reach road level I see there is someone in the passenger seat, but as I start to look away again, the passenger waves. The car slides off the road into our parking area. The door opens and someone who looks like Ben's brother steps out. The barley-coloured waves have been shorn to stubble; his chin is unshaven and he has a large camera slung around his neck. We exclaim and surround our lost sheep. He seems just the same.

He speaks airily, 'Apologies, Dan. I'm afraid I had to leg it for a bit.'

Imogen asks, 'Were you far away? We thought we saw you the day before yesterday in the zoo.'

He laughs. 'That must have been my alter ego. I was in Venice. See Venice and die.'

'Venice!' I exclaim. 'How? Why?'

'I've never seen Venice,' says Leon.

'Nor me,' adds Anita wistfully.

Ben grins. 'Well, Leon, why don't you go on the way home?'

'How d'you know I'm going home?'

Ben ignores him. 'It's only a day trip from Ljubljana. That's how I got there. You simply take a train. If the guys who are chasing you...' He pulls out a strand of my hair. 'Don't look so bothered, Grace... are umbilically attached to their cars, Venice is rather a cool place to hide. A thousand large, blonde, camera-toting tourists make excellent cover.'

'You mean it was true, all you told me?'

He looks suddenly sober. 'Every word. It's been rather incongruous to be spending my last days with all you upright citizens.'

He looks at the other's blank faces and reaches an arm round me, I feel Adam flinch, but after a quick squeeze Ben shrugs and releases me. 'Well, so you didn't tell, Grace. You have talents; what a waste! What Grace didn't tell you is that I'm a… bad man and one way or another I'm on the run. Actually I am sorry about the hassle I caused. I didn't ever plan to bring my past along with me, but it is superglued to my tail, so even after a few "second thoughts" in St Mark's Square I've decided to stick to my resolutions. I'm going on to the finish.'

'Adam and I are going home, Ben.' I tell him.

'Of course you are,' he says lightly.

Leon asks, 'Ben, don't you have parents? Do you want to send them a card or anything?'

'Parents?' he answers as if they're unheard of possessions. 'No, they died. There was an accident.'

I gaze at him, appalled. I distinctly remember him talking about them as though they were alive when he mentioned a letter for them with the bank. 'Ben, did you… what have you done?'

He gives a short laugh. 'Come on, Grace. That would have been a step too far even for me.' He picks up his bag and walks over to Imogen.

'I really don't know what to believe about Ben now,' I say to Adam.

'At a rough guess, nothing.'

Leon adds, 'It wouldn't surprise me if it's all staged, you know, a fake disappearing act.'

Before I can argue with this Daniel, whose face has registered only relief at Ben's reappearance, now says gently, 'I think we ought to go. Our car is waiting for us, beside the bus.' He puts an arm round Imogen and Vicky, but looks at those of us staying and says, 'You should be proud of yourselves; it is harder to live than to die.' Then he turns towards a black people carrier.

This is more difficult that I could possibly have imagined. I love Imogen, her tiny frame and silky white head are now, after a brief hug, ensconced in the car. I want to make a dramatic un-English scene, and pull her out. Adam is reading my brainwaves, and takes a firm hold of my arm. Soon it's too late, Imogen is boxed in by Ben and Vicky.

Vicky leans out of the window and beckons to Lindsay. 'You *will* talk to my husband – to David – won't you? You'll explain?'

Lindsay hugs her through the window. 'I promise. We'll go to Newcastle straight away.'

Bedrich and Anita have been hanging back talking to Leon. Now Leon leans into the taxi and speaks to Daniel. Daniel gets out and takes Anita and Bedrich's cases out of the taxi. His face is radiant; they are staying.

Last night Anita rang a priest, whose number Daniel had given her. I thought she seemed calmer today than yesterday and simply imagined that she had accepted her fate. Talking to the priest, and to Leon about his charity, seems to have tipped the balance of their complex moral equation. It's odd that their decision has only just emerged, but who am I to talk.

Now the three of them have the expertise to raise funds and work together to support full-time carers of children with all sorts of problems. They will make a curious, but effective, team.

Ben calls out of the window, 'Go and see Venice, Anita.'

For a moment we are all happy, hugging each other, asking questions, buoyant with relief at this reprieve.

Once again Daniel signals the end.

We have to let go of Daniel yet again. We all surge round him unable to believe that someone so valuable, so beloved, can choose to leave us behind. He has tears in his eyes, but in the shine of them I see also a resolve. Lindsay is clinging to his jacket still. He unlatches her fingers and holds both hands together for a moment, then presses them back against her chest and very swiftly climbs back into the taxi shutting the door. They're pulling away waving and smiling. Yes, smiling, while we stand forlorn, tears streaming down all our faces.

I must be hysterical, because next thing I'm laughing and the others stare at me. Hiccupping I try to explain. 'It's all the wrong way round. They are setting off happily to die and we are howling to be alive.'

Lindsay looks at me uncertainly. 'Do you think we'd be happier if we went too? Oh no, if we do that Daniel would have to return.'

With the thumb and fingers of one hand Kip presses his tears aside in a strange accustomed gesture. 'We've got important things to do. Grief packs down in the end. It feels crazy now, and it never exactly goes away, but you get sort of familiar with it over time.

Let's go back to that last village and have a coffee.' He tucks Lindsay into his shoulder and moves slowly towards the coach.

Kip is the youngest of us and yet experienced in grief. In Daniel's absence he is the *de facto* leader. Anita and Bedrich follow, hand in hand, then Leon. With the flicker of a smile, Adam takes my hand and we join the school procession.

We reach the coach and huddle towards the front seats, while Kip drives us to the nearest village with a café. We move to get off, but Leon walks to the back of the coach and bends down. He stands up with a peach and green scarf in his hands. Imogen's scarf. My tears flow again.

# On the other side of the world

Two young people are sitting side by side on a bed, their dark heads leaning together. Outside a green wall of spruce stretches across the Canadian landscape. Inside there is chaos; boxes, books and bags filled with clothes cover the floor. Spread out on the duvet are a DVD of La Traviata, a peach and green scarf and a scatter of un-written postcards – white horses, an African woman, a steam train. The girl holds the sheets of a letter; the young man a crumpled en-velope. She turns each page of the letter as she reaches the end; he occasionally puts out a hand to hold a page. Both have been crying. Now and then they gasp; occasionally they chuckle. At their feet lie pizza packages strewn with discarded crusts. On the wall their own faces look back at them from recent graduation photographs.

Unlike the rest of the room, the desk by the window is oddly square and neat. Between two bookends made of bright sweet tins, are a row of coloured and numbered ring binders and in front of them a computer tablet.

The young man looks up blinking and gazes towards the window where the sun, now setting, bathes his face and the room with amber light. He stands and stretches, then puts a hand over his mouth to hold it steady. He walks over and picks up the tablet.

The girl continues to frown at the letter. She says at last, 'Never. I can't get my head round that. We won't see them or hear them ever again.'

'Don't,' he says.

'All my life – all our lives – they've just been there. I know it's selfish and naive, but didn't think about them as... as separate... as making decisions without us.' She shakes her head a little, as if this act would juggle the concept into place.

Still holding the tablet, the young man returns to the bed and puts an arm around her. 'Shall we get some visas?'

'You mean go see this fabled country, the land of our concep-tion?' She pulls a wet tissue out of her sleeve, half smiling as she blows her nose. 'Where in the world is it?'

'Europe someplace.' He opens the tablet. 'There's a million maps in here.'

# Letter from Grace

Dear Twins,

I'm sorry about so many things I don't know where to begin, but not about you two. Dad and I had twenty-one years in which, unlike so many people, we knew we were happy. I was already pregnant with the pair of you when we left Slovenia, though I didn't know until I had a scan at twenty weeks. We were aghast as we watched the images of you floating there; both well-developed, firmly attached and determined on life. I lay squinting at that grey screen assuming, like a dunce, that this was some other woman's womb and that mine would appear, empty, any second now. Dad put his hand on my stomach. When he lifted it, trembling seismically and covered in the scanning jelly, the medics fell about. The sight of you blasted all our resolutions, but I am so infinitely glad we didn't hesitate.

The tablet and the folders on the desk contain the story I wrote about how I came to meet Dad. I wrote some notes as we travelled then added things I remembered as I waited like a stranded hippo for you two to be born. I was afraid Dad's uncle might catch up with us before you were big enough to understand and you have the right to know your story.

I was so busy from the day you arrived I never put the notes together until I ran out of time last year. I'm sorry it's so inadequate, but I want you to know that writing over the last few months has been wonderful, because I found that I was reliving those days, knowing, as I did not know then, that you two would come and I would have a good life.

The names in the story are the real names except for Dad's. We changed his name for a third time when we reached Canada before you were born. The name you bear is my mother's maiden name. The person you know as Aunt Aimée is not my sister, but Dad's. She also changed her name. Talk to Aimée but leave Dad's other relatives well alone. I don't know how much you remember about Grandma, my Mum. She visited from England quite a lot when you were babies. You were not quite five when she died, but you brought her great happiness towards the end of her life – thank you my darlings.

Now the difficult bit: if you are reading this it's because Dad and I have taken our lives. This action is not something I ever dreamed I would contemplate again once you two were born. To abandon you so young is an unbearable decision. Whatever we choose will be wrong in one direction or another. Dad, as you know, is sick, but so am I. They tell me I am in the early stages of a slow, dementing disease. The information from the hospital will be with this letter. I could stay a bit longer, but I will be ill for many painful years. I am able to make a choice now; later in this disease that choice will be taken from me.

You would both have looked after me like saints if I were still alive, but I would rather – and I know this is selfish and cowardly – remain in your memories as I am now. I could warn you; perhaps I should, but you will then need to try and dissuade me. You are such confoundedly clever creatures you might even succeed. I have to make this choice alone. We both love you beyond expression. Try to forgive and understand.

There's a world out there to enjoy and you two seem to have the knack of reaching out and grabbing it. We are relying on you to keep up this great enterprise. You have each other.

All – *all* our love, Mum and Dad

# Acknowledgements

This book has travelled a long way, with help, encouragement and tough love from many people to whom I owe an immense debt. From its early days onwards Jenifer Roberts, Paul Beck, Toni Battison, Paul Stevenson, Karalyn Patterson, Lis Hill, Achilles Tzoris, Barry Custance Baker, and Edwin, Eleanor and Amy Green all made substantial contributions.

Once Border Line became a complete story, detailed feedback and encouragement continued to come from these friends and also from Anthony Furness, Stephen Custance-Baker, Sian Miller, Peter Hewitson-Brown, Molly Greenwood, Janet Crofts, Mike Judge, Margot Chadwick and Hedwig Gockel.

Ewan Morrison via The Literary Consultancy, The Oxford Literary Consultancy, Kerry Glencorse and Sally Jenkins all made significant suggestions. I am also indebted to those agents who turned down the manuscript and told me why.

Penny Collins of Just Slovenia helped me to create a 'holiday' according to my own strange itinerary.

Peter Dolton and Anthony Furness gave me invaluable instruction in bringing the manuscript to print and my proofreaders, Mike Judge, Jo Leggo, Toni Battison, Kathleen France and Janet Crofts, did their utmost to eliminate my errors.

Without the warm, unstinting support of Edwin, Eleanor and Amy Green, this project would not have survived. I can only say thank you to everyone.

## Images from Slovenia

To see photos of some of the places and subjects mentioned in this story go to Hilary's website at:

### www.hilarycustancegreen.com

There are pictures of the Lippizaner horses, the Logar Valley, Slap Rinka, Lake Bohinj, the Black Lady, the Train Museum and many others.

If you have been affected by any of the issues in this story and need to talk to someone, please contact the Samaritans at:

**www.samaritans.org**

Available 24 hours a day to provide confidential emotional support for people who are experiencing feelings of distress, despair or suicidal thoughts.


If you are interested in the debate on choice at the end of life, please go to:
**www.dignityindying.org.uk**